The **Cheer Leader**

The Cheer Leader

A NOVEL

JILL McCORKLE

Algonquin Books of Chapel Hill • Chapel Hill, North Carolina • 1992

A special thanks to Rosanne Coggeshall and Richard
Dillard, who worked with me when this novel was in its
beginning stages; Liz Darhansoff, my agent; and Shannon
Ravenel, whose editing and sound advice have been invalu-
able. Thanks to Johnny and Melba McCorkle and Jan Gane.

ALGONQUIN BOOKS OF CHAPEL HILL
P.O. Box 2225, Chapel Hill, N.C. 27515
A division of
WORKMAN PUBLISHING COMPANY, INC.
708 Broadway, New York, N.Y. 10003
ISBN 1-56512-001-9 paper

© 1984 by Jill McCorkle

First paperback edition, May 1992.
Originally published in hardcover by Algonquin Books of Chapel Hill in
1984.

Library of Congress Cataloging-in-Publication Data
McCorkle, Jill, 1958–   The cheer leader.
ISBN 0-912697-11-3
    I. Title.   II. Title: Cheerleader. PS3563.C3444C44
1984   813'.54   84-16767

10   9   8

This book is dedicated to Max Steele, Lee Smith and Louis D. Rubin, Jr.
a small exchange for their instruction, encouragement and irreplaceable friendship.

The Cheer Leader

There is a picture of my mother that she keeps tucked away in her old scrapbook, yellowed pages pressing crumbled corsages, letters, gum wrappers. I used to sneak the book down often just to find that picture, to study every detail. Even now, I can see it: she is seventeen years old and it is her senior prom—she is wearing a strapless gown with a tulle ballerina length skirt. Behind her you can see stars, glittered cardboard—the theme is "Stardust." For years it bothered me that the man beside her was not my father. It seemed wrong that my brothers and I were not there, wrong that there was no knowledge of me behind those familiar eyes, wrong that there was no bump of a wedding ring under those white gloves, no thought that those gloved hands would one day change my diapers. It made me feel strange, very lonely, and I would cram that picture back between the gardenia crumbs, sneak it back to its place on the shelf in her closet, knowing all the time that I would have to look again.

And I did look again—again and again. I would spend hours sitting on the floor of that closet, my father's clothes all bunched together on the right, faint traces of tobacco—my mother's on the left, neatly spaced, hangers going in one direction like a parade of flat limbless people. Sometimes I would try on the clothes so that they wouldn't look so empty but usually I just sat with the picture box and spread its contents all over the floor. Then I would go through one by one and try to put them in chronological order so that I could see myself, my history, the parts that I could not remember. One day, I labeled all of those parts. I wrote B. J. (before Jo) in black magic marker; I drew a goatee and horns on the man at the senior prom; I put a neat circle around myself every time that I appeared. It seemed very important that all of that be done, even after my mother discovered my documentation and switched the hell out of me. Even now, those parts seem important. I call them pastshots.

There was my parents' wedding day—specks of rice frozen in midair; Great Aunt Lucille with a lace hankie up to her nose; my mother's mother with her hand lifted in a slight wave while my parents are caught in a blurred run towards the old black and white Ford on the street. I don't remember that car because it was B. J. My grandmother died B. J. Much of my father's hair thinned B. J. and yet, I know that it happened—I know that there was a moment when it was all real, even though what I remember is an old blue Rambler, going to the cemetery on Sunday afternoons to see my grandmother, Lucille looking much older and blowing her reddish snout into a jumbo Kleenex.

My favorite picture of my brother, Bobby, is one that was taken when he was two. He is sitting on Santa's lap in front of the old Wood's dime store and he is crying because he is scared. That picture was taken B. J. but it doesn't seem as foreign as the others. Maybe it's because it's Bobby and because I can remember him making that same face, crying that same way one other time.

This is Mama standing beside the old blue Rambler. When I was three and a half, I spray painted Jo Jo on the side of that car. Mama is fat and she looks upset just as she did when I painted the car. Bobby, who was three, is standing beside Mama and he is filthy dirty, mud all over his little overalls and face. They had called him away from his puddle in the sideyard where he had been making mud pies just to make the picture which Mama later labeled "just before Jo" which is what inspired my own system of documentation and the neat black circle around Mama's belly. I am told that Bobby could not wait for me to come out because he had always wanted a pet. All he had at that time was a fake snake named Buzzy that he kept in a jar of water by his bed. He wanted to name me Huzzy so that Buzzy and I would be related and for years it was tradition that this story be told on my birthday so that everyone could get a good laugh. Several years ago, that changed, and now they just make a toast to me, a year older, many happy returns.

MAY 18, 1957

This is my birth day. It is my debut but I don't have a long white gown, long stemmed roses, or an escort. All I have is myself and my Mama and the little plastic bracelet that assigned my name and sex, Spencer/Female—a picture of the beginning of my beginning, though there is not the slightest resemblance. This picture disturbed me, not just because I look so different, but because of what Great Aunt Lucille (who was not so great) told me on the day of her husband's funeral, that my mother threw up the entire nine months that she carried me, that she was so miserable, the most pitiful sight, that I almost killed my Mama coming out backwards the way that I did. "You ripped her wide open," Lucille said and blew her nose in a jumbo Kleenex. My mother said that Lucille shouldn't have told me that, that I was worth it all; but it was true. Now, when I think of that picture, I am reminded that I made my Mama vomit nonstop for three fourths of a year, that my whole life started in reverse, that Lucille was a bitch and is now a dead bitch. However, the picture did have one very useful function. It was the bit of proof that I clung to all of those times that Bobby told me that he was the real child and that I had been left in the trashpile by some black people who did not want me.

APRIL 1, 1958

Here, I am eating something that is green and comes in a little jar. Mama zeroes in on my mouth while making train noises, choo choo chugga chugga. Bobby is right there beside my high chair and he is holding long and rubbery Buzzy. "Buzzy loves you, Jo Jo. Buzzy wants to kiss you, Jo Jo. Buzzy wants a bite of your lunch, Jo Jo," and after rubbing Buzzy all over me, he dove Buzzy's nasty rubber head into the nasty green cuisine and it all froze: Buzzy's head always covered in green slop, Mama's spoon suspended on the invisible railroad track, her lips pushed forward in a "choo" while I sit helplessly, unable to control what is about to happen, unable to control the story that goes with this picture. I have felt that way many times.

MAY 18, 1958

It is my first birthday, documented by the one candle and the little "1" above the circle around my face. I am allowed to put my hands inside of the cake and mush up the good chocolate insides, squish them between my fingers, rub it on my face—so good for little Jo Jo for at this time, guilt was not associated with pleasure. Bobby is wrapping his gift to me (a girl snake named Huzzy) around my tiny wrist like an Egyptian bracelet. I am told that I never minded Bobby's attention; he was the dark haired creature who stood at the end of my crib when my diapers were being changed and made me laugh. I have always liked Bobby's attention and sometimes, still, he can make me laugh.

EASTER 1959

Bobby and I are sitting on the front steps with our Easter baskets on our laps. He is holding me so that I don't tumble down the steps in the few seconds that it takes Daddy to take our picture. Bobby had taken all of my red and purple eggs and replaced them with his white and black ones. He told me that he did that because he wanted me to have the "good" eggs. I loved him for that and yet, I hated to take all of the good ones because all I did was roll them around in my mouth and then leave them places where they would not be found for a long long time. I was feeling quite pleased when Mama yelled at Bobby for giving me all of the "bad" colors. I cried during the picture but then I forgave Bobby when he gave me all of the pretty colored tinfoil off of all of his chocolate eggs after he had eaten them. He also gave me all of the pretty colored tinfoil off of all my chocolate eggs after he had eaten them. My faith was restored and it made me smile such a sweet smile that Daddy had to take another picture. "A happy hoppy picture," he said, so I sat very still like a good Jo Jo when all the time I was confused by the fact that I did not know "good" from "bad," yet was content to roll both "good" and "bad" eggs in my mouth and deposit them in places where they would not be found for a long long time—infantile artifacts to remind me of myself on that particular day.

NOVEMBER 15, 1960

We are all in the front yard of the house on the corner of Walnut and 16th streets, Blue Springs, North Carolina. The house is red brick and the shutters were white then. There is a flat football on the roof of the house, thrown there by Bobby just two weeks before. He did not get a whipping because he had chicken pox. He is standing beside Mama and she looks upset. I am in Daddy's lap, a perfect circle around my face, and we are off to one side on the steps. The top of Daddy's head is cut off by Mr. Monroe, the fat man from next door, who took the picture. I am crying because I have just been switched for spray painting Jo Jo on the side of the old blue Rambler. At three and a half, I am told that I looked just like Lucille because of my dark auburn hair and wide green eyes. (I see no resemblance.) Already, I was starlet material because I had learned that if you will cry the first time that the switch hits (unlike Bobby) that it will not last as long and if you go further to pout and moan, then you can, indeed, hurt them worse than they hurt you. I also learned something else; you can get away with bad things if you are sick. This is a thought that has crossed my mind several times over the years.

MAY 18, 1961

It is my fourth birthday and I am sitting on my new red trike. Daddy tells me to hold up four fingers so I put them in front of my face (an age when obnoxious behavior is acceptable). Bobby is sticking his foot into my picture because a bee just stung it. He was trying very hard not to cry but he did anyway and it made me laugh to see him do that. I laughed and he pulled my hair until it almost came out but I did not fight back; I just sat there so that he would get in trouble (which he did). I had hurt him worse than he hurt me but I didn't enjoy it anymore when Mama switched him (in spite of the bee sting) and sent him inside. I made it up to him by letting him pull all of the roses off of my cake and then letting him blame me when Mama saw it with nothing but candles and a little ballerina. Looking back, I realize that this is the only time that I actually remember seeing Bobby cry. The time that he busted his head on the pier at Moon Lake, he just turned very white, and when Nancy Carson dumped him, he locked himself in his room, but I didn't see him cry. He didn't even cry in part three of "Lassie Come Home" when Timmy is burying Lassie's toys at the foot of that hill. No, but there was one other time that I can really remember seeing Bobby cry only it is hard to remember why. He was all grown up and we were down at the lake and he cried just a little, a quiet cry, and I didn't laugh that time because somehow it was my fault—somehow, I had made Bobby cry.

JUNE 1950

This is a B. J. that is out of line but I can't help thinking about it. It is a picture of my mother's mother, the same picture from the wedding except this time, she has been cut away from the group shot and blown up. Her dark hair is pulled back in a tight bun, and there is a slight smile on her face, her hand still raised in a wave. This is the only way that I know her and I have always felt slighted that she died before she saw me, that this is the only picture I can get of her. Every time that I have ever been to her grave, I see this face, beneath the dirt, inside that box, and it is a frightening thought because I know deep down that there is no trace of resemblance, that that slight smile that I have always wished had been smiled at me has long ago slipped into decay.

It is a very famous holiday but no one had taken the time to tell me about the historical figure that I came to admire so much. I am in Tiny Tots and I am afraid. This was my debut into social circles and although I did not know what I was feeling, I was feeling the need to be accepted and liked by the other children. I sat on a big red firetruck so as to call attention to myself in the picture but then a boy knocked me off and handed me the tamborine that he had been playing with. I did not know how to use it because I have never been musically inclined, so it was just as well when a girl that I did not know from Adam's housecat took it away from me. It was in this very scene that I was introduced into Survival of the Fittest but I did not feel very fit so I wandered onto the floor and started spinning with some other people to this song called, "I'm spinning, spinning like a top," but I got dizzy and had to sit down at one of those little tables. I was sitting across from a girl who wore glasses and she was doing something that Bobby had just taught me to do. She was crossing her eyes and I realized that for the first time I had found someone who shared an interest with me. "Hey, I can do that, too," I told her and crossed mine. The teacher saw me and slapped my hand, pulled me away from the girl and told me that what I had done was not nice at all. I cried the rest of the day, because I felt guilty, because I was worried that my eyes were going to cross and get stuck as punishment for what I had done.

SEPTEMBER 24, 1962

This is my Kindergarten class. The only difference between Kindergarten and Tiny Tots was that we had a different teacher and it was called Kindergarten instead of
Tiny Tots. We did the same things such as dance to "I'm
spinning, spinning like a top" and shake tamborines
(which I had mastered). I had learned that Killing with
Kindness is a good way to combat Survival of the Fittest
(a method that I clung to for years); I could get anything
that I wanted and maintain a sense of moral superiority.
I was becoming fitter all the time. I also learned that the
girl who had caused me to get into trouble way back in
Tiny Tots had a name, Beatrice, and often, I would try to
make up with her by telling her that I liked her dress
even when I didn't (a tactful lie which should be distinguished from damn lies and baldfaced ones). Beatrice
would have nothing to do with me when I gave these
compliments. This made me feel worse and I would try
even harder to make her forgive me. In the very second
of this picture (we are all lined up in front of the jungle
gym) I whispered to Beatrice that I liked her shoes (a
tactful lie, they are hideous brown patent leather ortho-
pedic looking shoes) and she would not even say thank-
you. I decided that if Beatrice did not want to be popular,
that was her red wagon.

FEBRUARY 2, 1963

This picture documents a holiday, the day that would
determine the weather for the next six weeks of 1963.

Everyone kept talking about the ground hog and I thought that I would like to meet this pig because we shared similar interests. Like the ground hog, I wanted very much to live in a nice dark hole where no one could see me and forecast the weather. I felt like everyone was watching me and spying on me and that is why, here, I am dressed as an old lady with a scarf on my head, Mama's high-heels, and a red bathrobe. Daddy thought that I was playing dress-up which is why he took the picture. I could not explain to him the very serious reasons that led me to adopt this costume. It was my disguise and it made me think wonderful poetic thoughts that I could not think at Kindergarten for fear that someone would hear me. Beatrice was a prime suspect because she was always so intent on whatever she was doing. When she shook the tamborine, she watched every single silver jingle (rhyme, alliteration, onomatopoeia) and when she fingerpainted, she studied her hands very carefully. Beatrice had new glasses that made her eyes unstick and I was convinced that if she chose to see what I was thinking, that she could do it. I wanted to make friends with Beatrice so that she would not do this to me, but she still was not interested in being popular. I was popular at Kindergarten but when I dressed in my old lady suit, I had a lot in common with Beatrice because I had very intense thoughts. I can't remember when I outgrew the red bathrobe and replaced it with a blue one. I can't remember when Beatrice decided that she wanted to be popular, can't remember when her eyes lost all semblance of intensity, can't remember if the ground hog saw his shadow in 1963, can't remember if he saw it this past year or not, but I can understand why he hides when he does see it.

MARCH 8, 1964

I am at Lisa Helms' birthday party and we are all in the first grade. She is the one in the center with the thin bird face, sticking out her tongue. This is a symbol of the future for at her next party, when we are all in the sixth grade, she will bring out an egg timer to see who can French kiss the longest. The boy on the far right, back row, with the black crew cut and simian features is Ralph Craig. He will win the future contest first with Lisa and then with Tricia McNair who will not move to Blue Springs until the third grade. (She will be a knockout with lots of sex appeal.) The girl standing beside me with long dark hair (she's the one doing horns over Lisa Helms) is my best friend, Cindy Adams. When we all leave the party, Lisa will give out the favors (which was usually the best part of a party). The boys will get plastic army tanks and the girls will get toilet water. I will pour mine into the commode that night only to discover that Lisa gave us rip-off favors; after one flush, it is gone.

Looking back on that event, I cringe at my ignorance. Beatrice never would have made such an error but then again, Beatrice didn't have the chance; she was not invited to that party. All of the other girls were coming to school with Lisa's toilet water behind their ears and for weeks, I was afraid that someone was going to ask me why I wasn't wearing some of mine. My Daddy thought the whole situation was very funny; my mother offered to buy me a whole Tussy kit so that I could get some more toilet water and still, it bothered me. It seemed that Beatrice and I were the only girls in first grade who smelled only of soap, clothes detergent and whatever we had for breakfast.

AUGUST 11, 1964

Here we all are back in the front yard. It is Bobby's tenth birthday and we all have on hats with yellow streamers coming off the top. Bobby is standing beside his new red bike and he is holding up both hands for ten. I hold up seven fingers; Daddy doesn't have enough fingers to hold up so he just smiles, and Mama (with a look of discomfort on her face) holds up little Andrew who cannot even hold up his head and therefore, cannot keep his hat on. It keeps sliding forward and he looks like a little slobbering aardvark. Mr. Monroe (who still lives next door and is even fatter than before) takes the picture and catches little Andrew's spittle right before it hits Mama's blouse.

Looking back, I can remember seeing that slobber hit Mama's blouse and run down her left bosom. She squealed and again got a look of discomfort. I realize now that this look did not come solely from the slobbered upon blouse but just from little Andrew in general. You see, (unlike me) Andrew was not planned or on the up and up. It was like playing Bingo and not really concentrating; covering all four corners and not even realizing; meekly yelling "bingo" as an echo to another bingoer and even though you have bingo, you lose. Mama was not prepared; when I am a Girl Scout some years in the future, I learn that that is something you must always be. Like me, Mama has changed her mind on a few occasions. In the future she claims that little Andrew (Andy) is a "blessing," "the sunshine of her life." And like Mama, I can honestly say that I, too (though it may be hard to believe), have screwed up once or twice.

JANUARY 15, 1965

This is the second grade class. I am circled on the front row where the short people stand. I look a little disturbed because Ralph Craig had just asked, "Why do cherry trees stink?" He did not even give anyone time to think of an answer before he said, "George Washington cut one." That was the worst joke that I had ever heard and it upset me that I had actually heard a "bad" and nasty joke, and especially about the father of the country. In due time, however, the joke did not bother me, because I had heard far worse, because I had suddenly realized that George was a person and naturally he had cut one; he had cut several. What has bothered me from time to time is that cherry tree in general and that whole little story about "I cannot tell a lie, it was I." I tend to think that the story itself is a lie. There is no proof, no picture of him standing there, guiltily, with his little hatchet. It is merely a way to provide insight into the father of our country.

I have heard another story about him that is shunned in the schoolroom. I have heard that he died of syphilis and pneumonia, the former which he got from someone other than Martha and the latter which he got on his way to see the carrier of the former. It seems to me that that is more historical than the cherry tree or the euphemistic approach that he caught his cold (and nothing more) while standing in that horrid little icy boat crossing the Delaware; yet, people just don't want to discover or accept a change in history, because it is easier to believe what everyone else believes. It is why there is religion, songs hit the charts, skirts rise and fall, the emperor made such an ass of himself strutting around in his underwear. It is why at one point in my life, those people close to me wore kid gloves, went out of their way to abnormally make everything seem so normal. No one had the guts to tell me that I was hanging by a thread, not for fear of my reaction as much as their own fear of an inconsistency, a change. It was far easier to say that I had had a "little upset," was "going through a phase." And so it goes, truth sacrificed for ease, which is why George will forever be the honest, truthful father of our country and why I was May Queen. It's all relevant. "I cannot tell a lie" is important and fucking out on Martha is not. "Little problems" are acceptable and so on.

OCTOBER 12, 1966

It was a very important day but we still had to go to school. This is a picture that I drew myself. There is the

Pinta, the Nina and the Santa Marie (just like in the song). The goodlooking man in the navy London Fog (he's on top of the Nina) is Chris and the woman on the other side of the ocean is the queen. Her little balloon of speech says, "Way to go, Chris!" and his says, "I have discovered America." I have discovered that I was not artistically inclined. However, when I drew the picture, I thought that I had done an excellent representation. The teacher said so, too (a polite encouraging lie). Now, I see that the entire picture is rather flat when the whole point was to prove roundness. Chris' arms are much too long (for this is not a picture of evolution, another favorite topic) and he should probably have a beard after being on that ship so long. The man most definitely deserves some sexy feature, a cleft in his chin, narrowed tempting eyes, or even a cigarette hanging out of the corner of his mouth. He deserves something but it is too late to rectify my past ignorance. Then, I spent much of my time wondering where the new world would be if Chris hadn't found it. Even now, sometimes, I think about all of that. Right out of the blue, I will think, "Columbus had balls" because he took a chance, because he did not base his beliefs on what other people thought, because he discovered the truth. I admire that because chances are hard to take, the truth is often difficult to face, because somewhere in the back of his mind, there must have been a slight doubt, a slight fear of finding himself clinging to the edge of the world, dropping into that pit of darkness that everyone else "knew" was there. And yet, he kept going after the bit of proof that was necessary for his beliefs.

Cindy is having a Halloween party and I am the one at the back with the white sheet on. I knew that my costume was not original but I liked the way that it felt inside of the sheet; I felt like I was in bed and dreaming the party. Tricia McNair, the new girl in the third grade, was one of four black cats. She is the cute black cat lying down in front of the group with her long black tail held up for all to see. For a new person, she was not the least bit shy and had been immediately accepted. Beatrice was an old person (she is the black cat wearing glasses) and yet, she still was not fully accepted. I have always thought that there should be some logical theorem behind all of that, some correlation between new people and old people, but I have never figured it out. Ralph Craig, whom you will recognize by now, claimed to be a stoplight which is why he has a red dot painted on his forehead. Tricia McNair, right after the picture was made, won the prize for the best costume which really wasn't fair to the other three black cats, but I didn't voice my concern. It was much easier to stay in my sheet and not call attention to myself. Besides, being a ghost was so unoriginal that I felt by doing it, I had been original. I suppose that deep down, I felt that I deserved the prize, not the physical prize, for what did I care for a tacky little plastic jack-o'-lantern, but the title, the recognition that went along with it. I consoled myself throughout the party first by congratulating Tricia McNair and then by telling myself that my turn would come. Besides, I was not yet ready to expose myself.

This picture is unexposed; it is very dark and it is grouped with all of the pictures from the Girl Scout campout. There are pictures of a bonfire, bags and bags of G.S. cookies, Cindy posed by a tree, Tricia swinging from a tree, Lisa with a Tootsie Roll Pop (oral fixation), but it is the dark one that I am concerned with. It could be another picture of the cookies or the bonfire, but since it is so dark and scarey looking, I see another picture: I am in the tent and everyone else is asleep. I have a dire need to use the bathroom but I am afraid to walk down the path to the latrine; I should have gone earlier when the whole troup went to shine their flashlights down the latrine to look but I was engrossed in a winning way conversation with the scout leader who I hoped would give me my cooking badge even though that very day she had caught me burying my food in the woods. (To get the badge you had to eat what you cooked.) She was no April Fool and I had missed my chance to use the bathroom. There, in the dark, perched on a ratty little cot, I sit, my legs crossed tightly, humiliated, guilty for not having one badge on my sash, and suffering that excruciating pain of not being able to use the bathroom. I couldn't go out beside the tent because I was scared of frogs, snakes, and whatever else might be out there, and so through the darkness, I endured the hurt, the little pee shivers that made me jerk involuntarily, the hurt pride of not having one badge. It was my first real experience with the pains of loneliness, failure, darkness; the pains which come when one denies those very natural bodily functions. I have felt this way on various other occasions (even when I did not have to use the bathroom and was not sitting on a ratty little cot in a Girl Scout tent somewhere in the mountains). The likenesses are that there have been times when I really didn't know where in the hell I was except in a bed, under a tent, under a sheet, an exposed ghost; and again, I did not always finish what I started. This is why I feel that this one mysteriously dark, unexposed picture is very important to my life in general.

JULY 4, 1967

It is a holiday and I am celebrating the fact that this country owes its birth to Chris Columbus, by sitting in the bathroom. I am wearing my new old blue bathrobe and it is just the right length because it reaches the tops of my bobby socks. The bathrobe was comfortable and the pink scarf that I wore on my head seemed to hold all of my thoughts together. I felt like a poet and so I spent hours making lists of words that rhymed so that I would have them when I was ready to let myself go. At that particular time, it was easier to fool everyone, especially Daddy who always got a real kick out of the "dress-up" pictures. Had he known then what he came to know later, he probably never would have laughed and teased me so, and thus would have robbed me of something very special. Teasing, when done properly, can be one of the finest indications of love, and it is quite sad when people decide that they will not ever do it again. Of course, I can't blame them. Who wants to feel responsible for hurting someone that they sincerely love?

AUGUST, 1967

In this picture, I am at VBS (Vacation Bible School) and I hate VBS because I have to see people that I feel I should not have to see over the summer. I am wearing a long purple dress and have just fished Baby Moses (a Chatty Cathy all wrapped up in a beach towel and put in a fruit basket) out of the bullrushes (a large azalea bush). Ralph Craig is Goliath which is why he has a rock taped to his forehead, his tongue out of his mouth and is lying flat on his back. Cindy is all wrapped up in long silky blue scarves because she is Mary and she is holding Baby Jesus (a Betsy Wetsy in swaddling clothes). Beatrice had wanted to be Jesus all grown up but the teacher would not let her. The teacher thought that it was acceptable for Betsy Wetsy to be Baby Jesus but that no one should try to play grown up Jesus. Beatrice got very angry and this is why she is all wrapped up in towels and lying on the ground right near my bullrushes. She had told the teacher that if she couldn't be Jesus, that she would be Lazarus and play dead just like Ralph Craig.

Even in this prominent position of the princess' maiden who discovered Baby Moses, I look somewhat perplexed. It is because Ralph Craig, before his death scene, came up and whispered a word to me that I did not know, a word that you would say if you used the name Buck in the Banana Nanna Fo Fanna song. I did not know that it was an ugly word, though I had my suspicions, so I did not tell the teacher. Too, as ugly as I thought Ralph was, I liked to look at him sometimes. I changed my mind after I asked my mother to define the word. Ralph had said that that was what he was going to do to me. It made me afraid of him and yet, I still had to look at him even though I did not want to. It was like he had a power; even Beatrice was in his spell because later that same week when he commanded that she pull up her skirt or get a busted nose, she obliged. I realized that being popular did not mean that you had everything. Beatrice had an experience (self-exposure) which I would not have for a long long time. This one incident at VBS caused a lot of trouble because it made me afraid of boys and what they had. I think it also had a hell of a lot to do with the knot that I would get in the pit of my stomach at the very mention of VBS.

SEPTEMBER 30, 1967

I am upset in this picture because I feel that I do not fit in. It is an odd thing because outwardly, I do fit in; I am one of the most popular girls in the fifth grade (along with Cindy, Lisa and Tricia McNair). It has been this way for some time, our four names always said together as if it is one name, TriciaLisaJoandCindy; I am third in line. We maintain this close friendship so that other people will not be forced to make decisions about whom they like best (that choice comes much later). However, I also learned something very important from all of this, something political; there are divisions within groups that have already been divided from other groups and ideally should be whole. They are not; nothing is whole; even people, without realizing, split themselves up into little parts. This theory is one that came to mind much later, for then I was simply confused by the issue. You see, all three of my best friends had asked me in private to be their best friend and I had avoided answering for suspecting that they had asked each of the other two the same so that they would eventually be everyone's best friend and therefore have power. For times such as that, I had chosen for my answer, huh. Not "huh?" but "huh," like "I see" or "Oh, yes," and thus had not committed myself to any particular belief. This tactic works, for the person then assumes your answer to be whatever they would like for it to be and yet, there is no proof of exactly what the response meant. It is confusing, but then it was the easiest way to maintain my position. Noncommittal is easy or at least appears to be for it allows you to stay on the up and up with everyone. The problem, of course, is that you eventually have no opinion that you can think of except that which is thought by others and you never know if what they think is true or false. Monkey see, monkey do.

I was disturbed by other things as well. For instance, sometimes Tricia tried to hold my hand and I felt that I was much too old for that. There was a motive behind it. Was it a subtle suggestion to the others that we were best friends? Was it a way to make Cindy and Lisa try harder to be her best friend? Or was it that strong human urge to expose and possess people who do not wish to be exposed or possessed? I was saving my hands for a future encounter with a male for that struck me as being normal and when done tastefully, with discretion, I thought could be a worthwhile event. Naturally, I did not reveal this thought for it was one of those very sound, very old, bathroom bathrobe thoughts that I had to save just as I saved my hands.

Here, Cindy is holding hands with Tricia and it is strange to see because Cindy was my friend first and yet, she doesn't seem to be bothered by holding hands with a girl. Nor, was she bothered when Tricia turned and spoke directly in her face. It was my belief that people just shouldn't do that and yet, I was helpless to make them stop. A reprimand on such an issue would have committed me to an inescapable opinion that would set up a conflict between myself and the other three popular girls, three to one, and I had no desire to be on the outside. I had ideas that I needed that position, that if I hung in there, one day, my name would come first. Although I clearly had thoughts and opinions I did not reveal, I felt that I had to do one silly thing so I would not be rejected and could fit into the popular picture. I said, "Boolahbuster! Boolahbuster!" and then I squatted down and made a frog noise. This kept me in for a good two weeks without holding hands.

We were sailing along on the Pinta, the Nina and the Santa Marie. This is little Andy sitting in the bathtub. He is surrounded by little plastic boats and stretched and tattered Huzzy whom he loves (in a way that I never did). On this very sacred day, Andy chose to play with himself (if you know what I mean) more than he played with the boats and I was quite distressed by this. Bobby saw a great deal of humor in the situation and Mama passed it off as a normal response. They did not see that little Ralph Craig glint in Andy's three year old eyes as I did. I thought that Mama should possibly beat him but she didn't and I had to console myself with the thought that after me, there was very little sense left for Andy to receive, sort of like, "where were you when they passed out the brains?" Of course, now I realize that that is not how it works and that Andy is quite intelligent in his little assey way. He was merely into blatant exposure while his sister was discreet, tactful, mysterious and sneaky.

JUNE 18, 1968

I am getting ready to go to Moon Lake with Tricia. She is wearing a hot pink two piece that shows her navel, an "inny." The rest of us are wearing one pieces with skirts around the ass. Lisa has a look of discomfort on her thin bird face because she has (just three hours before) started her period for the first time. She is very early, but I learn in the future that Lisa is early in whatever she does. She is the first person that I know of (in my age group) that has one and she will tell us all about it at the lake after we have all been swimming and she hasn't. Tricia will act like she knows all about it and Cindy will ask lots of questions. I will not say anything as I usually don't when I am perplexed. Lisa's descriptions will so link periods to tidal waves that I will spend the next two years of my life in constant fear even though my mother will try to soothe my prepubescent worries.

AUGUST 10, 1968

Here I am with Jeff Johnson. We are getting ready to ride our bikes up to the Quick Stop to get a can of boiled peanuts and two strawberry Icees. Bobby is the smart ass that takes the picture as a subtle way to give me hell for having a boyfriend. I don't really but Bobby won't listen to good sense so I make a face and Jeff just smiles this real nice smile that Bobby will call a sissy smile when the pictures come back long after Jeff is gone.

After Bobby takes the picture and blows a kiss to me when Jeff isn't looking, we ride to the Quick Stop. This day, I don't have to pay half for the peanuts or buy my own Icee; Jeff buys as a going away present because it is his last day in Blue Springs. Looking back, I am glad that Bobby took the picture (even though at the time I hated him) because otherwise, I would not remember what Jeff looked like that summer. He was about the same size as me (short) except he was much thinner and he had pale skin (a freckled sunburned nose that prompted me to call him Rudolph most of the time), soft pale hair and eyes like pale gray tissue paper. He was the kind of person who looks much better in black and white and thank goodness, that's what kind of film Mama always bought for Bobby because it was so rare for him to take a worthwhile picture. This picture is good though, and it makes me think of the few things that I knew about Jeff Johnson. He was two years older, from Maine, spending the summer with his aunt (Mrs. Monroe, wife of fat Mr. Monroe who took our pictures for us on holidays), and he was different from any boy that I had ever met. He didn't try to find out if you wore a bra or if you had ever kissed or if you had started your period, like Ralph Craig and a bunch of boys had done in the fifth grade when all the girls were given a book called *Growing Up and Liking It*. Beatrice had had to go home that day and if I had by then heard Lisa's description of periods, I probably would have gone home, too. No, Jeff Johnson was different; he liked to talk about fishing and bombs and poker and just the way that he talked made him sound so smart that on that last day, I confessed to him that I wrote poetry and thought that Christopher Columbus was the most wonderful person to ever live. That last day, he held my hand and it made me feel real strange but sort of good inside and he told me that he would send me a picture when he got his braces off. Just before we left that day, Jeff poured all the peanut juice out in front of the curb (our curb) and we watched it run through all the drink tabs and cigarette butts. I didn't look up but while we watched that juice, he put something cool on my finger and with my thumb, I could tell it was a ring of some sort; actually it was a pop top, but I wore it for a long time after that. Finally after a long time, I put it in a box with lots of other junk and forgot about it. I never heard from Jeff and Mrs. Monroe never mentioned him; I figured for years that he was still wearing braces and that was why. Naturally that was dumb, and I see it now; I also see that being in love and being dumb are often simultaneous actions which my future years seem to portray more blatantly than a silver pop top and one black and white photograph of a skinny Yankee kid with braces that no one else in the neighborhood would have anything to do with, and a summer nurtured by boiled peanuts and strawberry Icees. I guess the most important thing to point out is that I had actually engaged in hand holding, I had found someone, temporarily, with similar interests and I hadn't had to act a certain way. Even more important is remembering that after all of that, I never heard from him, not a single shitty little Yankee postcard, and I should have remembered that for future reference but unfortunately it was hidden from me by my subconscious who chose, instead, to remember that rubbery knee, sweaty palm, coronary palpitating feeling that I had experienced holding hands with Jeff Johnson, there in front of the Quick Stop in Blue Springs all summer when I was eleven.

OCTOBER 12, 1968

I am getting ready to go to the high school football game with Tricia, Lisa and Cindy. That week, we all had boyfriends; Lisa was going with Ralph Craig which I thought was sickening though I didn't tell Lisa, Tricia was going with a boy in the seventh grade which was par for the course since she had already gone with all of the boys our age, and Cindy was going with Myron Paul who was cute but always in the slow reading group (something that I had little tolerance for). My boyfriend, as of that very day, was Ray Peters. Myron had come up to me during lunch recess and handed me a note that said that Ray wanted to go with me and then there were three boxes: Yes, No, I'll let you know later, check one. I was just about to put No but Tricia, Lisa and Cindy all stood there telling me that I should, that he was cute, and that we'd all sit together at the ballgame as a group.

Needless to say, this was my first big encounter with peer pressure. Ray was standing beside the cafeteria door with his hands in his U.N.C. parka, staring at the ground. Myron went back with the Yes block checked, Ray looked at it, turned red and went into the cafeteria. I knew that Ray was not cute and not the kind of boyfriend that I felt I should have, and yet, I was not ready to stray from the group, even if it meant having a chubby boyfriend with large teeth. He was nice, though, and by the time that Daddy took this picture of me and Bobby, I had convinced myself that Ray Peters would make a perfectly acceptable boyfriend. Still, in the picture, I am slightly uncomfortable not just because Bobby, whose girlfriend is a junior high cheerleader and stacked, has just called Ray Peters "Porky Pig," but also because my training bra was slowly riding up to my neck. Prior to the picture, I had stuffed it with a pair of Andy's socks, then Mama made me unstuff it. She had said that I would grow, to give it time (a parental lie spoken out of love when you are in one of those dreadfully awkward stages, a parental prophecy which in my case, never came to pass).

My discomfort with myself and my anticipations of Ray (which both show up in the twisted smile) do not both come to pass. Only discomfort grows when Ray Peters slips his hand under my corduroy poncho (which is what everyone is wearing) and grabs hold of mine. His hand is plump and damp (so unlike that cool Yankee hand of Jeff Johnson from whom I am still waiting to hear). Then, as if that's not enough, Ray picks his nose a little when he thinks that no one sees, but I do and I am so horrified that I can hardly concentrate on the way that Bobby is all huddled up with the large breasted cheerleader just three rows in front of me. As if that's not enough to endure, I have to cope with the problem of my boyfriend's last name which all the boys (Ralph Craig in particular) make fun of. I take it as a personal insult and I realize that I do not want to be linked up with someone who inspires penis jokes.

The following Monday, I sent Lisa (because she enjoyed that sort of thing) with a note to give to Ray. I deliberated long and hard that previous Sunday night on just what to say in the note. I wanted to say, "Bug off, creep. I can't stand you," because I felt that he deserved it after the humiliation that I had experienced. However, something kept me from doing it, maybe I was too nice, maybe sometime during the night I considered his feelings, maybe I was too weak to take such a strong stand.

I wrote, "I am breaking up with you but we can be friends (a tactful lie) from: Jo Spencer." Again, he merely turned red and went into his classroom.

MARCH 8, 1969

I am at Lisa's house sitting beside a stack of 45's. Her mother took the picture and then she and Mr. Helms disappeared into the back room for the rest of the night. Lisa had to raise hell for several weeks to get such an agreement from her parents (something that I never would have done or even thought of doing). After they leave, the party really begins. I have found at an earlier boy/girl party had by Tricia McNair (Mrs. McNair made a check every twenty minutes) that I like to control things like record players while at a party. I am playing "Dizzy" by Tommy Roe because I like the way that it makes me feel. It makes me feel like I am moving all over even though I am sitting perfectly still.

"Come on, Jo," someone says but I ignore them. Ralph Craig and Lisa are apart now and breathing deeply. They French kissed for three minutes. In just a minute, he will kiss Tricia McNair and they will look like the pink gouramis that I saw in the pet store, their mouths twisting up and down, like the first fish that I ever caught at Moon Lake when I was six. That fish just lay there, wide eyed, open mouthed and dumb; he was dying and had a good excuse; I felt that Ralph and Tricia did not. Years later, when I was studying sixteenth century poetry, I found that "die" was often used as an orgasmic description, and thus, my analogy between the fish and Tricia and Ralph was perfectly plausible. They stopped at five minutes, a record which Ralph and Lisa tied before we went home.

"I'm so dizzy, my head is spinning." I am ready to go home and have been since I arrived. Beatrice is sitting in that circle and I am surprised. Usually, she avoids such scenes but I think that possibly, remembering her fascination for Ralph's nastiness, she wants to kiss. The Pepsi bottle stops on her and I can feel myself getting embarrassed for no good reason except I know that Beatrice is pleased and that Ray Peters doesn't want to kiss her. I stare at the little plastic bust of Beethoven that Lisa won for playing chopsticks or something very similar. There are giggles when they lean forward on their knees, and I know that Beatrice as intent as she is, does not realize that everyone is laughing at her. At that point, I had a strong urge to take up for Beatrice and yet, I couldn't speak out; I could not call attention to the fact that I was not playing, so I put "Dizzy" back on and kept an eye on Ludwig because I felt that what you can't see can't hurt you.

At nine-thirty, I said a quick good-bye and ran outside to wait for my Daddy. I sat on the curb in front of Lisa's house to remind myself that I had fun one time sitting on a curb. The street lights looked like tall skinny people with halos and I recognized the sound of our car before my Daddy even got to the third person. Just when I felt that I couldn't stay there another second, he stopped and I got in. I remember it so well because at that point, I told a lie. He asked, "How was the party?" and I said, "Fine, I had a good time." He smoked his pipe and it smelled like burning leaves and I wished that I could ride forever that way and that I'd never have to go to another party and that I'd never have to kiss but it wasn't long before I had forgotten that, too. The only part of the wish that lingered for a long long time was the part about smelling the pipe and riding in the car with him forever. Even now sometimes, that wish occurs to me.

MAY 30, 1969

It is a beautiful day and I am standing at the very end of the Holden Beach pier, watching the sky change from blue to apricot glaze to faint pink outlined in deep violet and I am struck by the poetic thought that it looks like a watercolored print being washed over. I am so immersed in finding a word that rhymes with color that for a few minutes, I stop watching everyone else doing the jerk down on the beach. They have all written boys' names in the sand and drawn hearts, arrows and other symbols of love. Even Beatrice has written Ralph and no one can make fun of her because she is the one having the end of school party and we are all staying with her mother and older sister in their beach house. Otherwise, I'm certain that Beatrice never would have written Ralph's name.

"Come on, Jo!" they yell and Lisa aims her camera at me; I am the dark speck bisected by the rounding horizon. I know that if I go down there, that I will have to write something in the sand. I would want to write Mark in the sand but I just can't let anyone know. He's in high school, in Bobby's class. They must never know because if they do, I have all suspicions that one of them may go after him and get him. Cindy wouldn't do that to me but Cindy is going with Ray and I want to tell her how I saw him conspicuously inconspicuously pick his nose that time. It is one of those dilemmas which I will find in the future is a "damned if you do, damned if you don't" situation.

Granted, it was a trivial matter and yet, the outcome then appeared as great as it has appeared other times when there was far more to lose. Still, I kept thinking, suppose I tell Cindy that Ray picks his nose in public; she would be embarrassed; if she really liked Ray, she would say that I was jealous. However, this is the way that people sometimes think as I discovered once when I thought that way. On the other hand, I did not want to be responsible for Cindy's humiliation if she happened to witness the picker in action. I could imagine her saying, "Did you know that Ray picks his nose in public?" and being the honest person that I am, I would have to say, "Yes." Then she would ask, "Why didn't you tell me?" and I would explain the "damned if you do, damned if you don't" theory, and she would say, "But, I would've believed you," which is exactly what everyone says after it is all said and done and there is no choice to be made. In situations such as that, I try to get by without saying anything and preserving my opinion. That is what I was doing on the pier, preserving my opinion and thinking big thoughts.

If I can just think of what rhymes with color, then I can join the party with confidence. Muller! You might say

I'm a muller when it comes to water color that paints the sky when the day does die, (not orgasmic) and duller! The color of the sky gets duller when I try to catch the pink spots. I stare so long, I see dots, like millions and trillions of forget-me-nots, and I am not forgotten, re-membered to the end, all I have to do is smile and every-one will be my friend until the end so help me, God is my witness that I'll never be hungry again by Joslyn Marie Spencer and with that touch of drama, I wave to the yell-ing crowd below and head down the pier, I'm coming! I'm coming! (I was not aware of the sexual implications) though my head is bending low, I hear their silly voices calling, our friend, Jo.

MAY 30, 1969 P.M.

This picture was taken after everyone stopped doing the jerk on the beach and started doing the pony on the balcony of Beatrice's beach house. Beatrice insists on playing "Julie, Julie, Truly Do You Love Me?" over and over on the record player because next to Ralph Craig, Bobby Sherman is her favorite person in the world. She has already told us that we have to watch "Here Come the Brides" whether we want to or not because it is her party. Nobody minds that because Beatrice has already assured us that we can eat whatever we want to and stay up all night.

In this picture, Tricia is doing the pony *right;* her way is no different but everybody acts like they are learning something because Tricia is just one of those people that has to have her way and be in the limelight. The dirty white tennis shoe attached to the skinny white leg that Tricia is about to land on belongs to Beatrice's mother who is squatted down beside a grill fixing hotdogs for us. Cindy keeps trying to do the pony but she keeps getting her hands behind her when they should be in front and vice versa. Cindy never caught on to things very quickly (like about having Ray Peters for a boyfriend) but she was always very good in math. Beatrice cannot dance at all but Tricia doesn't correct her like she does Cindy about her hands and me not bobbing my head at the right times. It is because Beatrice is having the party and her mother is standing there. Also Tricia wants to win our Miss Universe pageant that we have planned to have right after hotdogs and before Here Come the Brides. I have my back turned in this picture and it looks like I am doing the pony but really I am not. Everyone thinks that I am and this is why I hop from one foot to the other. What I am really doing is saying Mark Fuller in my head one hundred times on each foot so that he will want to ask me out when I am old enough to go. Looking back, I realize that that was a foolish wish to make, not because it never came true but because had it come true, I would have gone out with a tight jeaned, greasy headed, zodiac medallion wearing, undesirable, who always talked about how he hated to shave his face which was an ignorant (he thought subtle) way to hide the fact that he had very little facial hair, only about four hairs that sprouted from his chin that were just as greasy as those on his head which I'm certain were unnumbered. Why would God (with all the other hairs on other heads to count) bother with such a poor example of the human race. Mark Fuller should never have owned a razor.

MAY 30, 1969 (*Just before "Here Come the Brides"*)

Here, we are all in native costume. Tricia is in the center with a beach towel around her shoulders and tin foil on her head. Clearly, she is the winner. She is from Arabia and has on pajama pants like "I Dream of Jeannie" and a bikini top. She has half of a maraschino cherry stuck in her navel and it stayed there the whole time that she did a hoochie koochie dance to "Ahab the Arab." I am standing beside her with the plastic fruit because I am Miss Congeniality. I am from Spain and I am wearing my blue bathrobe with a red scarf tied around it. It doesn't look Spanish but I had decided that that was irrelevant since I did not look Spanish. I felt that I had done a wonderful job reciting excerpts from "The Highwayman" for my talent. I opened my arms wide when I said "the moon was a ghostly galleon," and looked up at the ceiling in a poetic way the whole time. I was somewhat shocked and displeased that I did not even place.

Cindy is very happy because she is second place. She has on Beatrice's mother's raincoat and she brought her white go-go boots and her Nancy Sinatra 45 just for this occasion. She always did "These Boots Are Made for Walking" at every pajama party but this was the one time that she placed. I was happy for Cindy and told her so though I could not stop wondering what I could do the next time so that I would be the winner. Nevertheless, I was Miss Congeniality and I almost always got that because I was always real nice about agreeing with people even when I didn't mean it so that they would leave me alone. Years later, this congenial act got old but my subconscious continued to do it against my will. I would be saying "eat shit" or "bite the big one" and all that would slip from my tongue was something like, "Yes, you look just like an Ethiopian Princess." I was very good at saying what people needed to hear to quieten them and it was this factor alone which I think ultimately led me to being the first name in the group, the most popular senior girl.

Lisa did not place at all since there are just five of us at the party but she doesn't care. Her name is Fifi and she is from France. All she did to herself was paint her thin lips like a Valentine, tease her hair and put on a bathing suit. For her talent, she sang "Frère Jacques" and did the jerk. She was not upset by the results because she was still in a position of authority, she was still the only one of us that had a period. Tricia said that she could feel one coming on and had brought supplies. I remember thinking that with her luck, she would probably get to use them, and advance another step beyond Cindy and myself. As a result, she did but Cindy told me later that she was faking. I had thought as much but it bothered me that I was the last to know.

Beatrice did not place either but she said it was because her mother and sister did not play favorites. That was a good excuse; however, I think she must have known that she wouldn't have won anyway. She was a hippie even though we told her that that was not a country and that she had to pick a country. Cindy was already from America but Beatrice said that it was her party and she didn't have to pick a country if she didn't want to. She just tied shoestrings around her head, held her hand with the peace sign, pulled her jeans below her navel (an outie) and did the hitchhiker to "Hitching a Ride." She ended up by doing the pony (which she couldn't do at all) after her record was over and her sister finally had to tell her to sit down. Having a party had changed Beatrice. It had given her just enough of a sense of belonging that she was willing to freely expose herself. She probably even thought that it would stay that way.

I was glad that I had my bathrobe especially after "Here Come the Brides" when we had a séance and Lisa saw John Kennedy's face in the T.V. Everybody started crying except me because I knew who John Kennedy was and therefore knew that he had no reason to get me. Besides, of all the parties in all the world, why would he have picked Beatrice's? I thought things like that all night long. Even after everyone else was asleep, I thought about people in China who were eating lunch and all of the fish swimming around all night with their eyes open; how everybody slept, even Mark Fuller and that was hard to believe, that we would do all the same things like eat, sleep and use the bathroom. I couldn't picture him using the bathroom because it just didn't seem that he would ever have to. It seemed demeaning but it also made me feel close to him when I realized that he was a person, had a mother who probably made him clean out the bathtub or do other menial chores. Later, of course, I realized that he was as much a part of any bathroom as the permanent fixtures; he was groutish and deserved to be sucked by a drain. However, then I thought that he was the one meant for me, the love of my life and I rubbed my finger where the pop top used to be. I decided to give up on Jeff Johnson, somehow sensing the futility of it all; I told myself that I would never again hold that cool Yankee hand; I told myself that one day Jeff Johnson would be mad as hell that he didn't get his braces off soon enough to hold onto me.

Mark Fuller was a person and Bobby Sherman was a person even though I couldn't imagine either of them ever vomiting. Beatrice was a person and that was easy to imagine because I just rolled over and saw her lying there with her glasses still on, shoestrings around her head, snoring quietly and not knowing that when we all went home everyone would give her hell for writing Ralph Craig's name in the sand, that things would be as they had always been. I knew that Tricia would probably say the most even though she was the least likely person in the room. She did not snore and I knew that she would wake up looking just as she had when she went to sleep, a frightened Miss Universe, and there was a second when I wished that John Kennedy would get her and then I remembered that we were friends.

MARCH 2, 1970

Bobby takes this fuzzy picture to make me mad because I am already mad. I am sitting outside on the porch reading *Where the Red Fern Grows* for the fourth time. It is my favorite book next to the biography of Helen Keller. It is about two coon dogs, Old Dan and Little Anne. They both die unexpectedly and it makes me cry every time so I read it when I am mad and upset so that I can blame my tears on the book. Bobby knows my trick so he takes my picture. It is fuzzy because I threw the book at him right when he clicked and he moved out of the way. The best page, which contained Old Dan's death scene, fell out but I don't even care. I am mad and upset because I have started my period for the first time and everyone has lied to me. It is not (thank goodness) as Lisa had described way back at Moon Lake; it is not an old and wonderful thing as Tricia said when she faked having one at Beatrice's party; it does not make me feel like a lady like that woman at school said back in the fifth grade and it does hurt (unlike what Mama said when I was worried over tidal waves). It makes me feel old and young; not old like a teenage lady who probably wears sunglasses but old like somebody that walks stiff legged with their legs spread apart like John Wayne, or young, like a baby in diapers. I had decided, while reading *Where the Red Fern Grows*, before Bobby took my picture, that as soon as he got the hell away from me and as soon as Andy took Huzzy and his first grade art project (a kite that looked like shit and wouldn't fly) into the house, that I would practice walking like a teenage lady who wasn't having a period. It was as much a secret thought as my bathrobe; it made me feel old but instead of rhyming good words, it made we want to rhyme bad words, filthy, horribly sordid words like pecker.

I thought that becoming thirteen would cause a change in me, that I would suddenly develop full rounded breasts like Bobby's girlfriend, Nancy Carson, or that I could just so easily go out and buy a pair of Foster Grants. It was very disappointing; I looked the same, felt the same. I was the same but it seemed that all of my friends were changing right there before me. I had a pajama party in celebration of the change that I thought would take place and here we all are, standing around my cake, my cheeks puffed up, ready to blow. I was having a reasonably good time until Bobby told the toilet water story, until I realized that my friends were suddenly looking at Bobby not as Jo's brother but as a male, someone to have a crush on. As it got later, things got worse. In my head, I was singing "It's my party so I'll cry if I want to" because that's what I felt like doing. I felt that I should be able to control what happened, what was said at my own party, but I couldn't. I did not want to hear what Beatrice had to say, that she had made out with Ralph Craig after school, that he had put his hands up her tie dyed shirt (which is what everyone was wearing). I was shocked and found myself mulling over the problem repeatedly. Beatrice had filled out, so had Tricia, Lisa and Cindy. I felt like putting on my bathrobe, hiding; I felt rejected by my friends, by my own body. All of them had engaged in such activities and I wondered if they were transforming because of this or if they engaged because they were changing. I could not bring myself to ask such a question and was not yet ready to engage in such myself, and so after much deliberation, I decided to get a padded bra. Of course, I eventually realized that that was no answer either. The only noticeable change was that I had to wait forever for the bra to dry or it would have sponged wet spots right up through my puckered crepe shirt, which is what everyone wore all through the eighth grade along with Indian moccasins and anything that resembled the American flag. That night when going to sleep beside snoring, semi-sexually active Beatrice, I had no idea what was ahead, all of the things that would reduce worries over padded bras and small breasts into trivial matters. And when I smiled before puffing up my cheeks and closing my eyes to wish for a voluptuous body, a good smile for a good thirteen year old Josie, I was so protected by my ignorance about a lot of things. This is why Andy was able to sit for years, happy as a lark with torn and tattered Huzzy; he did not even know that she was tattered and torn and I did not know that people can get that way without even knowing it.

JUNE 19, 1970

It is hot which is why the American beauty roses in the wreath in this picture are wilting. Just seeing this wreath again makes me smell all sorts of things; gardenias, roses, liquor, B.O. It is not a happy event because my great-uncle Bertram is dead. I do not know Uncle Bertram well and I have never really known him well except to have said "hello" and gotten a dollar the few times that I had seen him. Aunt Lucille (great-aunt and wife of the deceased) is standing beside the wreath. I have always been told that I am a dead ringer for her and people say that this day; they say "dead" ringer which I find in extremely poor taste. Everyone has always called Uncle Bertram a drunk, a crazy, until today and now, he is a fine man, a Saint. He is dead and I begin to see how being dead makes a difference in the way that people feel about you. Of course, then there is a problem with the fact that you don't get to hear it unless of course you're like Huck and happen to stumble upon your own service.

This is right after the burial service and Aunt Lucille has been crying her heart out. "You ripped your Mama wide open," she told me earlier that day. Now, she says that she is hot as hell and wants a gin tonic. It breaks the tension and everyone goes back to Lucille's house (we are staying in a Holiday Inn in Knoxville, Tennessee; if Uncle Bertram hadn't died, I probably never would have seen Tennessee which provides another interesting insight into what happens when people die). Lucille's house is small and she doesn't have central air and so what could have been nice floral fragrances become stifling and gag provoking. Bobby has himself a little drink when no one is looking and Andy is fascinated with the big fat yellow cat that keeps clawing his lily white hands every time he tries to get a pet. I have to go outside and swing so that I can't smell all the various odors and so that I can think about everything that has happened. The first day that I was in Tennessee (yesterday) I saw Uncle Bertram stretched out in his box; he looked blue—not blue like sad, just BLUE—and I had needed to leave the room. There was elevator music playing all around and I couldn't tell where it was coming from and there was a closet full of clothes in the hall that had no backs. It was possible that Uncle Bertram was naked on his underside and I tried to get a picture. It was like turning over a rock and finding moss there; Uncle Bertram's moss was on top. I realized that there was something wrong with that analogy but I didn't have time to think it out.

Aunt Lucille's voice comes through the screen behind my head in shrill "Berties" and I think that I will one day come back to Tennessee when no one has died so that I can fully remember this time when someone has died. Uncle Bertram is getting a lot of mileage out of this and so is Lucille. She loves flowers and I would like to write a poem about how strange funerals are and about how just because I am a dead ringer for Lucille that I will not grow up to be like her or act like her. Dead-red, bled, head, said. As I said, I want some red roses for a blue body. Send them to the deadest man in town. I see by your half-ass outfit that you are a dead man, you see by my outfit that I am not dead. Looking back, I realize that I learned a very valuable lesson: Don't look a dead man in the face. But it also led to many disturbing questions. For instance, if Bertram went to sleep like the preacher said, did his whole body go fuzzy like when your foot falls asleep? Did he turn blue like when you swing your legs without letting them hit the ground? Did he die in an orgasmic way? An organic orgasmic? The questions plagued me for a long time and even now, I have questions. Even now, I am intrigued by the thought of preservation and memory. When I hear "Bertram" the picture that I always see is the very last time that I saw him—in the casket, dead and stiff, an old man. Even though I can conjure up other pictures of him, slight memories, old photographs, that last picture is always in my memory. When I think of Lucille, now, it's the same way and it's interesting because she was born in 1900, the same year as Thomas Wolfe, yet Wolfe will always bring to mind a picture of that large somewhat handsome thirty-eight year old with his dark hair pushed back, and Lucille will always bring to mind a picture of a seventy-four year old shriveled bitchy woman with age spots on her wrinkled cheeks, yet they are the same age. Or does death change things like that? Bertram is the first to go of the three people that I know who are dead. Or is it four people? Bertram is the first to go of the three or four people that I know who are dead. The red roses of the blue body in this picture are repulsive just as they are in a future picture of Lucille's flowers, the second person that I have known who has died. I didn't go to her funeral for fear that I would be a "dead ringer" for the dead person. I don't even know who took these pictures, his and hers dead wreaths. It was a sick gesture and I see no humor in it at all.

SEPTEMBER 12, 1970

I am in the eighth grade and this is my first time cheering for the junior high team. I am wearing a cute little yellow and white suit just like the other ten yellow and white suits cheering with me. Beatrice did not make cheerleading, and it seems now that that could have been a dramatic turning point in her life. Here, she is being a good sport because she is wearing yellow stretch pants, a white turtleneck and a wildcat mask. She volunteered on her own to be our mascot and everyone agreed, knowing that she felt totally left out. As a matter of fact, the only way that she even got in the picture is because Bobby took this picture of me and I was on an end of the line because I was so short. That is where Beatrice was supposed to stand—at the very end. I remember a lot about that day. I remember feeling so proud when I looked over and saw Bobby standing with a bunch of his high school friends. I remember thinking how very All American he was, as All American as Wally Cleaver on "Leave It to Beaver." I remember seeing Mark Fuller with a "Kiss My Patch" patch on the ass of his filthy (not even Levi) jeans, and I felt confused because I realized that Beatrice was quite smitten with Mark Fuller's disgusting appearance. It made me realize that Beatrice had changed; that she did not pull her wagon so much as she got taken for rides. I realized that we no longer had as much in common as when she was so mesmerized by her fingerpainting hands and I was so faithful to my old lady suit. Beatrice could not think the same without her paints but I could think the same without my robe. I thought that we were all like trees, flexible youths, saplings, who grow up heavy and stiff, spread seeds and get chopped down and turned into notebook paper. I remember everything about that day because it was all so important. It was the day that Beatrice decided that she was in love with Mark Fuller ("as long as you don't still like him," she had said). It was the first time that anyone had ever been smitten with me (that I knew of). His name was Pat Reeves and he was a runner for the high school track team, very smart and a Bobby/Wally Cleaver carbon. I remember it all: losing the game 28–0, Beatrice running around awkwardly trying to get Mark Fuller's attention, Pat Reeves watching me, smiling at me, coming up after the game and introducing himself, walking me across the parking lot to where my mother was waiting in that old green station wagon. I can see his face so clearly, those wide hazel eyes fringed with long dark lashes (if he had been a girl, he never would have needed mascara) and straight dark hair, a wisp of which he used to have to wet down so that it didn't stick straight out (a little detail that always made me want to call him Alfalfa). He was always so calm as though everything he said or did was very controlled, in slow motion. Yes, I remember it all, and in the far corner of my mind, of the picture, there is a blue-gray almost autumn afternoon, a boy with thick red hair throwing a javelin in the clear field at the end of the school, spindly pine trees swaying over the top of the field house, their roots hidden by a building full of helmets and jock straps.

OCTOBER 31, 1971

This picture is dark because it was taken outside at night. We are all at Beatrice's house for a Halloween party. Nobody even dressed up; it was not a fun party.

I am sitting on a trashcan, away from the garage where everyone else is making out. Pat Reeves is beside me as he had been for over a year, and we still had a lot to talk about. We talked about poetry or the movies that we had seen, our childhoods, families. Being with Pat was comfortable because it was like being with Bobby. But, it seemed to me that something was missing, that I was at a dead end, missing out on the excitement that everyone else claimed to have. That's why out of the blue I decided to break up with Pat Reeves. That's why I spent most of the night staring at Howard who is the tall guy with curly hair smoking a cigarette and drinking a beer. He was in the eleventh grade and known as a "lady's man." I was impressed by this. Why the hell I don't know, but I was impressed, and I stared at him all night long, even before I broke up with Pat, even after Pat asked me "why?," looked back and forth from me to Howard who was talking to Lisa, looked out at that little spark of fire in the yard where Beatrice and Mark Fuller were smoking a joint, and then turned and walked away so slow motioned without saying a word. I didn't even feel sorry for him, just for myself.

JANUARY '72

Here, I should feel like something in my Jay Vee cheering suit. I'm in front of the bleachers kicking my legs and yelling "boogie woogie, right on, right on," but I didn't feel like anything. I felt like nothing. I wanted to lie down on the court and blend with the lines, get stomped.

48

At this time I had very mixed feelings about everything which made it difficult to concentrate on anything. I was a xeroxed either/or. All the time, an either/or. Either a cheerleader representing my school as fine moral fiber Or Howard's girlfriend and managing to fake my way through all the parties with an occasional "wow man" or "cool." I had not heard of *The Feminine Mystique* at that time and it is a blessing or things would have been complicated. My salvation was to look at all the people in the stands and to think how they all had lives and how they would go home to their own homes, sleep in their own beds. They were like ants or the amoebae that I had seen sliding around in biology, looking like everyone else but not being anyone else. It took a great deal of thought and it was a secret thought, the kind that could keep me safe.

JUNE '72

This is Bobby in his graduation robe. He looks very distinguished and we are all very proud of him. Nancy Carson is all scrunched up beside him smiling. Everyone thought she looked so pretty that night, except me. I thought she looked somewhat whorish in that tight red dress. Howard is in the background, slumped on the couch, and it looks like he is staring at Nancy's chest. "Howard is a doll" all of my friends said except for Pat Reeves who would not even talk to me. But Howard was not a doll and I had discerned this long before; I knew that very night with him slumped there, his hair falling in his eyes, that he was not the one for me, yet, I made no effort to do anything about it. It was perfectly obvious that I had no future with such a person, a person who was very popular in school, but a person who used double negatives constantly, a person who had shoplifted a radio. He did those kinds of things, things that Bobby or Pat Reeves never would have done. This is a good picture of Bobby, though, except for the fact that Nancy Carson should have been cut away, especially since she broke up with him just two days after the picture was made. He locked himself in his room for the entire night. He did not even come out when I went to his door and told him that Marcus Welby was on. We watched that show together every single Tuesday night and that is why it took years before I could forgive Nancy Carson that one.

JULY '72

This is Andy out in the backyard. He has big scabs on both knees and is dripping with water and mud. He had tried to make a slip and slide in our backyard by hoeing up the grass and wetting the dirt. It didn't work very well and right after Bobby took this picture, Andy got the worst whipping that I can ever remember him getting. It seems to me that Andy always had big scabs and even now, I expect to see Band-Aids on his arms and legs. Of course, that's ridiculous because he has changed since his slip and slide days. Bobby had to replant the grass and he was so quiet, that day and all summer. I knew it was either Nancy, or the thought of going off to school, but he shouldn't have been upset, ever, not Bobby.

AUGUST '72

I feel very scared without Bobby. We are on our way home from taking him to school and Andy and I are standing in front of a Tastee Freeze. Andy has a huge milkshake so that he will have to stop every five miles to pee but I only drink a small Coke because I am so very upset that Bobby is gone. I feel like he's gone forever and I realize for the first time that I love that dark haired creature who used to stand at the end of my crib more than I have ever loved anyone. It makes me see just how little I love Howard even though I've told him twice that I do. All I can think about is Bobby's face, kind of white like he wanted to cry but not crying just like the summer when he busted his head wide open at Moon Lake. I had cried then, too, but not Bobby, not Wally Cleaver, and I wonder why I don't love a nice boy, a smart boy who plays sports and keeps his hair clean and short like Pat Reeves. I think about Pat Reeves the rest of the way home and seeing the way the sun hits that Tastee Freeze sign makes me remember a very important thought: "One day, I will really fall in love," I think and by then it is dark.

FALL '72

It is hard to remember exact dates now because everything starts going real fast. I'm in the tenth grade, a cheerleader, honor roll student and for some reason, I still date Howard. Here we are after the Homecoming dance and we are in my living room kissing which is what we have in common. Mama leaves us alone after she takes this picture of us, me with my funeral mum corsage, and Howard tells me that my face looks like the inside of a kaleidoscope. This hurts my feelings greatly because I know that he must think that I'm very unattractive. Then he explains to me that the reason is because he does drugs. This makes me feel much better because I realize that it is his fault and not mine that my face looks screwy. I try to reform Howard by giving him a book called *Getting High on Life*. He says that is stupid, that he loves flowers and trees and me. He wants to touch my padded bra but I don't let him. I tell him that he should only take drugs if he's sick. He says I don't know where he's coming from, he wants nature to be intensified, he says that nobody is a virgin anymore. He says I am a nobody in so many words and this upsets me more because I am not ready to be exposed; I am too young to be exposed and so I must do a difficult thing; I must let Howard have his freedom, I must thrust him into that field that people play, where they sow oats.

I shouldn't have been upset about Howard because I knew that last night when he held my hand that things were not the same. You can tell a lot by holding hands; it is much more intimate than those parts which serve no other purpose except sexual functions. Those parts just sit around waiting for something to happen but your hands do everything. Somebody told me once that I couldn't talk if my hands were tied behind my back and that's probably true because I use them constantly. I don't just mean to do the little quote signs that a reformed hoodlum turned preacher did once in church when he said "crap" and "screw" to shock the congregation. I mean to kind of show each syllable, comma and period. When someone holds my hand I feel like they are holding on to everything that I've ever said or ever will say. If Howard felt any words that last night, they were in a different language; a colorful "groovy" language that I did not know nor have any desire to learn. It just wasn't right, not the way that I remembered holding hands with Jeff Johnson in front of the Quick Stop.

Howard had said that I was a virgin, a nobody and this truly infuriated me. I wanted to be "good" and "nice." I wanted to be somebody. Mary was a virgin and she was somebody famous but this made things worse. I had never really understood how all that happened, how Joseph had been such an understanding gentleman about the whole thing. It was just one of those questions without an answer, the kind that must be accepted. What I couldn't accept was ME and what I had in common with HER. Mary was chosen because she was so good and I needed to think of something fast because Jesus was supposed to come back and if there really weren't ANY virgins (as Howard had said) to choose from, I might be a possible choice. No, I had to do something. That's why I started smoking Salem cigarettes in my bathroom late at night, fanning towels and spraying deodorant so that no one would know. It was a bad thing to do and since I hid it from the world, that made me a lying hypocrite and that was even better. I could be both good and bad.

SPRING '73

The spring goes even faster than the fall. Pat Reeves has come back to me and we do nice things like go to the movies and play tennis. I am not in love with him but I am a May Court sponsor along with Tricia, Cindy and Lisa. I smoke cigarettes in front of them and say "damn" and "shit" a lot. This keeps me "in" without exposing myself. I make excellent grades and I am very fit. I am so fit that I buy an itsy bitsy teeny weeny chartreuse polka dot bikini for the summer that comes so fast it makes my head spin.

SPRING '74

I'm spinning, spinning like a top. My how time flies when you're so much fun!! Again, I am a May Court sponsor! Again, I am so "in." I am still completely unexposed and no one even knows this except me. They don't realize that in being identical to them that I am so unique, that I am merely using this as a disguise. It is such a way to stay fit, to survive! Beatrice is no longer even a little bit fit; she is a misfit and that must be where the word comes from, misfit, one who is not in shape, one not fit enough to survive among the rest, as a part of the rest. I am not even sorry that Pat Reeves, my loyal standby, is going to graduate and go away to school. Why, there are so many fish out swimming around all night with their eyes open, just waiting for me to throw my bait!

This picture has a date, July 7, 1974; however, I choose to simply call it Summer '74, because it could be any day, every day of that summer, when we would all go down to Moon Lake to lie out in the sun. Tricia, Cindy, Lisa and I are sitting on colorful towels at the end of a pier, and it makes me remember so many things, our bodies greased with Hawaiian Tropic, the smell of a banana and coconut blend. On the pier to our right when facing the lake (though they are not in this picture) were the college people, the All American bronzed beauties of Bobby's class, destined for fame, fortune, MBAs. To our left, at the far end of the lake, was a dock where the water was dark and slimy, where (as Blue Springs reputations went) dark and slimy people hung out. That end of the lake was shady and none of those people ever sunned; they all wore long jeans and long hair in spite of our swampy summers. I remember thinking how odd to see Beatrice at that end of the lake instead of with us, in the middle.

I liked to lie on my stomach and pull my towel up to my neck so that I could see through a crack in the pier down to the cool green water. It seemed so small that way, just a crack, and the surrounding voices would evaporate just like the water on my legs and I felt alone just as I had years before in my bathrobe. It was nice feeling small, detached, like I had escaped being similar to so many people, like I was not in the limelight of Blue Springs High which I most definitely was: chief cheerleader for the coming year, National Honor Society, a May Court representative for two years; the list went on and on, all of the good things of all the best years of my life, something like Gidget goes to Moon Lake. Yet, something was odd; something in the curve of the horizon that was blocked from my sight by the row of pine trees, by the very way that the world moved, not letting me see what was beyond. There was a time when such a sight would have brought to mind Christopher Columbus and the story of how he held an orange and watched a butterfly creep up the side, appearing slowly like the sails of a ship on the horizon, but it seems that then, I had other things on my mind. I remember thinking the words "All I could see from where I stood were three long mountains and a wood" and I couldn't believe that Edna St. Vincent Millay had written that when she was just a little older than I was then, the thought that someone so young would have had the power to describe something as big as a rebirth. Sometimes when I was lying there, I would get an almost sexless feeling. It wasn't that I wasn't feminine because I was (though never the frilly type) and it wasn't that I was masculine even though I was quite athletic and prided myself on being so. There was no reason for this feeling; I wasn't beautiful like Tricia but I wasn't unattractive. I was the one that always managed to merit "cute" which is really a half-assed thing to say about someone, though superior to ugly. It was a nothing feeling that seemed to spread over me: not feminine, not masculine, not heterosexual, homosexual, bisexual, not penis envy or any other such shit. No, it was sexless, asexual, like the tiny amoebae that I had seen under the microscope in biology, sliding, changing, splitting, totally independent, a single organism and yet, identical to the other millions. Was there an original somewhere in that green cool water where a population greater than the world fed and bred? It was such a big thought, something to hold onto, that all of the days seemed the same. This picture is a picture of every day of the summer of 1974.

LOOSE SHOTS

It goes faster and faster once summer ends. Here I am in my Varsity cheering suit. There is a big hairy arm around my waist but I have cut away the person that this hand belongs to. Here I am again at Christmas in my brand new coat and again there is an obstrusive hairy arm. What is that story about the hairy buried arm? Here, I am the May Queen. Finally, I wear the crown, a tin foil looking crown and I am wearing a strapless dress with a tulle skirt. Pat Reeves is behind me and he has not changed one bit, though I look different, something is different. The theme of the dance was something ridiculous like "Venus and Mars Are All Right Tonight" (you know, the Paul McCartney song) and there are these tacky chicken wire planets hanging all around. Here, I am in front of my college dorm that late summer day when my parents left me there and it almost doesn't look like me at all. My hair is long, longer than it has ever been, and I don't look as fit as I have before. I'm not even looking at the camera. I am looking at my hands like a complete fool, but pictures get that way, old and strange, some of them total misrepresentations of the given moment.

Even when we are beyond a change and can see it, there
remain parts that are unaltered and maybe for just a second or maybe forever we will get that same feeling that
we felt at that given point even though we know what is
to come. Didn't Marcel Proust on one depressing winter
day spoon a morsel of cake to his mouth and find a youthful pleasure even though that pleasure will move toward
youthful pain and eventually back to that cold depressing
day? Why do we often forget what we know of a past
future? Why was I always so frightened by the flying
monkeys in the Wizard of Oz even when I knew year
after year that Dorothy would be just fine, that it was all
a dream? Why, even after I discovered that they were
West Point cadets, servants of the U.S. of A.'s military
flying incognito, did those monkeys make me so damn
nervous? I feared for the lives of Lassie, Roy Rogers, Sky
King even though I knew full well that they would be
back the next week. Why am I always so hopeful when
Lana Turner returns (the mysterious Madame X) and
John Forsythe's eyes light up in the courtroom; the young
attorney (her son) is representing her in his first case and
he sees her only as the social zero from skid row which

she has now become? Why am I so hopeful when I know she is going to die and her son will never know that she is his mother? Why do I cry every single time that happens and why do I always hope that Natalie Wood will return from her sanitorium in Splendor in the Grass and find that Warren Beatty is *not* married and that they will resume as though nothing had ever happened? Am I ignorant or is it IGNOREance? How can Guy de Maupassant rip my gut out every single time I read "The Necklace" and why do I expect to read it just once and the words will have changed and the pitiful victim will discover that the necklace is paste before she works her ass off for the rest of her life to replace it? Why is irony so ironic? Why do I so often want to reconstruct my life, pretending that parts had never happened, wanting to go back to a time that seemed better. Why, even now, do I feel a sentimental stirring when I recall the summer before my senior year even though I know what is to come? It is a home movie, a romance, a horror film, playing in my head for free over and over. It begins slowly, as slow as that lazy summer where it begins.

His name was Claude Williams but everyone called him Big Red, I suppose because he was both of those, and too, a name like Claude never could have done him justice. He was not handsome in that perfect chiseled feature way that Tricia found so attractive, nor did he have that "Then Came Bronson" ruggedness that Lisa was so enthralled with. He did not have that boyish All American appeal that I admired so in Bobby, either. Red Williams was different and I was immediately attracted to his disheveled dark auburn hair, the thick irregular waves that stayed even when his hair was wet, his broad erect shoulders, the bleached hairs that covered his chest and long muscular legs, the large brown eyes that seemed oddly misplaced, too soft for his other features. I noticed him the very first day of summer vacation when Tricia, Lisa, Cindy and I went to Moon Lake to sun and swim, and I knew with that first glance that he was different from anyone that I had ever met.

The day itself was perfect, a blue cloudless day; there was a full turn-out of the college students who had returned to Blue Springs for the summer (another reason for our being there), and summer itself was a long lazy stretch in front of us, promising days just like that one, leading to our long awaited senior year.

"Let's get as close as we can to the college people," Tricia whispered as soon as we got there. She had waited weeks to see Tom Fulton again, a guy from Bobby's class who was now a Phi Delt at Carolina, a perfect face person whom Tricia had, in a spontaneous intoxicated moment, kissed at a Christmas party. We had all heard the story numerous times and were perfectly willing to go along with her. "I see him, he's here," she whispered.

"Let's just walk on over," Lisa said all too loudly and pulled her shirt over her head to expose a tight black bikini that made her rounded hips and full thighs look even whiter. "You like my new suit?" She did a turn, her shirt thrown over her shoulder. This brought a few whistles from the pier where the older people were set up but none of us had the nerve to look over and see who had whistled.

"God, make her stop," Tricia hissed and looked at me as if I could control Lisa; no one could control Lisa.

"You wanted to be noticed." Lisa laughed and waved her hand as a thank-you to whoever had whistled. "Look, Jo's brother is over there. We can say that we've come to talk to him."

"He'd kill me," I said which probably wasn't true, but I had to do something on Tricia's behalf, who by then had her head turned in the opposite direction and was walking towards a small empty pier close by. Cindy was right behind her and I waited uncomfortably while Lisa took her time rearranging the thin straps that supported her top heavy top. "Come on," I said and also looked in the other direction, towards the shady end of the lake where Beatrice and another girl from our class whom I vaguely knew, were stretched out on the hood of a car listening to a blast of hard rock. It startled me to see Beatrice down there in her tight jeans and tee shirt because I still always expected her to be with us, though that had all changed. I was startled more by whom she was talking to, bright green beach britches, the only person at that end of the lake with any skin showing. I wanted him to turn around.

"I don't know why Tricia gets so upset," Lisa said and waited for me to say something which I did not. "She wanted Tom to see her, didn't she?" I just shrugged and we walked on. For all I knew it would be one of those unbearable days where Tricia and Lisa weren't speaking and Cindy and I were caught in the middle. Tricia was already oiled up and leaned back with her eyes closed, and as I sat on my towel and waited for one of them to speak, I looked back towards the shady end. He was still there, hands on his hips, lifting his feet up and down as if he were walking in place. In the other direction was the college crew. Bobby was there, already tan, drinking beer, listening to the Beach Boys, and to my dismay, talking to Nancy Carson.

"Hey Tricia, wait'll you see what I've got," Lisa finally said and reached into her beach bag.

"Probably V.D.," Tricia mumbled and opened one eye.

"Oh, be serious. Voilà!" Lisa pulled out two cans of beer and handed one to Tricia. "They're a little hot but it's better than nothing."

"Thanks, where'd you get these?" Tricia sat up and opened her can. The silence was over.

"From home."

"You're going to get caught again," Cindy said and started coating herself with suntan lotion.

"Won't be the first time." Lisa took a big swallow. "Besides, I only took three. You don't drink and we know that the chief cheerleader isn't going to drink."

"That isn't why I don't," I said. "Tricia's a cheerleader, too. I smoke and that's against the rules."

"Aren't you the daring one?" Lisa asked and laughed.

She maintained that she had outgrown cheerleading, that she would rather be sitting in the stands with a date.

"Well, nobody ever even asks me if I want a beer," Cindy said. "I'm a cheerleader and I want to drink." She held out her hand and Lisa reached back into her bag. "You won't say anything will you, Jo?" Cindy sat staring at me, either waiting for me to answer or waiting to take that first swallow.

"Of course I wouldn't," I said and lit a cigarette. Now, he was sitting in the car, his leg sticking out of the open door. "I'm tired of being treated like a goody-goody," I said.

"Oh, I didn't mean it, Jo." Lisa reached back into her bag. "You know I think it's great you got chief. Look! I brought this just for our entertainment." She pulled out a *True Confessions* magazine and stretched out on her stomach. "It's hilarious."

I had just settled down to listen to Lisa's reading, preferring that to her cheerleader jokes or when she gave real true confessions, when I saw him again. He was jogging along the shore, turning to yell and wave to those at the shady end, where there was still a blast of hard rock and faint traces of pot when the wind picked up. Then he ran towards Bobby's crew where he was greeted by several loud yells. It was so strange to see someone who seemed to fit in with the distinctly different groups, but obviously he did, and I was impressed by that. I suppose I was staring and did not even realize it until Lisa interrupted me.

"I didn't buy this for nothing," she said and put her

hands on her hips. "I want total participation. The plot is difficult so pay attention." We all, for some reason, found that hysterical and got ready for the story. I angled myself so that if he decided to make another run, I wouldn't miss it.

"This is called 'Why I Can't Settle for Just One Man,'" she read and held up a picture for us to see, a woman in a leopard suit with about twenty hands reaching for her. "Jo, who are you looking for?"

"No one, just wanted to see what Bobby was doing."

"A likely story." Tricia sat on her towel and carefully positioned her long, already tan, legs, one knee up and the other leg stretched out model style. "She's waiting for Pat Reeves to get here."

"Really, Jo?" Cindy rolled over. Already the freckles were popping out on her nose.

"Hell no!" I said, attempting forcefulness, so that they would not start with the Pat Reeves teasing again. They all found it hysterical that Pat Reeves and I had dated for over a year and had never made out, just quick kisses at the door after a date. Lisa enjoyed that subject more than cheerleading. "I told him that I didn't want to see him any more." I hadn't told him that, yet, but I was going to.

"What did he say?" Now, Cindy had her hands cupped over her face to shield the sun.

"He said that he was relieved that she finally knew that he was a queer." Lisa shifted around and moved into the center of the group. "Now listen to this, 'I am a love starved woman.'"

"Quiet," Tricia hissed. "Don't read to everyone here.

I would die if anyone knew what we were doing!" She slung her head towards the older crew. "They might think we're serious."

"It's very serious," Lisa said and continued about this woman who got raped when she was working as a waitress at a truck stop. She did not tell her hayseed fiancé or the police because secretly, it was the most rewarding experience of her life. The scene was vivid with lots of panting and moaning and Lisa was reading more and more dramatically, hand to her chest then a wiggle of the hips.

"This is really Lisa's life story." Tricia flopped back on her forearms and tilted her face directly into the sun.

"Don't knock it til you've tried it," Lisa said.

"And who says I haven't?" Tricia just smiled and this brought Cindy's face from beneath her shirt that she had covered up with.

"So tell it then," Lisa said. "Was it that jerk you met at the beach? Was it Tom Fulton in the flesh?"

"I better wait for you to get a little older, Lisa." They bantered back and forth for awhile, bordering on their real true confessions, and then Lisa went back to her reading. The crux of the story was that this lily white totally innocent country bumpkin virgin thoroughly enjoyed the abuse that she received from the dark foreign trucker. I had just lifted my head to ask Lisa to please take a break, when I saw him again. He was walking that time, digging his toes into the sand, and then he turned and entered the water right near where we were. It was then that I noticed the hairs on his chest and his legs, noticed that his eyes were brown, that he had a full bottom lip that made him look like he was sulking. There was a moment when he looked directly at me, or I thought he did and it made me look away. Then, in that split second, he was under the water and all I could spot was his bright green bathing suit. Lisa was still reading and I turned back over on my stomach so that I could watch him. He was a graceful swimmer, long steady strokes, his arms clearing the water, his head turning for a breath in perfect rhythm. He was swimming out to the center of the lake to the tower where people went to dive or to escape the crowded piers.

"Her breasts exploded, heaving mounds of flesh." Lisa thrust out her own and panted. By then, he was at the tower, shaking his head. He sat on the edge with his feet in the water. It looked like he was staring over at our pier and I stared back.

"Jo Spencer, how can you not laugh at 'exploding breasts'?" Lisa yelled. "Have you ever in your life seen a boob explode?"

"How could she?" Tricia laughed and slapped me on the back. "She doesn't have any."

"Well, the trucker's loins are throbbing," Lisa said and held her hand to her mouth like a microphone. "Tell us, have you ever seen throbbing loins?"

"No," I said and without even thinking of the teasing that may be ahead, I continued. "Who is that guy over there?" I realized then that I was setting myself up. "I can't figure out where I've seen him before."

"Pardon me, but haven't we met somewhere before?" Lisa was still speaking into her fist. "Wasn't it you whose loins throbbed when my breasts exploded?"

"I can't believe it." Tricia shielded her eyes and looked over at the tower. He was standing with his back to us, looking out to the other side of the lake where there was a row of homes. "Jo has actually seen a guy. This girl who always asks 'who' when we see goodlooking guys."

"The space queen has landed," Lisa said and waved her arms. "Ahoy, stranger!" Luckily his back was still turned.

"I think his name is Red," Cindy said, at last, a serious answer.

"Red Williams," Tricia said. "My God, don't you notice anything? He graduated with your brother."

"Well, that's probably how I've seen him before."

"That and the fact that he was All State track and has throbbing loins." Lisa threw her magazine onto my towel. "You better read this and if you have any questions, just ask."

"Give it to Cindy when you're through," Tricia said but Cindy was already back beneath her shirt and was too lazy to give any more of a response other than, "bull."

"So you do want the scoop on Red Williams?" Lisa asked and I shrugged. "You have to say yes or no."

"I guess," I said. "You won't be happy until you tell it."

"In a nutshell." She started with the microphone bit again. "He's a runner; his real name is Claude; used to go with Snot Queen, Buffy Paige, and rumor has it that the affair ended when Buffy went to visit her aunt in New York to get rid of Little Red."

"I don't think that's true," Tricia said.

"Well, still," Lisa continued, "he has a devious reputation in that sense."

"What sense?" Cindy mumbled.

"In the sense of making breasts explode, singly, jointly, repeatedly." By that time, he was back in the water and swimming towards the older group, where Bobby I noticed was still talking to Nancy Carson. I hoped that Lisa would shut up but she was on a roll. "Buffy Paige has got the kind that explode regularly. Look, Jo, there he is."

"All I asked was who he was," I said. "I'll never ask again."

"Come on," Tricia said, finally getting a serious tone in her voice, "you asked because you think he's cute, right?"

"Right?" Lisa repeated.

"Right," I said finally to which Lisa clapped her hands, and for the first time all day, shut up.

Then he was gone, up through the trees, a lingering "See ya, Red," trailing behind him. The rest of the afternoon, I waited for him to come back, saying that I didn't have enough sun though my shoulders and nose were already touchy. Cindy, by then, was completely wrapped in her towel so that no skin was exposed, and Lisa, who, thank God, was on the last story, was unable to use her hips for dramatic effect because they had gone from snow white to lobster red. Tricia had merely tanned a shade darker, and since several of the college guys were still around, she wanted to stay, too. That night I was somewhat sorry, as I coated layer after layer of Noxema on my nose and shoulders, but not so sorry that I would dare miss going to Moon Lake the next day or any day. I invested in a large supply of sunscreen, deciding that Red Williams was worth it.

There were very few days that we did not go to the lake. We were there when it was overcast or chilly. Some days, we were the only people there except for those at the other end of the lake, for whom good weather was not a factor. The only days that we missed, as a matter of fact, were those when it was raining and then we spent the afternoons riding around in Tricia's car, smoking cigarettes, and talking about who had been at the lake the day before. During this time, I had learned several other things about Red. He worked construction off and on; he lived right on the lake all year in this little cabin that his parents owned. On Saturday mornings, he worked part-time as a mechanic at K-Mart Auto Center. Tricia would circle the auto center often, and I would hide in the floorboard, knowing that if he ever saw us he would know how I felt about him. I knew every page number where he appeared in all of Bobby's old annuals, and he had even signed the senior one, on the page with the picture of the track team. "To one helluva guy. Take it easy with Fancy Nancy. Knock 'em dead at Wake Forest. Red" I must have read that a hundred times, over and over, the long thin irregular letters, the curl on the "d" at the end of Red.

For one whole month, I had watched Red, some days disappointed by the fact that he did not show, other days, disappointed when he talked to Buffy Paige or one of the other older girls. There had even been days when I felt a twinge of jealousy when I saw him at the shady end of the lake talking to Beatrice or one of the others in their tight jeans and tee shirts, their heads wrapped in bandanas. But then, there had been the good days, those days when I was certain that he was watching me, certain that all I had to do was smile or lift my hand and he would acknowledge my presence. Of course, I never did that, I suppose out of fear that he wouldn't respond, that it would turn out that he was not looking at me at all but someone just past me, or Tricia or Lisa. It was during one of his daily jogs between the two worlds when he stopped and introduced himself. I had fallen asleep and was quickly awakened by the shaking of the pier and by Tricia's flirt laugh which was quite recognizable to all but a large percentage of the male population.

"You girls having fun?" he asked and it was funny because his voice was not nearly as deep as I had imagined.

"Just catching some rays," Lisa said and looked at me. She immediately went into action. "I'm Lisa and this is Tricia, Cindy and Jo." I opened one eye and nodded, certain that my face was getting redder.

"Yeah, you're Bobby's sister, right?" I was dumb-founded that he actually knew who I was. Tricia and Lisa were staring at each other and I could tell, were trying very hard not to laugh. Cindy remained very calm but kept trying to catch my eye so that, had I given her the chance, she would have either winked or mouthed something like "go for it." I just nodded and stared over at the row of pine trees. "Bobby's a good friend of mine. Real good guy."

"Thanks," I said and it didn't sound like my voice at all. It was that high squeak that I always heard when I taped myself on a tape recorder.

"Going back to Wake Forest?"

"Yeah," I looked up and his eyes were darker than I had ever imagined. I had to look away.

"He always was the smart one." Red walked closer and sat right beside where I was lying and dangled his long legs off of the pier. "What's he studying? He was here at the first of the summer and I haven't seen him lately." Tricia was laughing again and I didn't know why. I started getting uncomfortable, afraid that my suit was riding up my crack or something. "Let's swim," Cindy said and Tricia and Lisa immediately went along with her, leaving me alone with him.

"He wants to go to med school." I sat up so that he wouldn't be so close to me, just in case my suit was riding. "He's working in Winston-Salem."

"Oh yeah, Nancy told me that." He had talked to Nancy; maybe he had talked to her about Buffy; maybe there was still something going on, maybe there really had been a Little Red. "Why'd you wrinkle up your nose? Taking up for big brother against the wicked ex-girlfriend?" He caught my nose between his big fingers like he was stealing it, like old men do to little children. "Is that it?"

"No, not really." I kept getting a picture of Red and Buffy Paige in one of those loin throbbing, breast explod-ing, scenes and it made me even more uncomfortable.

"You're here every day, but I never see you at night."

"We just come to sun." Cindy, Tricia and Lisa were way out in the lake by then and I almost wished that they would come back. He was staring at me, the fuzz on the tops of my thighs, my unpadded bathing suit. He laughed and his eyes narrowed into slits like laser beams that went right through my suit.

"Yeah, I've seen you diving. You're pretty good."

"I like to dive." I looked away like I was embarrassed and maybe I was but I realized that I had been right; he had been watching me and I had felt it every single day during that slow motioned minute when I spiraled from the tower before I disappeared into the water.

"Let's swim out there." He jumped in and the water was just up to his waist. "Come on." He started splash-ing all around me and I had the oddest feeling. I wanted to go but I didn't. I wanted him to freeze, to stay right there, but I wanted him to leave so that I could think through it all and figure out just what I was supposed to do. Finally, I did the only thing that I could do; I slid in feet first.

We swam side by side and everytime that I switched

strokes, he was right there beside me, doing the breast-stroke, his head up above the water, watching me. "By the way, my name's Red," he said one of those times.

"But really it's Claude." It surprised me that I said that. I immediately thought that he may be self-conscious about his name, that maybe I had made him angry. My philosophy of life delivered by Bambi: If you can't say anything nice, don't say anything at all. I shouldn't have said anything at all so I did freestyle with my face in the water and when I turned to get a breath, he was laughing, or maybe it was a distant motor boat, or maybe it was in my head.

There was no one else at the tower and I was both sorry and relieved. Sorry, because if some of the boys from my class had been there, they would have laughed and joked and asked me to dive with them and Red would've seen what a likable person I was. Too, I was afraid to be alone with him. I was relieved only because Red might have thought the boys in my class were silly and then he would have been reminded of the age difference. I couldn't think of one thing to say. How did Tricia and Lisa do it so well?

"Let's sit here a minute and rest." He sat on the edge of the lower level. I had already started up the ladder but came back down and sat beside him. Tricia, Cindy and Lisa were already back on the pier and from that distance, they looked like small children. I couldn't see their faces but I knew what they were doing. They were watching me, talking about me, and it made me as uncomfortable as when Red scooped water into his hand and sprin-kled my face. Then he did the same thing to my legs and just watched the water bead up from the oil that I had put on and slide down. "You're not shy are you?" he asked and looked at me so hard with those laser eyes that I had to look away and shrug.

"You know I've been watching you all summer." He laughed and slapped me on the back and then didn't move his hand. I had heard of such moves, had even en-countered them with Howard but that time was different.

"I knew," I said. "I've been watching you, too." I had to look at him with that honest statement. Soon, I felt just as I had years ago when I told Jeff Johnson all about Co-lumbus in front of the Quick Stop. I wanted to tell Red how I liked to read Millay and Dickinson, how the best feeling in the world was the one that I got when I played old sad songs and thought, how I was intrigued by the fact that every hair has its very own follicle. It seemed that it was happening, that I was falling in love, that I could tell him anything, but I had to be sure, had to see what he was going to say.

"So you're going to be a senior?"

"How did you know?"

"I find out what I want to know." He moved his hand across my back until it was on my other shoulder. "You don't have a boyfriend, do you?"

"No, do you have a girlfriend?" I wanted to ask about Buffy but decided that would have to wait, too.

"No." He laughed again and rubbed his hand up and

down my arm. I felt like my whole body had gone numb like when my foot falls asleep. "I have lots of friends that are girls but not a girlfriend."

"I thought you did."

"Thought wrong." He kicked his feet. "I thought you might still like Pat Reeves. Used to see you playing tennis with him all the time."

"We're just friends," I said and I wanted to ask him when he had seen me, the exact days, but then I didn't feel like talking about Pat.

"He's a pretty good runner, nice guy. He always talks about you like you're his girlfriend, like he's crazy about you." Suddenly it dawned on me that maybe Red wasn't interested, maybe he was out there with me only to promote Pat Reeves.

"Well, he's not. He's never been my boyfriend," I said and I couldn't believe that Pat would have ever made it sound like he was my boyfriend; we just dated. He had never even really kissed me, just slight brushes against my cheek or mouth. And Pat had never mentioned that he knew Red Williams; all Pat talked about was going off to school, to Duke no less, and most of the time when others were around, he acted like I wasn't even present; he pretended that he wasn't crazy about me, though he was.

"So, tell me about you," Red said and it made me jump to realize that I had been sitting there thinking in front of him.

"What do you want to know?"

"Well, what do you like?"

"I don't know." I wanted to jump in and swim away.

"Bet you're a cheerleader."

"Yeah."

"Smart like Big Bobby."

I shrugged because that's what people always asked me and teachers seemed to expect it of me. Bobby was very smart, the scholarly type, and I had learned that if I said nothing at all that people would merely assume that I was the same kind of smart.

"Tell me about you," I said and he did. Talking wasn't a problem for him just like running back and forth. I admired that. His parents were from Blue Springs and he had always lived there. He was an only child and had moved down to Moon Lake right after his graduation. He thought that eventually he would go to school but for the time being, liked things as they were.

The things that he talked about didn't really interest me, yet, I was perfectly content to sit and listen, to watch him. He talked about running and how good it was for the respiratory system, how he liked the tired feeling that he got after running or after working a day of construction, how he loved to work on cars but didn't want to be an assistant mechanic all of his life. He wanted to save money, maybe go to school, maybe one day own his own garage and just run things. Then again, he didn't want to rush getting old because he liked living at Moon Lake and there were so many things that he wanted to do; he wanted to spend a full summer hiking on the Appalachian Trail; he wanted to learn how to play an electric guitar because he was really into hard rock. He was a perfect blend between Bobby and those carefree people at the other end of the lake. I wanted to tell him that I had never been into hard rock and had stopped pretending that I was when I stopped pretending that I liked my red, white and blue pants. I could have said it was just like pocketbooks and sunglasses. I wanted to have both, but for the longest time felt that I was too young and had not earned the right. Tricia and Lisa were very natural pocketbook carriers and sunglass wearers. They could do it so easily. I probably never would have even made the conscious effort to carry a pocketbook except that once a month I had to for personal reasons and if I hadn't carried it all the time, people would have known the personal reason. That's how it was with red, white and blue pants, hard rock, words like "groovy." I didn't have the right to be a part of that because I was too young, didn't have a cause. I thought that Red possibly did have a cause and I admired that; I envied it.

I wanted to tell Red that I faithfully played all of my Daddy's old albums: Frank Sinatra, Judy Garland, Bunny Berigan, and that I always pictured myself in some dim smoky room slowdancing to "Stardust" in one of those nice strapless gowns with a tulle ballerina length skirt. I wanted to tell him that I had always wished that I had belonged to the previous generation where there were rigid rules and convictions, where certain appearances were upheld just like in cheerleading, team sports, the Olympics, National Honor Society. I almost told him all of that but then thought better considering it was our first meeting. For some reason, I felt like I had known him for a long time, felt that I had staked some sort of claim on him. I didn't even dive. We just sat and Red held my hand, rubbing his thumb back and forth on my knuckles. I swam breaststroke all the way back with my head out of the water and I watched him. I stopped only to blink and the sun was so bright on the water that it almost blinded me and the longer that I looked, the more dark spots I saw all around Red.

I was certain that Red would call me that night; I could just feel it and too, I had received all kinds of hopeful bets and promises from Tricia and Cindy on the way home. "Maybe you and Red can get me a date with Tom," Tricia said and I loved hearing "you and Red." Cindy was adamant that yes, he would call. Lisa was the only negative bettor in the group. "Give him time," she said. "He'll play it cool for awhile. Now, he needs to see you with someone else."

"Then he'd never ask me out."

"That's where you're wrong." Lisa looked at me with her most serious grown up look. "Then he'd want to ask you out even more. I told Ralph to meet us at the lake tomorrow and I'll just call him and get him to bring some of the other guys along."

"Not Ralph again," Tricia sighed.

"There's nobody else to date around here," Lisa said. "He's not so bad."

"I'll date nobody." Cindy turned the radio down and faced the backseat where Lisa and I were sitting.

"C'mon, Jo, it's worth a try," Lisa continued. "You're friends with all the guys and any one of them would love to go out with you."

"That's what she's afraid of." Tricia pulled into Hardees which had recently become a part of our going home. "Anybody want anything?"

"I'm on a diet," Lisa said which made us all laugh. She was always on a diet and never lost any weight. Cindy and Tricia were already out of the car. "Just get me a Coke," I yelled and then turned to face the road. It seemed that I saw brown Toyotas everywhere I went, and I kept expecting to see Red in one of them. Lisa talked on and on about how to play it right; Tricia talked on and on about how she was going to give up on Tom if something didn't happen soon; Cindy kept talking about what it would be like to be seniors at the high school, people standing while we walked into assemblies, being able to leave the grounds for lunch and so on. All I could talk about was Red, rub my thumb over the back of my hand just like he had done.

Red did not call for a whole week. All of those days, I saw him at the lake and he would speak or even stop by our pier to talk, but he never asked me out. Once, he even grabbed me up and jumped into the water and then just held me there, his hands on my waist. But then he would be gone, off to the other end of the lake or over with the older people where Buffy was a constant attraction. It was the middle of that second week since the day at the tower, when Pat Reeves showed up at the lake and came over to sit with us. He was talking, mostly to everyone else, about going off to school, and I was watching Red, waiting to catch his eye. Finally, he came over, looked at Pat, back at me and grinned, winked. I could have died. Then, he just stood there, waist deep in the water, and started talking to Pat about running, tennis, Duke. Red even suggested that he and Pat play tennis sometime. "What about tonight?" Red asked and I wished that they would go somewhere else to talk.

"I'm going out tonight," Pat said and looked at me for the first time. "I came to see if Jo wants to go to the movies." I could feel my face getting red and I knew that I couldn't look at Lisa, Tricia or Cindy. I couldn't look at anyone except Pat, because it was so unlike him to say something like that in front of other people. "Well, what do you say?" It was like everyone was waiting for my answer.

"Well, Bobby's coming home tonight," I said.

"So?" Pat asked. "What does that mean?"

"My mother is fixing a special dinner."

"That makes sense. It will take you at least until eleven o'clock to eat, won't it?"

"It might," I said and tried to make a joke of it. Pat didn't laugh, Red did, but Pat didn't, and I probably would have felt embarrassed for Pat, probably would have said that I'd go to the movies if Red hadn't been standing there. Besides, Pat never should have done that to me, never should have put me on the spot after all of those months that he had acted like he could care less about me, had even told me that he might date other people when he went off to school.

"You're going to miss a good one," Pat said and stood up. Even in shorts and an old faded Izod, he looked like he was all dressed up to go somewhere. "See you around." He was almost at the end of the pier when he turned back. "Call me sometime about tennis," he said to Red and then to me, "tell Bobby hello for me; tell your Mama not to burn the chicken like she did when I came for a special dinner." Then he was gone.

"You broke his heart," Red said and pulled himself up on the edge of the pier. "Guess you wouldn't want to go anywhere tomorrow night either."

"I might," I said and I braced myself for what was to come. It didn't even bother me that Tricia, Lisa and Cindy were sitting there taking in every word.

"A friend of mine is having a party down here tomorrow night. Sounds like it'll be a good party." He dipped his finger in the lake and drew a circle on the dry pier. "Want to go?"

"Yes," I said without even pausing that way that Lisa had always told me to do. "I'd love to."

"Okay, I'll call you tonight." He patted me on the head and slid back into the water. "What time's the special dinner so I don't interrupt?"

"Oh any time is okay." I sat perfectly still until he was back on the shore and heading up to where he had his car parked. My whole body felt like Jello.

"You did it, Jo," Tricia squealed and grabbed my hand. "You have a real date with Red Williams!"

"Boy did you ever screw up," Lisa said and shook her head.

"No she didn't," Cindy said with this admonishing tone that I had never heard her use before. "She got just what she's been wanting."

"What are you going to wear?" Tricia asked. "Tom might be at that party. If he is, you have to tell me everything that he does, every person that he talks to, okay?"

I nodded and then turned to Lisa. "Aren't you just a little bit happy for me?" I asked.

"Yeah, yeah," she said, "it's just that I feel so sorry for Pat Reeves, I mean how embarrassing."

"Make up your mind, Lisa," Tricia said. "The whole time she's dated Pat all you've ever done is call him a queer."

"But he's a goodlooking queer," she said. "Why didn't you ever tell me what a goodlooking queer he is."

I did not even say my usual, "He's not a queer. He's a nice guy." I didn't care anything about any of that. All I could think about was Red. I had a date with Red.

My mother thought that Red was too old for me. "And especially being down at that lake at night," she kept saying. But as he had often done, Bobby stepped in and helped me out.

"Red's okay," Bobby said. "It's just a date. It's not like she's going to marry him." Bobby carried a lot of weight that night all dressed up in his khakis and pink button-down shirt, Phi Beta Kappa bound for Bowman Gray. "I know all the people that hang out at the lake. I might just go myself."

"I wish you would," Mama said and went back to the kitchen where she was frying chicken (Pat Reeves had been right) leaving us in the den where Andy Griffith was on T.V. That was my favorite show and I was so nervous that I couldn't even watch. "Thanks Bobby," I said. "She's got to let me go."

"I might go," Bobby said again and I could tell that he really wasn't doing it for me. He was thinking of Nancy Carson, I knew, and even though I did not think that she was worth his time, I was glad that he was thinking about her. "Thanks for trying to help me, Bobby, but you know Nancy might be there."

"Why do you say that?"

"She's always at the lake. Every single day she's there."

"Jo could just ride with you, Bobby," Mama yelled over the splattering grease. "It would save Claude a trip." It made me cringe to hear her call him Claude and I would've said something but I was afraid of pushing my luck. "And ya'll could ride home together, too."

"Who's she usually with?" Bobby asked, lowering his voice.

"Girls." I was getting to him.

"What time does Jo have to be in?" he yelled. He was now walking around the room, his hands deep in his pockets.

"Between eleven and eleven-thirty." Mama came back into the den.

"Eleven? The party won't even get going until eight. In Winston-Salem I don't even go out until eleven." Bobby raised his voice but still managed to keep his All American appeal.

"Just this once," I said. "Please!"

"Aren't any of your friends going?" she asked.

"They weren't invited or they would be."

"I don't like the idea of you being on that road that late at night. There's not a thing between here and the lake."

"Hardees," I said to which my mother put her hands on her hips and stared towards the kitchen where there was still the splatter of chicken frying.

"I know," Bobby said and walked over to the phone. "We'll just stay at Bruce Pittman's place for the night and come back early Sunday morning."

"Not Jo!" Mama said. "Besides, we won't see you at all."

"Yes you will." Bobby was dialing the number. "We'll be home in time for church." He winked at Mama and she just shook her head. He could get away with anything. It was just fine with Bruce and his sister Sally and finally, since "Bruce's parents are nice," and "his sister Sally is a 'nice girl' and just finished college at Meredith," Mama said "yes" with the agreement that I would be at the Pittmans' and Red would be gone no later than eleven-thirty. Bobby told her that he would see to that. It never even crossed Mama's mind to tell me to make sure that Bobby was by himself, without Nancy Carson, at a particular curfew time, and that was a bone that I would have liked to pick. However, I was not in any position to take any chances. When Red called, I could barely hear him because there was loud music and voices in the background. I told him that I was riding with Bobby and that we were going to spend the night at the Pittmans'. "That's fine," he yelled. "See you then." And it was fine; everything, including the charred chicken and the thunderstorm that lit up my room throughout the night, was just fine.

After much deliberation, and with Tricia and Cindy as my advisors (Lisa had plans to go with Ralph to Fat Mama's who was a bootlegger in the black section of town), I finally decided to wear a pink cotton sundress that had a ruffle across the top.

"Are you sure this isn't too dressed up?" I asked.

"You know how Buffy always looks." Tricia was flipping through the clothes in my closet. "That is perfect. Pull it down on your shoulders," she said and came over and tugged the flounce down.

"You look fine," Cindy added.

"I wish ya'll were going. I'm not going to know anybody."

"Yes you will," Tricia said. "Besides, all you need to know is Red and remember."

"Watch out for Tom," I finished and she nodded. "I'll call you as soon as I get home."

"Lisa said that she and Ralph may go down there," Cindy added and laughed. I hoped not. Lisa talked enough when she was sober.

"Not if they've already gone to Fat Mama's," Tricia said and it made me cringe. I didn't want to hear about it, didn't want to picture a drunken Lisa and Ralph. Everyone, even Cindy, had been to Fat Mama's, except me.

"She's going to get into trouble." I took off my dress and hung it back up. I had three hours before time to go.

"Nah, her parents are gone. Cindy and I are going over there later." Tricia put on her sunglasses and took her car keys out of her pocketbook. "Good luck!" I walked to the door with them and then watched as they drove away. For some reason I felt oddly left out. It was the first time that I had been the only one with a real date.

I started getting nervous when Bobby and I were halfway to the lake. He had been quiet the whole time. "Are you thinking about Nancy being there?" I finally asked.

"Why do you ask that?"

"Just wondering."

He was quiet again and then finally, he started talking. "Yeah, I guess I'd like to see her." I didn't say anything. "You don't like her, do you?"

"It's not that," I said. "But you know, she did dump you."

"That was a long time ago." He stared straight ahead. "By the way, what's going on with Red?"

"Nothing. I just met him." For the first time it registered with me that Bobby actually knew Red, that he could probably tell me a lot about him, and about Buffy. "What do you think of Red?"

"He's okay." Bobby shrugged. "He used to be sort of wild, don't know if he still is or not."

"Wild like how?" I held my breath waiting for Bobby to tell me something really awful.

"Ah, just hanging out with a rough crowd, partying all the time."

"I don't think he's that way now," I said. "Besides I'm not that way and he knows me."

"Good, as long as you can take care of yourself." Sometimes he sounded more like Mama than Mama. And I could take care of myself. I knew all of the rules that had been preached better than I knew the pledge of allegiance: Stay in a group; don't drink anything (like a Coke) unless you open it and fix it yourself, and on top of that, act like a lady. I kept thinking about those rules that my mother had stressed and I could not help but wonder again why everyone didn't have rules.

When I got there, I stayed in a group. That wasn't hard because it was in a mobile home that belonged to one of Red's friends, a guy named Dwayne who clearly was from the shady side of the lake. The room had thick red carpet, heavy Spanish looking chairs and a sofa, mirrored tiles on one wall and a Playmate pinup on the door leading to the kitchen. I looked at the mirrored wall and from that angle, I could survey the group. The only people that I knew other than Red and Bobby were Beatrice and Mark Fuller who were sitting in one of the chairs together. I was the only girl in a dress; everyone else was in jeans, Red included, and I felt very conspicuous and out of place. I looked like I was on my way to revival and everyone else was going on a hayride. I was thinking that Bobby must be feeling just as uncomfortable as I did but he was talking to Tom and some other guys from his class. Then, Buffy and Nancy came in and for the first time, I was glad to see them. They had on dresses, too.

"What's the matter?" Red asked and at first I thought that he was still talking to Dwayne.

"I feel sort of dressed up."

"Don't worry about it." He put his arm around me. "You look great." He pulled me closer than he had at the lake that day and I was all scrunched up against his chest. He had on a white Izod that made him look more like Bobby and his crew than like his friend Dwayne, who was wearing a filthy workshirt, and I could not help but wonder if Red always dressed that way or if he had done it for me. I liked to think that he had spent as much time as I had getting ready. He pulled me towards the kitchen where some people were dipping this stuff out of a trash-can and drinking it.

"What's that?" I asked when Dwayne started laughing and spit a purple mouthful on another boy's shirt.

"Little bit of everything. Want to try it?" Red was pulling me through all the people and one girl, Beatrice's friend, was swaying back and forth with her eyes closed and sloshed some of her stuff right down the front of my dress. My mother was going to die when she saw it, and worse, when she smelled it.

"No one will notice." Red was scooping me a cupful.

Never drink something at a party unless you fix it yourself. I had remembered another one. "Don't you want it?" Red was whispering in my neck and his grip got firmer around my waist.

"I can't," I blurted and he gave me an odd look so I had to think of something fast. "I'd much rather have a Tom Collins." I had never had one before but I had heard of it and it was the first thing that came to mind. Pat Reeves had told me once that he liked Tom Collins. He had even mixed me one one time but I didn't drink it. I had already decided that I was going to drink this one. Red maneuvered us over to the counter and I watched him mix it about half and half and the first swallow made my whole face pucker. After that it was easy and I felt like talking. I pushed my way back through to find Bobby just so he'd know that I was having a little drink and that there was nothing to worry about. Actually, I wanted his approval which I did not get because he was standing in the hallway with Nancy Carson and they were whispering what seemed to be serious things. Bobby was drinking some of that purple stuff and that was all I needed to see. Everything was just fine.

Red waved from across the room. "How did you get away so fast?" He was pushing through to where I was. I waved and stood waiting for him to get there.

"Hi Jo. Didn't know you were here." Beatrice was standing right beside me. "I'm really surprised to see you down here." She kept staring at me and her eyes looked funny. "Where's the rest of your little crew?" Mark Fuller was right beside her and he was staring, too, first at my calves and then at my chest. I didn't have anything to say and just stood uncomfortably while Mark and Beatrice continued their perusal.

"Hey, I better hold on to you, not gonna let you get away again." Red put his arm around me and I was so relieved to see him. "Do you know Beatrice and Mark?"

"We're in the same class," Beatrice said. "We just never see each other. We used to."

"Hey, Red, let's go outside for a minute," Mark said and tossed his long hair towards the door. "Your little girl will be fine with Beatrice."

"Maybe later." Red gripped me tighter.

"Yeah," Beatrice said and rubbed her hands up and down the front of Mark Fuller's shirt and then down around his thighs. "Besides, if you're going to smoke a joint, I'm going, too. I bought the stuff, you know."

"That's not it," he said and grinned at Red. "I need to talk to Red about something, something private, you know?" He was staring at Red now and he was so ugly that I couldn't bear to look at him. "Come on, Red. She ain't gonna disappear." He leaned right in my face. "Poof!" he said and I looked away. I told Red that I didn't mind, even though I did, just so Mark Fuller would leave.

"I'll just be a minute," Red whispered and kissed me on the cheek. Then I watched him push back through the crowd of people with Mark Fuller right behind him.

"So, what have you been doing Beatrice?"

"The same," she said and stepped closer. "I didn't know you dated Red."

"This is the first time." I looked around but I didn't see Bobby anywhere.

"God, he'll be right back," Beatrice said and laughed. "What's in the cup? Kool-Ade?"

"I see you're still dating Mark," I said because I couldn't think of anything else.

"Yeah." She laughed again. "Remember when you had a crush on Mark?" I nodded and it made me cringe to think that I ever had, that she would even remind me. "Of course, I'd never tell him that," she continued. "He might have a thing about cheerleaders."

"It's obvious that he's crazy about you," I said which wasn't obvious but again, I couldn't think of anything else to say.

"I think so," she said. "Red acts like he's got the hots for you too. Of course, that's how Red is. Everybody loves him."

I was trying to figure out exactly what she meant by that when Red and Mark came back by way of the kitchen. Red handed me a new cup. "Your brother's got a heavy duty conversation going on out on the steps."

"So?" I asked and had to look directly at Red because Mark and Beatrice were staring at me again.

"Thought you'd like to know." He laughed. "She watches out for big brother."

"That's the cheerleader for you," Beatrice said and stepped closer to Red. "You know you're out with the chief, don't you?" She wrapped her hand around the back of Red's neck and pulled him closer.

"The chief, huh?" He looked at me and smiled. "That's real good."

"Yeah, listen to this." Beatrice got her other hand around Mark Fuller and pulled him in close to her other side. "All you have to say, Red, is you can do it, you can do it, you can, you can, and she probably will!" Beatrice did not look at me once during all of that. Then, she let go of Red and wrapped both of her arms around Mark Fuller and pulled him towards one of the chairs.

"Let's go in here." Red took my arm and started pushing our way back towards the kitchen. I looked into those mirrored tiles and I could still see Beatrice, her head thrown back, laughing, and she was chanting, "team's gettin ready, gettin red hot. You get it?" she yelled and leaned into Mark, "Red hot, she's gettin Red hot!"

Red must have heard her, too. "She's a little messed up," he said when we finally got to the kitchen. The only person in the kitchen was Dwayne and he was stretched out on the floor right beside the trashcan. Red hopped up on the counter.

"I've never seen her that way," I said and tried not to look at Dwayne.

"She's almost always that way." He pulled me over to where I was standing directly in front of him and he wrapped his legs around the back of my knees.

"I can't believe it. She's so different." I stared out the window where I could see a pier stretching out into the lake like a long black line.

"That's what drugs will do," he said and smoothed my

hair. "That's what I like about you. You're so different from the other girls." He had his hands cupped around my face. "You don't even drink, do you?"

"Well, I am tonight." Seeing Beatrice had made that little light-headed feeling go away and I wished that I could get it back.

"Yeah, but you're different." He took my cup and stretched across the counter to get two of the bottles beside the sink. "Sort of old fashioned in a nice way." The counter top was white with little gold specks and none of the specks formed any kind of pattern. They were just there and I was just there and didn't know what to do. It seemed like a good time to tell Red about all of the things I liked to think about, the old songs, a ballerina skirt, but then, that didn't even seem important. He apologized for leaving me alone with Beatrice; he told me the truth, that Mark had wanted him to go out and smoke a joint, to talk about how Mark was getting sick of Beatrice. And, he told me that he didn't, that he never would have done anything to make me feel uncomfortable, that he never would have done anything to change what we had going. His legs were wrapped around me again and his hands were on my shoulders, his face was getting closer and closer; the words "what we had going" going round and round in my mind. I kept sipping that drink, never moving the cup away from my mouth until he did it for me.

The next thing that I knew, it was after twelve and we were sitting out on the pier where it was cool and we kept kissing and I kept holding my crinkled up Dixie cup. I felt so safe and lazy that I probably would have stayed there forever except that Bobby would be worried about me and it was Red, not me, who said that it was time for him to walk me down to the Pittmans'. The lake looked so different at night, so dark; it looked larger. "It seems so much bigger at night," I whispered.

"What?"

"Bigger, the lake looks so much bigger." I looked at him and squeezed his hand, wanting him to stop and just sit down on the shore with me.

"Time for you to get some sleep," he said. "I've already kept you out too late."

"No, no you haven't, but it does look bigger, you know?" I wanted to stop talking but I couldn't; I wanted to find a way to ask when I would see him again, if I would ever see him again, but we were there.

"Hey, Bobby," Red said real loud and I looked up to see Bobby and Nancy sitting in the Pittmans' swing. "Hope I didn't keep your little sis up too late." He didn't even kiss me good night, just held my hand and winked at me. I realized that he wanted Bobby's approval as much as I did; he didn't want me to get in trouble for being late. He understood all of that; he understood my rules. He had even said that that's what made me so different.

Bobby didn't have much to say so I went on inside and watched Red from the window. I watched until he got smaller and smaller and when he was midget size, he turned and went back to where the party had been.

"Looks like you had a good time." Buffy was sitting on the couch, drinking a beer and flipping through a

Glamour magazine with her long glazed nails pausing gracefully over the pages. "You better not take Red too seriously."

"We're just friends." I felt funny even talking to Buffy. She was Bobby's age; she was older and she made me feel very young, very unattractive. Her long black hair was perfect and mine, when I caught a glimpse of myself in the window, was flat on top and frizzy on the sides from when I had gotten so hot in that trailer. The little bit of mascara that I had so carefully applied was under my eyes.

"Sure," she said, "that's what I thought when I first fell for Red." She tossed back her hair and sipped her beer. "You better watch out that's all I've got to say." She was doing it again and what could I say? "You're jealous. It's your fault you let it get hot and heavy. You don't know what you're talking about." But, I said nothing because that was the best way, the easiest way. As it turned out, I didn't have time to say anything anyway because Bobby and Nancy came into the room.

"Ready Buff?" Nancy asked and leaned against the doorway. Bobby could not take his eyes off of her and I noticed in him a weakness that I had never seen before. He looked as helpless as Pat Reeves so often looked, a look that I could not imagine ever seeing on Red's face.

"I've been ready." Buffy stood up. She tossed the magazine and when it slid to the floor she didn't even bother to pick it up. She was just that cool.

"You don't have to go," Bobby said. "Bruce isn't home, yet."

"I'm so tired," Nancy said. "And I know that Buffy is, aren't you?" Buffy nodded and Bobby seemed to shrink back. "It's been so good to see you, Bob." Nancy kissed him quickly on the mouth and he bounced back, best all round as ever.

"Yeah, maybe we can get together again some time when I come home." Bobby shrugged. I was proud of him. He had bounced from beggar to nonchalant.

"Maybe," Nancy said. "Buff and I are going back to Meredith in three weeks. I just can't wait to get back." That was a subtle punch in Bobby's gut but he didn't even blink.

"God, yes," Buffy said. "You know it's hard times when you go to a party like the one tonight. Talk about red-necks!"

"Amen!" Nancy said and for some reason I took it personally. I thought that Dwayne was a red-neck, too, but the remark was said to encompass Red and thus, to encompass me. It was like I wasn't even there and I had to say something.

"Do ya'll know Sally?" I asked. "She just finished at Meredith."

"Of course we do," Buffy whispered. "I had to talk to her most of the evening while I waited on my friend." She punched Nancy in the arm. "She's weird," Buffy mouthed to me and Nancy laughed. "Amen!"

"Your sister's cute, Bobby," Buffy said and walked onto the porch. "You better give her a good talk about you know who."

Nancy looked at me and smiled as though she were on

my side and then she mussed Bobby's hair like he might be four years old. "See ya Bob." He looked four years old and I watched him watch her and listen to the shrill girlish laughter that followed them to Nancy's car and then stopped suddenly with the closing of the door.

"I'm tired," I said, hoping that Bobby would say the same. Already there had been too long a delay in being able to think over my night.

"She's something, isn't she?" Bobby asked and shook his head.

"She sure is," I agreed, knowing that Bobby would take that the way that he wanted it to be.

"Did you have fun?" He was still staring out the window to where he had been sitting on the porch.

"Yeah," I said, "Red is really a nice person."

"Well, just watch out." He turned from the window. "You know he's got quite a reputation."

"No, I didn't," I said, knowing that Bobby had been spurred on by everything that Buffy had to say. Buffy never should have let the situation get out of control. No, I was different and Red could see that. Red could protect me and I would be perfectly safe with him.

"Well, he does," Bobby said. "I think he's sort of crazy."

"That's what Buffy and Nancy say," I said. "But he's not that way. You didn't think so, either, until you started listening to them."

"I hope you're right," he said and got that stern look on his face. "Just be careful." I wanted to say "you be careful, beggarman, fool" but I didn't because I love

Bobby, because I didn't want him to tell that I came in late, because now I had a cause, a reason to do whatever I did. Red was different from what Bobby said and I'd have to prove it. There was no need to tell anyone or even try to explain because time would explain for me. Red didn't want anything to mess up what we had going; we had something going and it was going to be perfect.

"Don't worry, Bobby," I said with complete confidence. "You know I think that Nancy is really crazy about you."

"Why do you think that?" he asked and could not hide the pleased look on his face.

"I just do." It slid as easily from my mouth as "Yes, you look just like an Ethiopian Princess."

"Night," he said when I turned to go and under the pretense of waiting for Bruce, he returned to his seat in the swing, no doubt to savor some hopeless and ludicrous fantasy about Nancy Carson.

When I went into the room, Sally was still up reading something like chemistry. She was going to start graduate school in just a few weeks. Sally really was a nice girl, very smart, though totally unattractive with her straight chopped hair and wire rim glasses that were too small for her full face.

"What do you want to major in, Jo?" She finally asked after I told her that the only school that I was interested in was U.N.C. She was worse than the guidance counselor at school.

"I don't know."

"Well, what are you interested in?" She stuck a box of Ritz crackers towards me and I shook my head. It was starting to throb a little.

"Have you had any chemistry?"

"I had a reaction tonight," I said and that was so unlike me. Sally's nice girl eyes behind the tiny frames were giving me the once over and I could tell that she was thinking that I was very immature. I didn't care. All I wanted to do was climb in that other bed and go to sleep, pretending that I was still kissing Red. It was a puzzle; I wanted a mature, smart girl like Sally to think that I was silly, and I wanted a silly, snooty girl like Buffy to find me very mature, intelligent and sincere. Clearly, there was something wrong in that and I started thinking that there must be an inbetween between the silly beauty and the smart wallflower, between an All American like Bobby and a careless, funloving red-neck. Red was the inbetween and it came to me that so was I. I thought first about how I would explain to Tricia that I really didn't keep an eye on Tom Fulton, what I would tell my mother about that stain on the front of my dress, but then I went back to Red, and I fell asleep with a picture of him in my mind, a successful businessman who has a carefree look about him and has earned the right to be that way, and of myself, a glamorous wife and mother who nonchalantly is always nominated and elected to various titles and positions, but who reserves herself and time for her husband and home. The picture was sharp and clear each time that I awoke to that wonderful hazy darkness that promises more sleep, more dreaming time, and not once did I ever consider anything negative, that Red could have gone back to that party and gotten up with someone else, that he had fallen asleep without a thought of me, for my feelings were so strong that I knew it had to be the same for him.

For the rest of the summer, Red and I were inseparable. I still went to the lake with Tricia, Lisa and Cindy, but as soon as Red got there, we would swim out to the tower to sun so that we could be alone, or we'd just go up and sit in his car, maybe ride to Hardees or to the other side of the lake where there was a thick wooded area with lots of dirt roads. A few times, I even walked down to the shady end of the lake with Red. I didn't want to and everyone was shocked that I did but I felt that I owed it to Red; after all, he had gone to parties with me at Tricia's or at Lisa's, not to mention the fact that he was very tolerant of the teasing that they had suddenly begun to dish out. "Had any good pot lately?" Lisa would ask in a very matter of fact way, and I couldn't tell if she was trying to irk me or make Red feel funny or both. Even Cindy had begun to make comments here and there like about how Red always stared at girls' breasts when he was talking to them, or how the pupils of his eyes looked funny sometimes.

"Even I break a date every now and then so that I can spend time with my friends," Lisa said on the way to the lake one day. "No guy is that important."

"If a guy really likes you, then he understands that you want to be with your girlfriends once in awhile," Tricia added. They were ganging up on me and I looked at Cindy to see what she was going to say. After all, she was my oldest and closest friend. She just looked away.

"But what about the pact?" I asked. "The pact where you can break a date with the girls at any time if there's a guy involved."

"Break one," Lisa said. "To do that, you at least have to make one."

"I thought ya'll would understand," I said and I felt for a minute like I was going to cry. I had never been ganged up on before, ever. "I've always understood when ya'll were dating someone. I didn't think you thought any less of me."

"Who's had a date lately?" Tricia asked. "I've given up on Tom Fulton, no thanks to you, of course."

"I told you, Red doesn't even really know Tom."

"Yeah, well you didn't even look out for me that night you went to the party." Tricia was staring straight ahead, gripping the wheel. "I would have tried to help you out."

"We did help her out," Lisa continued. "What about all of those days that we circled K-Mart? What about the past few weeks when you've wanted to ride by and put a note on his car or something?" She stared at me and I could no longer keep the tears back. Cindy had gotten very quiet and was staring out the window. I suddenly realized that they had probably been talking about me, making fun of me for weeks.

"I'm sorry," I said. "I had no idea that ya'll felt this way." Part of me kept thinking that they were jealous, that if they all had boyfriends, they wouldn't be doing that to me. And yet, it also crossed my mind that if I had to choose between them and Red that I would choose Red; at least Red understood.

"You won't even go out with us the nights that you're not out with Red," Lisa said, her voice softening. "Hell, you've never been to Fat Mama's!" She laughed and I could tell, now, that she was sorry that she had made me cry.

"But I don't like to drink."

"God, we're not going to pour it down your throat." Tricia was not ready to lighten up. "You could just go, but no, what do you do, sit home and wait for Red to call from God knows where."

"He's usually tired after working."

"Yeah," Tricia said and she glanced at Cindy and then at Lisa from the rear view mirror, like maybe she knew something.

"Well, we can't afford to go out every night," I said. "And he can't come over and sit at my house and watch T.V. all the time." Those were Red's exact words.

"Well go to the movies with us tonight," Cindy said. "It's got Robert Redford and Paul Newman."

"'The Sting'?" I asked and Cindy nodded. "Red and I saw it the other night."

"It figures," Tricia said but then finally, she began to let up. "We can see what else is on, though."

"No, 'The Sting' is good," I said. "I wouldn't mind seeing it again."

"Then it's a date!" Lisa said and by then we were at the lake. They weren't mad at me anymore or at least weren't saying those things to me, but I still could not get over what had happened and I could not help but feel a little uncomfortable, a little resentful. I didn't see Red anywhere and I guess it was obvious that I kept looking for him.

"Wonder where he is?" Lisa asked and I just shook my head as if I didn't care. I didn't fool them or myself.

"Hey, I see Red," Tricia said. "He's down there in that car."

She pointed to the shady end where there were several cars parked. "I think it's him, there, in the backseat of that blue one." I followed her finger and it was him. I wanted to go down there right then but I waited a few minutes. Surely, he would see me. I waited and waited and not once did I feel like I had even caught his eye.

"He must not see you," Cindy finally said which obviously wasn't true. It was an overcast day and there was no glare; we were just about the only people on any of the piers.

"Yeah," I said, "I better go tell him that I won't be seeing him tonight."

"Why don't you just wait until he . . ." Tricia caught herself and stopped.

"Yeah, tell him we're going to have a night on the town," Lisa said and turned on her transistor radio. I could feel them watching me all the way down the pier and then down the shore. Red still had not noticed me and as I got closer, I could hear the music coming from the tape deck of the car. Beatrice and Mark Fuller were in the frontseat and Red was in the backseat with Beatrice's friend. I started to turn back before he saw me but then, I would have had to face Tricia, Lisa and Cindy with some explanation. I stopped about ten feet from the car and just waited. Finally, he looked and saw me.

"Hey, where did you come from?" He got out of the car and walked towards me. Beatrice, her friend and Mark were all watching and I knew that my friends were watching from the other direction.

"I've been here about an hour."

"Sorry, Jo, I had no idea that you would come on a day like today." He was looking all around, everywhere except at me. "I was going to call you in a little while. Just been sitting around with some friends."

"Yeah," I said and stepped closer. His eyes were all red and he kept drumming his fingers on his stomach in beat with the music. "I came to tell you that I'm going out with the girls tonight."

"No you didn't." He grabbed my hands. "You're just mad, that's all, because I'm a little stoned."

"No." I shook my head and I could feel the tears brimming up again.

"Hey, baby." He lifted my chin and kissed me on the nose. "You know that I'd never do anything to upset you. Don't you?" I nodded because I wanted to believe that; I wanted everything to be just fine. "Forgive me?" He pulled me closer and kissed me. "You know that I'm in love with you and there's no one that I'd rather be with." He stared and nodded his head up and down waiting for me to do the same. He had never actually said that he loved me before. I nodded. "Is there anyone that you'd rather be with? Maybe Pat Reeves or your big brother? Cindy? I know you'd rather be with Cindy, her face covered in zinc oxide?" He laughed and kissed me again. "Well?"

"No," I said, though I wasn't quite sure, though I had this horrible urge to ask Red if there had ever been anything between him and Beatrice's stringy haired friend. No, but that was ridiculous.

"I know," he said, "I'll make it all up to you. Tonight. We'll have a special night, just the two of us." He was talking faster and faster. "You know, talk about us, really talk. You love me, too, don't you?" I nodded again and he kept talking, about when he'd pick me up, about what a good time we were going to have, about how much he loved me and then I was alone, watching him get his shirt out of the backseat. None of the people in the car seemed to even see me standing there; they just kept talking to Red, asking him to come back once he walked me down the shore, asking him if he was going to a party that night.

He lifted his hand to Tricia, Lisa and Cindy when we got back to the pier but he made no move to go any closer. I was relieved because I didn't want them to see his eyes, to judge him on this one time. He kissed me and then turned to go. "See you around seven," he yelled and then left.

"What's this?" Tricia asked when I sat back down on my towel.

"I'm sorry," I said, "but it's very important that I see Red tonight." I kept trying to pull this one thread out of my beach towel so that I wouldn't have to look at them. "Red just told me that he loves me," I said, thinking that that would somehow merit the pact about breaking dates.

"Do you love him?" Cindy asked and I nodded. "That's great, Jo." I knew that she was trying to break the tension, just like she and I had always done when Tricia and Lisa were fighting. It wasn't working.

"Hey, maybe we can go to the movies tomorrow night," I said and looked at Tricia. She just shrugged and got out her car keys.

"I'm ready to go," she said, "there's no sun, anyway. I don't even know why we came today." She looked directly at me and shook her head. "Besides, why would you want to see a movie that you've already seen? I mean why would you ever do that?"

That special night with Red was the night that I broke one of my rules, for instead of going out in Blue Springs to the movies which is what he had told my mother, we rode down to the lake and spent the time just sitting in his cabin, talking and kissing, lying side by side on his couch. I was worried that first time that my mother was going to find out, that I was going to get into trouble, that Tricia, Lisa and Cindy would never forgive me, but then it got easier, because I was with Red and because everything seemed so perfect. By the time that school started, I felt relatively little guilt about saying that I was going somewhere else and then going down to the lake with Red. It was that important to me, especially since I couldn't see him on school nights and my Friday nights were taken up by cheerleading. Every now and then, Red would come to the games but usually not, and I didn't blame him; he was too old to go to high school games; he would be glad when I was through with all of that and he had me all to himself. Tricia, Lisa and Cindy had just about stopped asking me to do anything with them because they knew that I would either be with Red or waiting for him to call; and yet, the four of us were really the only ones aware of the change. Around school, we were always lumped together; we sat together; we ate together; we were chosen for just about everything, dance committees, school representatives, and somewhere in all of that, my name had suddenly emerged at the top of the list and it was Jo, Tricia, Cindy and Lisa, maybe it was because I was chief cheerleader and then Tricia and Cindy were still cheering that it turned out that way, or maybe it was because I had never dated any of the guys in our class and had merely maintained friendships, unlike Tricia and Lisa who had made several enemies. Maybe it was just my turn, or more probably, maybe it was that I was not trying for any of it, that suddenly all of the things that I had wanted and looked forward to were not important in comparison with Red. It seemed that so many things were changing. Red even said that our relationship was changing, growing, and that we had to do something about it, that he had been so patient with me and so on, the ultimate crux of the conversation being that he wanted to make love.

There were so many times that autumn that I wanted to go to Tricia and ask what she thought, to Lisa or

Cindy, and even though I knew that they would be there for me, I also knew that they would say that Red was putting pressure on me, that if Red really loved me that he would understand, or worse, I was afraid that Lisa would look up with that certain knowitall look of hers and say, "What's the big deal?" And it was a big deal, especially when I gave in. But then, ultimately, it was no big deal at all except that I couldn't take it all back: a dreary Sunday afternoon (I kept thinking "of all days"), an old couch with busted springs, the uncomfortable position, the discomfort of my body being perused, the patronizing "it's okay" that Red breathed into me the whole time.

"Is that it?" I asked when he had rolled off of me because I really didn't know. How was I supposed to know? He kicked the couch and took me home, a long silent drive, at the end of which he promised, "It'll get better for you; it takes experience." I wanted to ask how he knew that, who he had been with that was experienced enough to enjoy it all, but I just got out of the car.

I kept thinking about how Lisa had lied to me when she used to tell us how wonderful it was and I even started wondering if she had done anything; I even started wondering if there was something wrong with me. I kept thinking about all of those movies where the girl does it and then goes and stands in front of the mirror to see her new self, all transformed. The only change that had occurred was that then, that was all that Red wanted to do, help me to get the experience that I needed and I went along with him because I loved him, because I suddenly felt the same sense of commitment that I used to have for my friends, that I once had for Blue Springs High, that I felt when I rescued our dog, Jaspar, from his mother who wouldn't feed him years ago. I could see the payoffs from those things; the closeness that I had had with my friends, the honors that all seemed to be falling my way in school, even Jaspar, because he was a good dog who did what I told him to do most of the time. I could only wonder when that was going to pay off; I imagined it would be when Red asked me to marry him.

Yes, that was really the change, for instead of being up on all the new movies which I had been since I dated Pat Reeves for the first time, my free time went to gaining experience. I remember one time in particular or maybe it was many times rolled into one memory. It was just before Christmas. I was in Red's room, his hands were going up and down on my back and the stereo was playing in the next room where Mark and Beatrice and two people that I didn't know were smoking pot.

We are in his room; the door is closed. I am in here because Red realizes that I am very uncomfortable around those people. Beatrice makes fun of my friends who I am no longer even certain are my friends. Red says that they are not my friends. Red says that my family is so odd, that I need to break away, that Bobby isn't the perfect person that I think he is. But he loves me; I'm his. It doesn't bother him that I'm a cheerleader because he used to do silly things like that when he was in high school. Red says, "It's all right. You can't help it. I still love you. You've got me. I may be all that you've got but you have me." I can't think of anything, not one good thought; I can only listen to the soft voice of Art Garfunkle singing "Disney Girls" and think how very much like that girl I am, or used to be, while I watch Red unbutton my shirt, while he tells me that he is all I've got, that it's all right.

"How many girls have you ever been with?" I feel like I have to know even though at this point, it really doesn't matter.

"I don't want to tell you."

"Why?"

"I don't want to upset you. Besides, they didn't mean anything. I didn't love any of them."

I feel cold like I have never seen him before, like I don't know him, don't know anyone, shouldn't have ever broken a rule. My clothes are on the floor and he is on top of me, always on top of things, breathing heavily. My mother's face is etched clearly on my mind. She is wearing a strapless dress with a tulle ballerina length skirt and she is dancing a slow dance around and around to "Stardust," to "Disney Girls." She is in my place and were the roles reversed, she would not be in this place, not now. I close my eyes and concentrate on the music, wait for what I know is going to happen. The bed rocks rhythmically, like this blue captured wave that Red has on his shelf that goes back and forth, back and forth. There is a tightness in my stomach, my legs, my head.

"Jo, Jo." He is gasping my name in short little breaths

and I watch his eyes, somehow foreign and frightening like the eyes of a dead man, scrinching up, feel the sweat of his chest making me sticky. "I love you, Jo."

I stare back and I realize that I am crying and I don't know why. He could have been saying "Abraham, Abraham" and I could look just like Richard Nixon and it wouldn't matter. His heart and his brain and all the really important organs are concentrated between his legs and when it is all over and he has left a thick white puddle on my stomach, I realize that he has nothing more to say or think. It is all there, thick and bland, a future promise, and I wipe it away with an old paper towel that is on his windowsill. Out the window is the lake, the pier that cuts through it, the very place where we sat the night of our first date, in the summer. Summer seemed to be years ago.

I liked being in school those last weeks before Christmas break, not the time before or after or in between classes but that time during the class, those fifty minutes when no one was talking except the teacher, fifty minutes of outlining history chapters, or working long trigonometry problems. I wasn't very good in trig, not like Cindy, but I enjoyed doing neat work, taking it all one step at a time. I liked the hours spent reading Shakespeare. It was easy to be in class; it was easy because my grades were as good as they had ever been and sometimes I could even afford to not pay attention at all, to think of nothing, or to think of how it was going to be when Red did all of the things that he said he was going to do, go back to school, get a good job, marry me. I had already been elected most popular senior girl. Everything was easy in school and all I had to do was be very quiet and agree with whatever anyone said to me. All I had to do when Tricia, Lisa and Cindy found me crying in the school bathroom one day was to say, "Yes, I'm fine. I don't feel very well. Everything's okay."

"You haven't felt well for a long time," Tricia said. "We're still your friends you know."

"Is it Red?" Lisa asked. "I overheard Beatrice tell someone that he had gone to Raleigh one weekend to see Buffy. Did you know that?"

"Yes," I said. "But it's not true. That's not it." But that was true, that was it. Why, all of a sudden were they there to ask all those questions anyway?

"I'm just going to go home," I said. "I hate to miss class but I think I've got the flu."

"You had the flu two weeks ago," Cindy said and then was sorry that she had said that. I could tell from the way that the three of them kept looking back and forth that they had been talking about me. "Well, what I mean is that you must have a bad case. I think you should go home."

"Don't tell anyone," I said while washing my face, "but there have been some problems at home. I can't go into it because my parents would kill me. Please, just don't say anything." They just stood and stared first at me and then at each other and I left. That was a lie, too, but so what? It seemed to me that everything was a lie and the only comfort on that day had been the drizzling rain that glowed on every grease slicked puddle in the high school parking lot, and all the way home all I could think about was James Agee's little Rufus in *A Death in the Family* when he is so proud of the hideous cap that he wears and his aunt feels sorry for him because she knows that he looks ridiculous and that people are going to make fun of him. Still, she doesn't have the heart to tell him. I began thinking that maybe Red was my hideous cap and that Tricia, Lisa and Cindy just didn't have the heart to tell me. I thought, too, that there might be another part of me in that book, a part that wished that out of the blue I would hear that Red had been in a serious accident and I could cry and do the proper amount of grieving and then begin all over as though I had never known him, never fallen in love with him, never been exposed. Or maybe it was none of that, maybe it was just a thought, the book and the drizzly day, to take my mind off of the lie that I had told my friends, the lies that Red had told me, the lie that I would tell my mother again when she suggested that I spend more time with my friends, that they were excluding me, that Red was my only friend, all that I had. I would tell her all of that and I would cry just as I had done before and she would hug me and say that things would work out and I would wish in that moment that she would say that I must stay there forever, that I must not see Red or anyone else ever again, that I could go back and start all over.

I was looking forward to the Blue Springs High Christmas dance. It was going to be special because all of the senior superlatives would be called onstage during the night. My mother had even let me get a new dress for the occasion. It was emerald green with a lowcut neckline and a little slit up the side. I should have known when I stood at the checkout and watched my mother write that check that I never should have gotten it, that Red wouldn't even see it, though somehow, I had thought that I could convince him to attend a high school function so that everyone could see us together and stop wondering "what's going on with Jo?"

"Jo, you know how I feel about these things." He is in my living room talking loudly as usual and I don't want my parents to hear him. "You go on and have a good time."

"But I won't have a good time. I'd do it for you, Red." I can feel myself getting ready to cry, the pulse in my temples. "I go to parties with you that I really don't want to go to."

"I don't make you," he says which is true; he has never made me go; sometimes I think he'd rather that I not go. "I'm sure one of your little boyfriends that are always calling on the phone would love to take you, Miss Most Popular." He laughs and hugs me as though it's no big deal.

"They're friends, that's all." I want to pull away but I don't want him to see my eyes start to water. "They have girlfriends. Besides, wouldn't it bother you for me to go with someone else?"

He laughs again and rocks me back and forth like a limp rag. "Not one of them. Hell, why should I worry, unless, of course, you're planning on hopping in the sack."

I can't believe that he has said that. I can't think of what I need to say back so I watch a drop of water splash on his collar and spread out into the green material with a tiny smudge of mascara in the center like a nucleus.

Red pushes me away and lifts my chin. "Jo, you're acting like a baby again. You know I can't stand it when you act this crazy way." He smooths his long fingers under my eyes. "I'll tell you what I'll do to make up for it."

"What?" I sit holding my breath, hoping that he has just been kidding and will say that he will go.

"A bunch of people are going skiing next week and want us to come along."

"What people?"

"Scott and his girlfriend, Wanda, and three other guys that you really haven't met." I am relieved that he did not say Mark and Beatrice, but Scott and Wanda are just about as bad. They are the pair who are always in a catatonic state. I am scared of them.

"I don't know, I'll have to check." I was so happy just a few hours ago, knowing that I had two weeks of vacation to be at home, to be with just Red and make things just fine like they were in the summer.

"Well, if you ask your parents like that, you know that they won't let you go." He rubs his hand up and down my back. "We need to get away, Jo. Just think, all that time for us to make up for lost time. You won't have to worry about getting home on time or your mother finding out where you are. I hate myself lately for what I've done to you. I don't know what I'd ever do if I lost you. Don't you know that?"

"Yes, Red," I say and I think about it; I think about that night at Moon Lake when the lake was so big and dark looking; I think of that rubbery knee, sweaty palm feeling when we sat on the tower that first day, when he told me that he loved me; there was too much time, too many times, to let go. "Okay, I'll try. I'll go." Red leaves and I just sit for a long while trying to remember exactly what had happened, why he wasn't going to go to the dance with me. But, that will all be different someday, someday next summer when I'm out of high school.

"Jo?" My mother sticks her head through the door. "I thought I heard Red leave. What are you doing?"

"Nothing."

"Is anything wrong?" She walks in and sits down and I try not to look at her because I know that my eyes look like a raccoon.

"No, not at all," I say and I can tell that she doesn't believe me but she doesn't have the heart to say so.

"Did you tell Red about your new dress?" she asks. "Or about how you'll be called up on the stage?" I shake my head. "I told your Daddy that I wish we could sneak in and watch."

"Please don't." I grab her arm. "It's no big deal."

"I'm just kidding," she said. "We wouldn't dare embarrass the Most Popular girl."

"I didn't mean that. I just mean it's no big deal."

"Did Red say that, that it's no big deal?" She asks lots of questions lately, peculiar questions.

"No, he thinks it's great." I smile and sit up straight, perk up.

"Well he should! I'm glad he does." She hugs me and there is a second when I want to crawl up on her lap, to ask her why things get so difficult sometimes. I just pat her on the back. "Let's get your dress hemmed." She gets up and waits for me at the door and I follow her into my room where she pulls the dress, still in the box, from my closet.

"Here, slip it on and stand on the chest."

I do and she steps back to look. I am trying to think of a way to ask her about skiing. She will not want me to go, but if I do it just right, like Bobby, she will let me.

"I think we should get you some new shoes." She pulls out the soft skirt and lets it fall back around my legs. "Then I won't have to cut off so much. We don't want to ruin that slit." She makes a face and laughs. I look as pitiful as little Rufus in his big loud cap and she knows it but she doesn't have the heart to tell me. The phone will ring, "Big Red is dead," they will say and I will wear a black dress and never leave this house, this woman fixing my dress.

"I saw some downtown that will be perfect, just the right height heel." She talks on and on the whole time that she is pulling pins from her mouth and flipping around the skirt of the dress. It is almost like she is the one going to the dance, like she is most popular, like she is the one who would know exactly what to say, what to do. "What kind of flowers is Red going to get for you?"

I just shrug. "Red wants me to go skiing over the holidays, too."

She looks up and pulls the last two pins from her lips. "Just the two of you?"

"Oh no, a bunch of people are going and it's going to be loads of fun." I step down off the trunk and pull the dress over my head. It feels good not to have to look at her and I want to stay inside of the dress until it is over, until I have an answer. Scott has a sweet mother, the lady in lingerie at Penney's, though that is no reflection on Scott, but I can tell my mother that; Wanda's father is a well-known dermatologist in town.

"We'll see. We'll ask your Daddy."

"Please." Begging seems like the right thing to do.

"Do you know any of the other people?"

"Oh yes," I say and I tell her about Scott and Wanda. I tell her that I don't know the other three but that Red wants me to meet some of his friends since he's always with me and my friends, like at the dance. "He's so nice to all of my friends, but you know what's going on. They're so jealous of him." The only way that I can say all of that is to concentrate on carefully smoothing the material of the dress back in the box. It must be smoothed just right, straight folds of green running parallel.

"We'll see," she says again. "I still don't understand what's been going on at school to keep you so upset. You know, Cindy called twice last night while you were at the movies with Red."

"I don't know either," I say. "If they were all dating, it would be a different story."

"Maybe you should have them all over to spend the

night over the holidays." She is worried, I think. I have never worried her before.

"We'll see about the other," she says and sighs. I know that that is a probable yes which it is the next day. It is the hardest yes that I have ever gotten because I have to say that one of Red's friends has a house in the mountains and that the boy's parents will be there the whole time. She doesn't even call to check; I don't even know if the name that I used is correct. The last name of the driver is Bond but is his name Barry? Larry? Carey? It doesn't matter because she trusts me. She trusts my good sense and judgment; she tells me that all the time. If I say "motel" one time, I will blow it all, and I don't, though there is one minute that I almost do, on purpose. I almost blow it all on the night of the dance.

"Look, Jo," Mama calls from the kitchen. "Red had your flowers delivered."

It is late in the afternoon and I have already washed and rolled my hair. It is getting longer, now, just the way that Red wants it to get. I get to the front door and Mama has already taken the white box and she hands it to me. "Open it, let's see."

I know before I open it, a nosegay with red rosebuds and baby's breath. I had called in the order myself and gone by earlier that afternoon to pay for it so that there would be no tracer.

"How pretty!" Mama squeals. "Red has good taste and it's high time that he starts doing special little things for you."

"Nobody does special little things anymore," I tell her

but seeing that she is so excited for me, I try to work up some enthusiasm because I know what question is bound to come. "Wonder why he didn't just bring them himself?"

"Didn't I tell you?" My temples are pounding and I am convinced that she can see my front rollers moving in and out of my head.

"What?"

"Red has to work at the auto center. He tried his best to get out of it but they couldn't spare him what with holiday traffic and all so I'm going to ride with Cindy and Myron and Red is going to meet me there." That rolls off very smoothly.

"Here, I'll put these in the refrigerator for you." She looks so disappointed when she leaves the room and I don't know if she's disappointed for me, in Red, or for herself. I have to press my hands to my head to make the curlers stop jumping.

My Daddy took several pictures of me in my new dress and shoes before I left that night. I was anxious to get there and get it all over with. Cindy asked me where Red was as soon as I got in the car so I had to explain all about him working so that he could earn extra money for our skiing trip and how he was going to meet me later. That was easy enough because later I would just assume to everyone that he must not be able to get away. It got easier and easier the more that I thought about it and by the time that we got to the school and walked into the gym, I just about had myself convinced that it was all true. I could see Red slaving over the hood of some car, while I was standing there, in the gym, red and green lights blinking and flashing, pine trees wrapped in cotton, the huge star suspended and glittering over the stage. I had helped make the star, had spent several afternoons wrapping pine trees, but it had looked nothing in the bright light the way that it looked that night.

"You girls did a great job," my English teacher said. "I don't know what we'll do without you hard workers next year." Tricia, Lisa and Cindy were all standing close by. Next year sounded so far away, too far away actually and I could not help but think about that for awhile. Who was going to wrap those pine trees next year? Cindy must have already told Tricia and Lisa about Red working because the only thing that they said was that they hoped he got there in time for the presentations. All three of their dates asked me to dance right away, but I preferred to just sit at one of the tables in the corner of the gym where it was dark, and listen to the band, a soul band who sang a lot of Gladys Knight songs. I put the centerpiece in my pocketbook first thing. It wasn't anything spectacular, two tin foil bells and some holly leaves, but I wanted something to remember.

It was during "Midnight Train to Georgia" that I saw Pat Reeves on the dance floor. He was with a girl who was a year younger, a girl who I thought was not his type at all. She was the perfect debutante, not cute, but given the right clothes and adult jewelry, and given that certain air of superiority to anything smalltown, she could somehow beguile people into thinking that she was cute. They danced round and round and she was tittering, though I couldn't hear the titter, and waving to everyone that passed, while Pat moved around like a stiff corpse. He was having an awful time.

When the dance ended, she hurried off to a group of girls and they left to go to the bathroom. Pat was standing by himself off to one side of the gym by an open door. Suddenly, I felt like I had to say something to him, to speak and have him speak back. I had to push through several people and it seemed that everyone wanted to talk, to ask "where's Red?"

"Hi Pat," I said when I finally got there. "I didn't know you were going to be here."

"Yeah." He looked at me once and then looked out the door. It was cold there but felt good since the gym was already so hot and stuffy. He turned back but instead of looking at me, looked behind me, looked all around. "Where's Red?"

"He had to work."

"That's a shame." Now, he looked at me, his jaws clenched.

"Good band, isn't it?"

"Yeah it is." He stuck his hands into his pockets. "I am about to die for a cigarette."

"You don't smoke," I said because he had always given me such a hard time, threatening to tell my cheerleader advisor or worse, my mother.

"That's what college does." He stepped outside into the darkness. "Want one?"

"Why not?" I followed him outside and we stood off to one side in the dark. I had never smoked at school before and that made me want one even more. Pat gave me one, a menthol which I hated, and then he cupped his hands around a match to give me a light. We just stood and inhaled, exhaled, and what had been an uncomfortable silence started becoming more comfortable.

"Your date's cute," I said, trying to say something nice.

"Yeah but she's a jerk." He said that so seriously that for a moment I didn't say anything and then we both started laughing.

"So why are you here?" I leaned up against the cold brick wall right beside him.

"I was coming home anyway, my Mom's birthday, so when she called, I just said, 'why not?'"

"So how is school?"

"Great. It's nice to be out of Blue Springs, make new friends, come and go as you please." He thumped his cigarette and it landed in the cold brown grass, a tiny red glow that slowly faded. I could not picture myself coming and going as I pleased. "So, how are things with Red?" It surprised me that Pat would just come right out with that, that he would look directly at me, those large hazel eyes not even blinking. I had to look away.

"Fine, just fine."

"I never did understand why you just weren't honest with me when you started dating Red." He lit another cigarette. "I mean I looked like a real ass in front of all of my friends. I thought there was something between us."

"I'm sorry," I said and put my hand on his arm. "I really am sorry, Pat."

"Hey, don't get all dramatic." He laughed and shrugged. "It's not like I was madly in love with you or anything. I just thought we were good enough friends that you would be honest with me. You know, no big deal." He was talking faster and faster, another thumped red glow into the darkness, just about a foot from where the other one had landed. "I mean I didn't sit around and mourn for you or anything."

"We better go in. Your date will be wondering where you are."

"Yeah. Hope I didn't hurt your feelings." He stood by the door and waited for me.

"Oh no," I said and shook my head. "Red should be here soon." I walked in front of Pat and back into the gym. When I turned around, he was waving and I saw his date walking over. "Bye."

"Yeah, it was good to see you, Jo." Then he walked onto the dance floor to meet whatever her name was who was standing there with her hands on her hips, obviously pissed. Pat Reeves couldn't stand her; he said that he had never been crazy about me.

For the rest of the night, it seemed that I kept seeing him. Everywhere that I looked, he was there. Even when I walked up on the stage with the other superlatives, standing beside Tricia who was bestlooking, beside Cindy who was most school spirit, I saw Pat, leaning against the gym wall, his hands in his pockets, whats her name clinging to his arm. I even saw him when Cindy, Myron and I were leaving; he was holding open the car door for her and he saw us. He saw Cindy, Myron and me, just the three of us, and he lifted his hand to us which I pretended not to see.

Red came over on Christmas eve and told me that they had decided that we should leave on Christmas day to go skiing because the traffic wouldn't be bad.

"Christmas day?" I asked.

"Yeah, isn't that a nice present?" He didn't even notice my alarm at leaving on Christmas day, the sudden decision, or if he did, he pretended not to. "Here's your other present."

"Here's yours." I got his present from under our tree and waited for him to open it. "You first." I watched him rip through the carefully creased aluminum paper.

"A watch?" He pulled it out and stretched the band between his thumb and forefinger. "Jo, you shouldn't have."

"I knew you didn't have one." I couldn't tell if he liked it or not.

"I used to. I just never wore it. Finally sold it." He put the watch on his wrist and kissed my forehead. "I'll wear this one, thanks."

It was my turn and I sat staring down at the tissue paper; it was square and flat with a bulge in the center. Carefully, I pulled off the tape and pulled the paper open. It was an album by Black Sabbath and a bottle of cologne that smelled like concentrated gardenias. I kept reminding myself "it's the thought that counts," but at the same time, I kept wondering how much thought could have possibly gone into that. I hated that spooky, druggie sounding music; I hated Tussy smelling cologne.

Christmas mornings at my house always began with Andy making the rounds and waking everyone up. Then he would let overgrown Jaspar into the house and then we all had to wait until the coffee was perked and Daddy had had a cup. That morning, I was anxious to get the routine moving so that it would all be over by the time Red called. As usual, he had not given me a set time and as it turned out, he didn't call at all.

The doorbell rings just after we finish opening presents. Mama is fixing a big Christmas breakfast while we all try out our new goods. Andy is outside plowing up the yard with his new minibike; Bobby is trying on oxford cloth shirts in every color of the rainbow even though they all are the same size. He pauses every now and then to flip through pages of his very own copy of *Gray's Anatomy* or to show us all another picture of Christine, who is the blonde beautiful Phi Beta Kappa from Greensboro and the Miss Right of his life. Not once has he mentioned Nancy Carson. I am modeling my coat and flipping through my new books, one on Degas, the other a poetry anthology, and I do not even get to do one full modeling turn, to read one sonnet aloud over the sizzling pop of my mother's bacon, before it rings.

"Why didn't you call me?" I open the door and Red walks in.

"I figured you'd know that we'd want to get an early

start." He flops down on the couch and I notice that he isn't wearing his watch. Good, I won't have to wear that cologne. "Everyone's in the car waiting. Are you ready?"

"No, I'm not even dressed." I run to my room to dress and finish packing. I hear Mama invite Red to stay for breakfast. "No, thank you." He can be so polite. "But it sure smells good." Red makes the rounds saying "ho-ho-ho" to Bobby and Daddy and it makes me feel strange like he has no business doing that. Bobby doesn't have much to say to Red and that makes me feel strange, too. I would be extra nice to Christine if she came over. I was always nice to Nancy Carson even though I couldn't stand her.

"Jo, do you need some help?" Mama is in the doorway. "Thought you might want to take this heavy flannel gown that Grandma Spencer sent. It's going to be cold up there."

"Yes, I do." I take the gown and cram it into the already stuffed suitcase. All of a sudden, I have that feeling that I used to get during fire safety week at school. "What would you take with you if your house was burning down?" I look around my room: scrapbook, pictures, the pink rhinocerous that Bobby gave me on my eighth birthday, the Bible that I got when I was born, toe shoes, letters, collected verses of Millay, Dickinson, Wordsworth, *A Death in the Family, Lord of the Flies, Where the Red Fern Grows, To Kill a Mockingbird, The Biography of Helen Keller,* Grandma Spencer's locket . . .

"Honey, I think you've got all that you need for one

night." Mama is in the same place, spatula in hand, her Rudolph apron tied around her waist. "They're all waiting for you?"

"I'm ready." I press in the locks on my suitcase and pick it up.

"You be careful," Mama whispers. "And if you need us for anything, just call. Never hesitate to call."

"I know, I know." I kiss her quickly on the cheek and go to the front door where Red is waiting. My parents follow us onto the porch. The people in the car all turn and give big friendly smiles and waves. Red has coached them.

"Be careful," Mama calls. "Have fun," and she has that scared look on her face that she gets from time to time, the time Bobby busted his head, the time Andy broke his arm.

"I'll take good care of her. Don't worry!" Red has coached himself.

The car starts and my parents get smaller and smaller and I feel like I am getting smaller, too. Bobby isn't on the porch and I have a horrible feeling that I will never see him again, that while I'm gone something horrible will happen, something that wouldn't happen if I stayed. My parents and Andy are too small to see now and it is a sad feeling, maybe what Mama is feeling—the same way that she felt when I graduated from Kindergarten, when I hugged her around the waist and gave her my last finger-painting. She had looked that way then.

"What's wrong?" I had asked.

"You're growing up." She had smoothed my hair over my head the way that she had always done before I fell asleep. "Soon you'll be as tall as me, maybe taller."

"I don't want to get big."

"Sure you do. It would be sad if you didn't." She had knelt so that we were the same height. "I want you to."

"Well, I'll never leave home!"

"You'll change your mind."

I felt a gnawing homesickness before we ever got on the highway. There are seven of us all together, three in the front, four in the back of this ancient Cadillac that ? Bond owns. Red and I are huddled in the backseat with Scott and Wanda and the back window is covered in heavy plastic. The edge right near my head keeps flapping and letting in quick spurts of cold air. The road gets longer and longer, and I keep thinking about how warm it is at home, how safe I feel at home.

Now, the road gets curvier and I keep tapping the driver on the shoulder. He has long hair, an earring in one ear and does not speak in complete sentences. "Could you please slow down?" I whisper.

"What say?" He is passing a transfer truck so I close my eyes, grip Red's leg and say a quick prayer in my head.

"Gary's (Gary?) a good driver," Red tells me and puts this little white pill in his mouth. He thinks I didn't notice. "Why don't you have a drink?"

"I'll have a drink," Wanda says and pulls a bottle from under the seat, takes a big swallow and passes it. I should be drinking, should get drunk but I am afraid of wrecking, afraid that I will die without having sense enough to think of something really profound, something so profound that maybe I won't die after all. Instead, I get sick.

"Red," I say and grip his leg tighter. "I'm going to be sick."

He laughs with his mouth wide open and he looks like one of the faces they show before the early morning horror films on Saturdays. I have never seen this look before. He laughs and laughs and I feel so cold; my hands are so cold.

He doesn't make Gary pull over until I am all sweaty and gagging. I have just enough time to get beside the ditch beside the highway. The grass is cool and wet and it feels good to my hands and knees and it feels good to put my face against the cool grass when I am through. Everyone in the car is watching me and I can't forget the way that Red laughed. I try to think of something better like when he told me that he loved me.

"Come on, Jo. We're almost there." Red is picking me up so I clutch the grass and carry two handfuls the rest of the way and I keep pretending that I am still beside that cold overgrown ditch, away from these people, by myself.

I have never skied before and the rest of them have so I suggest that they all go ahead and ski and leave me on the beginner slope. I want them all to go and ski and ski and ski and to let me find a warm place to sit and drink a cup of coffee, smoke a pack of cigarettes.

"I'll show you what to do." Red gives me these boots

to put on and even when I stand up straight, I'm at an angle. He clamps me in the skis and then we walk sideways up to where the moving chairs are. I feel weak from being sick and my legs feel like they do when they fall asleep and there is no control. We sit in a chair and start going higher and higher. I start feeling queasy again so I try to concentrate on the bright toboggans zipping below. That makes it worse so I stare at my blue wool gloves, the snaps on my coat.

Before I know what has happened, Red jumps from the chair and is screaming for me to jump out; the chair is going higher and higher and I am yelling, "Stop! Make it stop!" just like I had done once at an amusement park when Bobby had talked me into riding this one wild ride. That time it had stopped; my Daddy had made it stop and he had bought me some popcorn and taken me home. Red can't do that; he doesn't love me.

"Damn, Jo!" He is getting smaller and smaller. "I'll wait right here but next time jummmmp!" I can barely hear him and it feels good, the air feels good and I can sit forever until my Daddy makes it stop.

When I come back around, he is still waiting and I jump feet first. I slide off of the ramp and all I can see are specks sliding, getting smaller and smaller, a cluster of organisms at the end of that sloping white sea. I scream and grab hold of a skinny pine tree and squeeze it until I can hardly breathe. Red is pulling my arms away and I don't know how he does it, but he gets me loose and the next thing that I know, I am sprawled out just a few feet from the tree, covered in snow and freezing.

"Get up and try." Red pulls on my arms. I feel helpless so I stand up and inch my feet so that the skis are straight and I start moving, slow at first, and then faster and faster, so fast that the trees off to one side look like a green stripe painted on white. I keep my feet straight, frozen that way because I don't know what else to do and I don't want to fall. It is in that very second that I realize that I don't know how to stop and it is just that second that I notice the woman just a few yards in front of me. All I can do is scream as loud as I can but that doesn't help because I run her down and turn a somersault off to one side. I turn to see that the woman is all right (she is standing there in her fancy pink suit glaring at me) and all of a sudden, a kid in a red suit is coming right at me. I scream again but not loud enough because he plows into my hip. It doesn't hurt, it doesn't hurt, my whole body is asleep.

My hip is bleeding; I can see it and I am wet all the way through to my long underwear that I borrowed from Tricia. The gray haired ski patrolman is standing over me, fussing me out for not saying "skier on your right" or "skier on your left." I want to explain to him that I don't know how to turn but my throat is dry and his face is getting blurry. There are little black organisms rapidly multiplying all over his face and I can barely see his mouth saying something about a little cart coming to get me. I can barely hear Red say that he will wait for me at the bottom. Swing lo, sweet chariot—I am a blood clot, wet and sticky, sliding down the cool white marrow, down—the air hitting me, making me turn brown, and then black.

When I came to, I was in this room that looked like the sick room at my elementary school. A big nurse was sticking adhesive tape to my skin to hold a white gauze bandage on my hip. I remember looking around and expecting to see Mr. Sauls, the principal, or my Mama coming down the long hall of the school to take me home. Instead, enter Red, and he is followed by Scott and Wanda:

"She can leave whenever she's ready," the big woman calls and walks out. I wish that she had not said that and that I could spend the night here.

"See, you're okay!" Red has already inched his big hands under my thick wool blanket and is feeling around my bare thigh. He must have seen my pants and soggy underwear thrown over the chair at the door.

"Tough break," Scott says and shakes his stringy hair.

"Yeah, what a freak accident. Isn't it?" Wanda nudges Scott with her elbow and then proceeds to put her hand down the back of his jeans. "Me and you haven't even had the time to talk some girl talk, yet."

"Hey yeah," Red says. "You girls have a lot in common." He smiles at me and then back at Wanda. It is a trick. "Wanda loves to read poetry, too."

"Sure do," she says. "Who do you read?"

I shrug. I am uncomfortable here in this bed, a hand on my frozen thigh.

"Wanda is in love with Todd McKuen." Scott says and puts his hand down the back of her jeans.

"Rod, Scott," she says and glares at him. "How many times have I got to tell you, it's Rod!"

"All right, all right, baby. Cool your jets." Scott steps closer and pulls Wanda up with him. "It really was a freak accident. I was in the chair lift and only caught the very end. What happened?"

"Jo's not real athletic." Red's hands are still roaming and he winks at me. "She can cheerlead and ballet but otherwise she's kind of spastic." He laughs and Scott and Wanda chime in and it sounds like the idiotic chorus. Scott and Wanda laugh themselves right out of the room and Red laughs his other hand right under the blanket so I fake a gag and say "feel sick" kind of like Gary would say. Red moves away because nobody wants to be around someone who is about to throw up and I have to remember that; it is a lesson that I will use again.

I use it again that night at the motel when everyone is getting ready for bed. We are in a room with Scott and Wanda and the other three boys say that they are going to go out and "scout" and that they will stay wherever they end up. It bothers me that we have no transportation and that I have no idea where the hell I am besides on a mountain in a cheap motel called The Ranger's Cove. What bothers me even more is that Scott and Wanda think nothing of taking off all their clothes and sprawling out on the bed to watch T.V. Red says that they are a little spaced, a little out of it, and I agree.

"Jo, you're so inhibited," Red says when I come out of

the bathroom wearing the flannel gown from Grandma Spencer. He has turned out all the lights and there is just the dull gray of the T.V. Scott and Wanda have passed out with just their feet under the sheet and Red is sitting with the sheet just up to his waist.

"I'm cold that's all." I cut off the T.V. and climb under the covers.

"You won't be cold for long," he says and this is where I gag. I gag and gag until he leaves me completely alone, won't even talk and I know that he is mad. It occurs to me that I have felt this way before, here, in this bed, not knowing where in the hell I am except in this bed, under the sheet, an exposed ghost. It is a scarey feeling, a lonely feeling and I must do something to make it stop. I must find a new cause.

I don't really remember much about the next day or the ride home. Red still wasn't talking to me which meant that no one else was talking either. They had all said that they were burned out from the night before so I guess that's another reason for the quiet. Whatever it was, I was glad because it gave me plenty of time to think about what I needed to do. I must give up my mission, my cause, in saving Red and turning him into that gallant, successful businessman and husband that I had once pictured so carefully. I must find something new, a new secret thought. I guess I thought the whole way home but I never really came up with anything concrete. All I knew was that I felt a surge of strength, a flicker of hope.

All I know is that when we rounded the corner and I

saw Andy riding his minibike round and round a tree in our front yard, I started crying. I don't know what I thought could have happened in less than thirty-six hours but everything was the same—the trees, the front walk, my bedroom window.

"What's wrong with you?" Red was shaking me and rubbing his bandana all over my face. "Your parents are going to think that I've done something to you."

I just shook my head back and forth. I didn't know exactly why I was crying, why should he? "What's wrong with her?" I heard Wanda whisper to Scott. Everyone was looking and Gary was driving slower than I had ever guessed that he knew how.

"She's afraid that I'm mad at her," Red said loudly and hugged me close. I hated him right then. "Isn't that right?"

We were stopped in front of my house so I nodded and jumped out quickly. Red had a firm grip on my arm and twisted it when I tried to get away. "You know I'm not mad at you anymore."

"Hey, Jo's home." Andy parked his bike, ran up on the porch and knocked on the window until Mama came outside.

"How was the trip?" she yelled, and waved whatever she was knitting.

"Great! Jo never really got the hang of it, got a little too brave for her first try, had a little accident, but she's okay. We had a great time, didn't we?" Red was staring at me so I nodded.

"Oh yeah, it was a ball." I ran up to the porch and then

turned and waved at Red. I watched him get into the car and then the car got smaller and smaller and it felt good just like being in the moving chair. I felt like I needed to do something big, join a club and become the president of it, rededicate my life or something equivalent, though I had never been a believer in rededications. If everything that they told you when you dedicated the first time was true, then there would be no cause to redo it. People did not give God credit for having good sense, and Red had never given me the credit that I deserved.

It had been a month since I had seen or talked to Red. He had only called once right after the skiing trip to say that he needed some time to "find himself." It was very appropriate that he should do that, since finding oneself was as popular as tee shirts bearing the names of rock groups. At first it didn't faze me; I was almost relieved that the lies had stopped, that the old bathroom, bathrobe thoughts had returned. I was constantly seeking a definition of love since I now had some experience on the subject. I spent a great deal of time reading what others thought of love, looking for that definition. It seemed that roses were of some importance: "A rose is a rose is a rose," "O my luve's like a red, red rose," "It was no more or less, really, than we had expected: rose after rose after rose," "O rose, thou art sick!" Too, I discovered that love can be a very depressing thing. It maketh thou heartsick with grief, it maketh thou feel like shit. That's how I began to feel most of the time but I could not tell anyone; I had to smile like a good Jo Jo because they could not have taken it. They could never have understood.

My friends said how good it was that I acted normal again, that I seemed so happy like the old Jo. Tricia even had Cindy, Lisa and me to spend the night at her house in my honor. Lisa even baked a cake and wrote in that yellow gel stuff "Welcome Back Jo" as though I had been off somewhere for ages. They were so glad that Red was out of my life, so happy, that I never could have told them the truth, that I missed him, that I did not know what to do without him. I had to find something to do without him, which really wasn't difficult when I tried.

I was made co-chairman for making all of the plans for the May Court dance and though I was accused behind my back by several girls in my class of trying to use this all out, pert, winning way of mine to be elected the May Queen, it did not bother me for I knew that the entire role was a disguise, a way to keep myself from ever being exposed again. The truth is that I was elected May Queen; the truth is that that wasn't enough. It still upset me to even hear R-e-d's name, to think of him. I tried very hard to control it, especially the day that Beatrice let me know in a subtly blatant way that Red had been down at the lake with Buffy, that he had also been with a real shady girl named Martha who had been married for four weeks and then divorced. I told myself that if he was after scum, that he had no business with me. I told myself that one day when he was all mangled up and dying that my name would be the only murmur from his pained sorry lips.

Still, it bothered me. It bothered me mostly about Buffy because I could see what Red would see in her, what most guys saw in her, what I, had I been a male would never have seen in her because I would have been much too smart for that. Red was not smart enough, not like Bobby, not like Pat Reeves. And, just the thought of Pat Reeves made me feel better. I kept thinking that maybe Pat hadn't really meant all that he said that night of the Christmas dance, that maybe he had really cared and was just covering up, that maybe he still cared. I had nothing to lose. I wrote him a letter, telling him that Red and I had broken up, that I never should have dated Red in the first place, that it would be nice if we could get together some time. I must have read that letter a hundred times before ever mailing it, afraid that I would get a note back that said word for word what Pat had said that night outside of the gym. I mailed it on a Monday and Pat called me on Wednesday; he came home that weekend.

He came home almost every weekend in February and March and we did all of the things that we used to do, went to the movies, played Password with my parents, took long walks around the neighborhood. Sometimes, if Tricia, Cindy and Lisa, or any combination of the three, did not have dates, we would ask them along to go for pizza or to the movies and Pat didn't even mind. Not once did Lisa ever call him queer; Cindy liked to talk to him because she wanted to find out about college math courses; Tricia simply liked him because he did have those perfect chiseled features, something that I had never even noticed. He even seemed genuinely pleased that I had already been named May Queen. Of course they always named the Queen early so that there would be time to get her picture in the annual. Still, Pat seemed impressed and he didn't even make any high school cracks. It seemed he thought that I was an exception to any rule, that I was the first and only queen ever named. Of course, we never made any commitments; we simply dated and he even told me he might date other people at school. I told him that was fine because I knew that he wouldn't and he didn't. He just kept writing long letters, appearing at my house on Friday nights, seeing me to the door after a date. There were a couple of times when we kissed, really kissed, and I would have to peek only to find those large hazel eyes staring at me, at which the kiss would turn to a friendly hug, a kiss on the forehead or cheek. I knew those times that if I told him I loved him that he would say the words back to me, that a commitment would be made. There were times when I was tempted but then, I couldn't do that.

It had been three months since Red and I broke up and though I tried not to think of it, I was very aware of the time that had passed. I needed to do something. I found an old purple dress that my mother had worn one Halloween and put it on. I teased my hair out, put on red lipstick, black gloves and dug up my mother's old lizard purse which I carried with me to Parker's drugstore. I walked all the way, just swinging my purse and taking my time because it was a beautiful Saturday morning. The booths in the fountain area were overflowing with shoppers and salespeople but I managed to find one empty stool at the counter and squeezed right in. I ordered a cherry Mountain Dew and sat there sipping even though I knew that everyone was staring at me. I decided that the only way I could drink my drink without budging from that green vinyl stool was to pretend that I was the only person in town who was normal. It worked and when I walked outside and saw the way that the sun made everything look so sharp and clear, I decided I was going to be that way from then on. No acts, I was Joslyn Marie Spencer and I was no either/or.

Cars kept stopping to look at me but it didn't matter, nothing mattered. Why, those people should be ashamed of themselves looking the way that they did; copies, copies, copies. Didn't they know that they were seeing an original person? Get your eyes full and then fill your pockets!

"Jo? What are you doing?" Out of the blue day, Red steps out of K-Mart's auto center. He has gotten a haircut and it looks nice that way, a "nice" cut like Bobby's, like Pat Reeves. He wipes his face on the sleeve of his shirt and starts walking towards me but I pay him no mind. I just keep walking and swinging my lizard purse behind me. "Hey, wait up!" He runs up and grabs my arm the exact same way that he grabbed it that last day we were together, only this time, it is a softer, more tender grab. His eyes are softer; his hair is short; his clothes are neat except for the grease splotches. "What's this? Some kind of initiation?"

"You could say that." I smile at him and it doesn't even

hurt me. I don't even feel my cheeks puff up like a chipmunk and my lips spread, my teeth shine.

"You look great," he says. "I've been wanting to call you."

"So, why didn't you?" I open my purse to get my red lipstick and put some more on. I can apply it without looking.

"I was afraid that you would never speak to me again after the way that I hurt you." He looks down at the toe of his tennis shoe and scuffs it back and forth like a pitiful little boy who has done wrong. Yes, he is trained well. "I've been so dumb. I wanted to surprise you, to show you the new me."

All work and short hair makes you dull, I think, and I want to say it aloud to test out the sound of that but I'm not ready for such a display. I choose to say, "I see you got a haircut."

"Yes, but that's not all," he says. "Jo, I realize how foolish I've been. I know how you feel about my friends, so many of the things that I do and I see that you're right. You are the only thing that matters to me." He takes hold of my hands and pulls me out of the road so that cars won't have to keep going around me. "Please, let's start all over."

"Well, I don't know," I say. "I've been getting along just fine. I'm the May Queen, you know. In just five weeks, I'll be crowned the May Queen."

"I know," he says and I don't even get a chance to ask how he knows before he launches into a long speech about how he's changed, seen the light, the truth will set you free, hallelujah, praise the lord, and he's going to prove it to me, to Bobby, my parents, my friends; he knows it won't be easy, but he's going to try. Somewhere during that speech I see myself as the winner, the crusader who has saved a fellow man from the shady side, accomplished a mission all by dressing up and going to Parker's drugstore for a cherry Mountain Dew. Was this what I had been waiting for? Was this an answer? Who knows but I said yes, knowing that if I was wrong that I had mastered the art of pretending that I was the norm, the original, the correct.

It seems that everything happened so fast. I had forgotten that Pat Reeves was home and that we had a date that night. When he got there, just fifteen minutes before Red was scheduled to arrive, I couldn't think of anything to say but the truth, which as they say, hurts. Pat Reeves accused me of using him; he accused me of having no interest in him whatsoever. He said that he hoped that I would be very happy with Red, and when he left, he looked at me one good time, as if I might laugh and say it was a joke, tell him that I had changed my mind, and then he turned and left, leaving the front door standing wide open. I had to ignore all of that, pretend that that never happened, tell myself that I had done the right thing no matter what anybody else had to say, believe that Red was sincere, believe that he really did work every night except Friday and Saturday which he quickly adopted as the nights he would eat at my house and watch T.V. That was, he said, the way to win my parents' confidence. Maybe, he said, he could go running with

Bobby when Bobby came home; maybe, he said, he could take Andy out and teach him how to high jump or how to keep his minibike tuned up. He was trained very well and I had the greatest feeling of hope that everything was just fine. I had always heard, "You may shit on me once, but no one gets the chance to do it twice." I gave Red that second chance, just like Pat Reeves had given me.

I feel very guilty about not seeing Red on a Friday night but I have to work on the May dance decorations with Tricia, Lisa and Cindy. "Do what you want," Red says. "if it's that important to you, I guess I'll just have to understand."

"I really need to," I say and I have this awful feeling that I am going to cause him to go away again. "Maybe I can see you later."

"No, I don't want you driving down to the lake at night. I'd worry about you." His voice is filled with concern and this makes me feel much better. "Go and do what you have to do. I'll see you tomorrow."

"Thanks, Red," I say because he is so understanding these days.

Beatrice stops by the high school for just long enough to run in the tissue paper that she is supposed to bring. "Here, Jo," she says and hands me the paper even though there are plenty of people closer to her. It always surprises me that Beatrice always, in some small way, helps out with all of the dances and school functions that she makes so much fun of. Sometimes, she acts like she wants to be friends in an odd way or maybe she feels guilty and uncomfortable because I've seen her messed up so many times. She is probably afraid that I will talk about her.

"Thanks," I tell her. "Aren't you going to stay and work?"

"No, I've got plans," she says and puts her hands in the back pockets of her jeans and stretches. I hear a few people laugh but it doesn't faze Beatrice. "Big plans," she says loud enough for everyone to hear. "I thought you'd be going to the party, too, Jo, or are you and Red on the outs again?" She stares and her eyes look funny, like they're crossing again; she has bags under her eyes like she's been crying.

"No, we're fine," I say though I have to climb up a ladder and adjust the chicken wire planet that we are constructing. "I just needed to be here tonight."

"That's a shame," she says. "Scott and Wanda throw really good parties. I'm sure Red must have told you that they're using his place to have it."

"Oh yes," I say and then I watch Beatrice swing down the hall with a confidence that I have never seen in her. I suppose that Mark Fuller has made her that way. All of a sudden, I fell like I have been socked in the stomach, that it is all happening again. Cindy, Tricia and Lisa follow me into the bathroom because I am crying. I have been crying since I crawled down from the top of that ladder without putting one piece of tissue paper into the chicken wire, red paper for Mars. We are constructing the Universe; our theme for the dance is about space though I can't remember the exact words.

"What is the theme for our dance?" I ask so that they will forget I'm crying.

"Jo Spencer, look at me!" Lisa says and her voice has that strong but soothing maternal effect. It makes me cry more. "Red has you upset, doesn't he? That's been the trouble lately."

"Is that true?" Cindy stands back as though I'm contagious and whispers.

"There weren't ever problems at home, were there?" Lisa is very persistent like a mother. "All those things that we've ever heard about Red are true, aren't they?"

"All what things?" I ask and what I really want to know are the exact words about the universe. What are those small words that will forever bind the class of 1975 when aliens dig up a big chicken wire planet?

"Jo, you know. Don't act like you don't!" Lisa swings me around and makes me look in the mirror. "Look at you, your eyes. They're always puffy from crying." It is noticeable; I can't believe that I have not noticed this myself, that my friends have and didn't tell me.

"That's no way for the Queen to look," Tricia says and tries to get a laugh.

"And dieting," Lisa continues. "Look at you, a size seven. I wear elevens, do I look fat?" Lisa steps back and I look at her. No, she doesn't look fat at all. I shake my head. She is tall and can carry it. I am short and cannot. I can't carry weight. I look back at myself and it is obvious that I cannot carry my weight. There is simply too much of me; there is way too much.

"Does Red do that to you, too?" Lisa continues. I have to think about that. Does Red do that to me, too? If it's one thing I can't stand, it's a girl who doesn't take care of her body, Red says. Don't you ever get that way, Jo. No, no, I will never get that way.

"I just like to watch my weight," I say.

"Well, you can watch it without starving yourself," Cindy says a little bit louder.

"Really, Jo," Tricia says and puts her arm around my shoulder. "What have you got to be upset about?"

"Dump him!" Lisa says. "There are loads of guys that want to go out with you, Pat Reeves for one!" That is hard to believe. Pat Reeves doesn't care about me; he said so one time. They just want me to be without a boy-friend. They don't know all I know about Red; they don't know what Red can be like I know.

"You hate Red, don't you?" I turn around so that I don't have to look at myself. "You've always hated Red!"

"It's not that so much as we hate what he's doing to you!" Lisa is crying which is dumb. Grown up mother types don't cry, or do they? Did my mother cry when I told her that I was ugly or did I cry? What are those words about the universe? No, none of that happened and the truth is that I don't cry, ever, not really. And none of this is true. I can go right down to the lake and everything will be fine.

"I have to go to the lake," I say. "Red is expecting me."

"Jo, don't go," Lisa pleads. She is begging and Cindy

is begging. Tricia doesn't say anything. "You'd have to be crazy to go down there alone," Lisa says and grabs my arm.

"But, I told him that I'd go." Yes, now I have myself together.

"I'll go with her," Tricia says and hands the tissue paper that she has been holding to Cindy. "Let's go, Jo, before it gets too late."

"Thanks," I tell her and I face Cindy and Lisa whose mouths are wide open. "I'm okay, ya'll. We'll be careful and we'll be right back."

"Call me," Lisa says and then looks at Tricia. "Please don't stay down there long. I may have my nights on occasion but nothing like what goes on at the lake at night."

"I hope everything's okay, Jo," Cindy whispers and Tricia pulls my arm and I follow her, down the long silent halls of the high school, through the parking lot to her car. It is a silent night and we listen to the radio all the way to the lake. Tricia keeps saying that she is doing this only for me, that she doesn't think we should be doing it. I listen to her but it doesn't bother me because I know that Tricia will see the truth, that everything is fine and then, I'll have a witness.

The cabin looks dark except for the small candle burning in the front room and the gray silence of a T.V. with the volume turned down. I walk in because I have done that before. Scott and Wanda sit, their glazed eyes staring into the candle. Tricia's hands cling softly to my sweater. "I don't like this," she whispers. "He's not here."

"Well, hey," Wanda says and looks up. "Come on in."

"Where's Red?" I ask. "Isn't he here?"

"Somewhere," Wanda says. "He's somewhere."

"Nah, he left," Scott says and I can tell he is lying. "He wasn't feeling well."

"I thought there was a party," I say. "Beatrice said that ya'll were having a party."

"Beatrice?" Wanda asks and holds up a glass of burgundy wine. "You can't believe a word she says. Have some? We can make it a party."

"No thanks." I walk to the door leading to the other room.

"Don't, Jo," Tricia says. "Let's go." She hangs by the door where it's dark.

"Oh, I thought there was just one of you," Wanda squeals. "It's like personalities splitting apart. That really gave me a rush."

"Everything gives you a rush," Scott says and twists her nipple.

"Jo, please!" Tricia's voice is almost shrill, almost like a warning signal and I want to turn around, to get in her car because I know what I am going to find. I know, deep down, I know. I just don't know who it's going to be and at the same time I am thinking, "It can't happen again. What Bobby told me were lies or did Bobby tell me anything? Did anybody tell me anything? Did it happen? Is this happening?"

I turn the doorknob slowly and gently push the door open. I try to ease any creak that the door might make.

"Hey, Mark's in there." Scott jumps up and weaves like a top in slow motion to get his balance. I push the door open and for just a second all I see is the light that goes back and forth like a seesaw, a captured ocean wave that rolls under fluorescent blue light. That tacky light holds my attention, my breath, against the rustle of sheets, feet on the floor.

"I tried to stop her, Red." Scott pushes past me and stands in front of Red. Now, my eyes are focused and I see him, sitting on the side of the bed, no shirt, his jeans pulled down below that hideous inny navel. He is alone.

"What the hell are you doing here? I told you not to drive down here at night." He acts as though I am out of place, as though I have no right, no cause. There is a minute second of relief but no, it's not good enough—there are sounds; there is a light, just a thin crack of light, coming from under the bathroom door. Red sees me looking.

"Somebody's sick," Red says very calmly. "I was just waiting to make sure they're okay." They are? They're?

"Oh God, I'm sick," the muffled voice rings in my ears like some haunting nursery rhyme. "Somebody help." I know that voice, now, I know that voice.

"You are sick," I say to the closed door. "You're all sick." I want to slap Red, to spit on him but I am afraid. How could I have loved this person that I hate so much. The fear comes over me like a wave, rocking, shaking like that blue captured wave.

"Ah, leave him alone," Scott says. "The boy's had a

rough night, got a little messed up because he had looked forward to seeing you tonight. He's just trying to help out a sick friend."

"Yeah," Red says and flops back on the bed and covers his face with his hands. "Your May dance was more important than me. I can dig it but you can't expect me to sit home and watch T.V. everytime that you have something better to do." He is making it sound like I have always done this to him. No, I haven't done anything, nothing at all and I want to scream it but I can't get the words out. Nothing; then there are moans in the bathroom, a stammering, "help me."

"Boy, she's out of it," Wanda says and flops down on the end of the bed. "Who invited her anyway?"

"Nobody," Scott says. "She invited herself after Mark told her to fuck off; ugly little screwed up bitch."

I hate them, hate them all; I hate Beatrice but not enough to ignore her, not enough not to spite them or maybe I do hate her. I go to the bathroom door.

"Jo, I'm leaving," Tricia says and turns around.

"Wait for me. Please, wait." I am crying and I can't control it. "Please, I'll be there in a minute." I push open the bathroom door and I hear the front door slam behind Tricia and I can only hope that she will wait for me.

"Come here, Jo," Red yells and jumps up off the bed. I slam the door and lock it. It is bright, a stark white bulb without a cover, a shower with no curtain, gold specks on dirty white, hairy drain.

"Jo, I'm sorry. Nothing happened." The words are slurred and lost in the echo of the toilet.

"I don't know what to say."

Beatrice gazes up and it occurs to me that there is no trace of intentness left in those eyes. Or if it is there, it is hidden by a film, the black of her pupils so large that they look like a deep deep blue, like a helpless blind dog. I want to slap her, to choke her but instead, I reach and pull her hair out of the commode, flush.

"Get up," I say. "Get up," and I shake her shoulder but it is like rubber, her neck is like rubber.

"I can't," she mumbles. "I'm so sick."

"Please." I pry her hand from the seat and it goes limp in mine, cold and clammy like her face, the white walls.

"Jo, I need help. I need something."

"What? What do you need?"

"Something."

"Come on, get up. Wash your face." I pull on her arm but she only sits back and slumps against the wall. "We'll take you home."

"I can't go home." She closes her eyes and her head drops forward. "I can't go home like this." She grips my hand as hard as she can and I could so easily break it off, snap her wrist, her neck. She looks up and her eyes look wild, foreign and frightening like I have seen before, another time. "You've got everything, do you know that? You've always had everything—even in kindergarten— perfect princess—perfect cheerleader—good at it all— goody goody—get anything you want."

"That's a lie, Beatrice."

"Jo, get out of there!" Red is beating on the door.

"Come drink some wine!" Wanda screams.

"Get the hell out of there. Do you hear me?" He pounds again.

"You see, I've never had anything, you know? I just wanted a little of what you have, Jo." She slumps lower against the wall, her stringy hair pulled to one side. "You see, I've never really had anything, never really fit in with you and your friends. That's why for all of this, you see, because I don't have anything especially since I don't have Mark."

"I see," I say or do I? Do I even care? I feel as cold and distant as the white light.

"I'll knock this damn door down!"

I want to leave, to get far away. "Don't be mad. Don't hate me," Beatrice mumbles and lowers her head to the floor. I open the door to leave.

"Why didn't you let me in?" Red steps forward. "I can explain everything. Nothing happened, baby, I'm sorry."

"Yeah," I say and look at Beatrice.

"Leave her alone. She'll sleep it off." He nudges Beatrice's foot with his toe. "She's always screwed up."

"What about you?" I ask and I can feel my scalp bristling. "Are you always screwed up?" Before I can even finish, he has both of my arms and pins me to the wall. He has that same blank look and he is right in my face.

"Nothing happened. But don't you see . . ." He shakes me. "Something could have happened and it would have happened because you weren't here, because there are things more important to you than being with me. You never want to be with me." He shakes me harder and I have to think of something else, something that can make me feel like this isn't happening. "You don't care a thing at all about being with me, really being with me, and all of a sudden, she comes up and she wants it! Yeah! You know some people really do want it! Everybody's not like you, Jo. Everybody's not frigid and unfeeling. You're fucked up all by yourself. Don't you see? The crying, the way you never say anything—you're crazy! Only a crazy person would be like you. You'd like it if you never had sex, if you never had; you want to pretend that nobody knows that you have. Well, let me tell you baby, they know, everybody knows!"

The smallness comes back, like being wrapped in cotton, so fragile; I can't feel my heart, my breath, can't find a thought, can't cry—numb and black spots—light too bright.

"Even Beatrice, your friend there that you'd like to save, she thinks you're crazy!"

"No, no she doesn't." I look and Beatrice has stretched out on the floor, her pants are wet and her face is as white as the porcelain. I see another face, shoestrings around the head, the old thick glasses resting on her nose, snoring quietly through the night at Holden Beach while I lay awake, even then, awake and trying to think of something that could make some sense.

I see; I see. I see the moon and the moon sees me. God bless the moon and God bless me. "And then the windows failed—and then, I could not see to see." Tricia drove very slow all the way home and talked so low like a lullabye that everything disappeared. Yes, I was okay.

I could handle it. It was just a matter of letting go, giving up, throwing in my guns and hanging up the towel. I told Red that I never wanted to see him again and I suppose that I cried but I really don't remember. I really don't even remember when I got crowned May Queen and Pat Reeves, as a favor he said, stood behind me as my escort. But it happened. I have an old brown negative of us standing there and if I hold it up to the light, I can see our bodies, brownish blood red forms. He, in a suit with a smile on his face. She, in a strapless gown with a tulle skirt and maybe a smile on her face. She is a little overweight, just a little, but everyone tells her that she is the prettiest that she's ever been. Perhaps that was true. It seems to me that I did a lot of thinking, a lot of worrying and somewhere in the midst of all of that, there seemed to be a fear—a fear of being sought out, hurt, squashed like a spider on a sidewalk.

But I had little time to think, for after graduation, the summer bled and ran faster than any other summer ever had. It bled and ran into fall and a forest full of colored leaves, the prettiest that I'd ever seen, and I would crunch, crunch, through them on my way to class where I would sit quietly like a good Jo Jo, do my work like a good Jo Jo, and go back to the robin egg blue room that I shared with a girl named Becky who was very nice and had the slowest Alabama drawl that I had ever heard. She was very funny and had already made friends with everyone on our hall. She kept asking me to go out to eat, or just out, but I wasn't ready for that, yet. I was still thinking

quite a bit, about Red, about how he was going to be
sorry for what he had done to me. I saw Pat from time to
time but he had made it perfectly clear that we were just
friends, that he was dating other people and that I should,
too. It sounded like a lie to me but I told him that that
was just fine. I didn't want to date anybody.

Tricia and Lisa had both gone to Meredith and they
really liked it there. They called every now and then but I
never really saw them. Cindy had gone to Davidson and
it was very hard, she reported, but she loved it because
there were so many more guys than girls. And how are
you doing, Jo? Fine, just fine. Beatrice's grades had gotten so low that she had had to go to a technical school
right near Blue Springs. I never heard from her. As a
matter of fact, I had never even spoken to Beatrice since
that night. She had sent me a note in school one day via
this red-neck guy that I didn't know from Adam's housecat and it was something about how she was sorry and
how Red had told her that he would never love anyone
else but me. Let's be friends, it had said, I want more than
anything to be your friend, you know, like we used to be
way back in kindergarten and grade school. I hadn't an-
swered her because I was so busy what with helping to
choose the cheering squad for the next year when I
would be long gone, what with having to get ready for
college, getting sheets and towels that were pleasing to
the eye but also of durable quality. And graduation night!
That took so much planning and we all sat together and
cheered and cried and said little things like "friends til the

end, I'll keep in touch, Oh silly! How could I forget you?" and when I walked out of that school for the last time, I expected it to fall down and crumble behind me. Instead, it seemed that something had crumbled up inside of me and I didn't even remember having felt that way until I went home for Thanksgiving and found that Beatrice had slit her wrists and bled like a stuck pig.

Everyone talked about it, probably everybody in town between bites of turkey and dressing, talked about it, wondered why she would try such a thing. I did not eat my cranberry sauce or those sliced thin white pieces of meat. I did not want to eat those candied yams with the brown sugar on top either but I did because everyone knows that is my favorite. I didn't want to go to the hospital but I did. I sat in a plastic chair and did the Word Power in an old *Reader's Digest*. Mark Fuller was waiting to see her, too, and he shouldn't have been. It was his razor blade that she used, his bathroom; it was his fault. Her mother was standing by the door, twisting her hands and talking to the doctor; she probably thought it was her fault. Her mother was nice to Mark Fuller and she shouldn't have been; she was nice to me, squeezed my hand and thanked me for coming, and I wanted to say "you're welcome," wanted to smile or say something cheerful but there were no words, no right way to say "I am so happy that your daughter did not bleed to death. I am so very sorry that everyone thinks that she is crazy." I got all the Word Power words correct. That meant that I was a master, exceptional. Beatrice did not want to see

Mark Fuller; she told her mother so. Her mother said, "I'm sorry," and Mark Fuller stared down at the floor like he was hurt, like HE was hurt. "I'm sorry, Jo," her mother said. "She doesn't want to see anyone." I said, "I'm sorry," though I was not, there were no words that I could have said. Beatrice did not want to see me; she did not want to be my friend anymore. She had changed her mind since she wrote me that note way back when the very leaves that I had crunched through up that hospital walk had just turned green. Mark Fuller did not speak to me; I did not give him the chance. He sat in the end chair near the elevator and I stayed in mine and read Points to Ponder. There were none that struck me as something that I wanted to think about. I wanted to ponder the fact that Beatrice's mother was so nice to Mark Fuller when it was his fault; he made her do it and then he came in and found her before she could finish. I wanted to ponder the fact that Beatrice did not want to see me, that she was going to get so far behind in her school work, that she would have to always wear long sleeves, that once she got well it would all be over and everybody would go right back to being the way they had always been, like everybody had done after her pajama party that time, or worse, things would never go back to the way that they were before and people would only remember that she had done that to herself. She may as well have been dead.

The elevator bell rings and it seems it rings and rings and rings, turns into a long moaning buzz inside my ears. Red gets out and lifts his hand to Mark Fuller to which

Mark shakes his head. Red gets this sad look on his face like he cares. It is difficult to get up from that plastic chair but I do when I see Red getting closer. I get up and I walk down that hall to where it says "stairs." I stare at "stairs," my feet moving so quietly, so softly.

"Hi Jo," Red says and puts his hand on my arm ever so lightly, ever so slightly. He strokes my hair which is now very long, very much the way that he had always wanted to see it but it hadn't had the time to grow for him to see it; now it's grown and it doesn't matter. "Didn't expect to see you here."

"Why? I cared." No, not right. "I care."

"I know you do. We all do," he says and for some reason, I forget the time. I think that it is old times and I hug him and press my face into his shirt to hide, get safe. He strokes my back up and down, up and down. No, it isn't that time; it's this time.

"I've got to go," I say and stare at "stairs."

"Jo, can I see you some time?" He is begging but so did Beatrice. She begged the night when he kicked her foot and said she was screwed up. She begged but nobody cared, but I cared and I can't listen. No, I can't hear because of the buzzing. No, he can't see me because I am so busy. I am going to the movies with Tricia, Lisa and Cindy. I am going to go home and get the new *Reader's Digest,* do exceptional on a new Word Power, find new Points to Ponder.

I didn't tell Becky about Beatrice; no one should talk about Beatrice. Becky said that I was acting funny and did I want to go out to eat and talk about it? Who was that boy that had called me long distance? Acting funny? Just because he keeps calling me to say how he has realized how much he loves me? How we can work things out, have a future. That's funny? A future of razor blades and wide mouth laughs? I have taken my final exam for the semester and gotten all C's and that's funny? "But you're through," Becky says. "Let's go celebrate. I go home tomorrow."

"I can't go out," I tell her. "I'm not ready for Christmas." I must sit up all night and read. I get *Winesburg, Ohio* and begin it for the third time. I like the story about hands very much. I makes me feel sad but sort of good inside because it is a feeling that belongs to me. Yes, and I like the story that tells how some people must live and die alone. I feel like that person; Beatrice is like that person. Am I like Beatrice? Was I ever? Did I ever wish anything bad on her and will I almost die because of it. My eyes hadn't crossed way back in Tiny Tots when I accidentally made fun of her but that time, I had made up for that sin. I had made it all up by being nice in such a fit way. But no, I'm not fit anymore, not fit to go into that room. Must get thin, stay small, stay very little so that people can't see me. The phone rings and it is him again. He wants to see me over the holidays, says he's seen Beatrice and she looks so good. Compared to what, I ponder, compared to what? You can't see me, I think, because I am so small. He wants me back, wants everything the way that it was. How was it? I ask but he doesn't know the answer. It is just one of those questions without an answer. I want to see you, he says and I hang up and go back to read. I can't read, though, because my head's too full, my body too heavy. His voice keeps saying the same old stuff, same old shit; you're crazy, Jo, fucked up. I have to get out, run down the stairs, get outside where I can breathe. I love you, Jo Jo, Buzzy wants to kiss you, Jo Jo. It is so cold that the air shoots straight up my nose and into my brain. I must walk fast. Young girls shouldn't walk around by themselves at night. I don't want you driving at night. I can't go outside of the tent, can't walk to the latrine because it's dark and I am so small. I've got to see you, Jo. I hear it; I hear him and it's getting louder and louder. He's here somewhere, in those dark bushes, behind a tree. He's coming for me.

It is cold and I can feel the blood in my heart freezing into clumps, pumping, squeezing my chest, constricting, breathe, puff, puff of fog. There is a magnolia tree. Run to it. He's coming closer and closer. You can do it you can do it you can you can. I run around and around and the huge magnolia leaves are brushing against the ground like brooms, brushing against my legs. He is coming, calling my name and it echoes up against the huge brick dorm, up to the lit rooms. I must crawl under the branches and hide. My knees are cold and rough and I wait, barely breathing, wait. I climb the tree slowly; I see myself: I say put this foot here, hold onto this branch and I get up higher and higher so that I can hide and get warm. I can see the windows, my room, that robin egg blue like two wide eyes. All the windows look warm and the girls are

162

inside painting their nails, playing albums, watching T.V., studying for one last exam as though nothing has happened, as though Jo Spencer has never been born, as though she does not feel her scalp being peeled away like the skin of an onion.

His voice gets louder and louder; it disrupts her reading. She watches Becky putting on makeup. Becky is pretty and Becky is smart; Becky has lots of fun and remains cool and calm. Something is wrong with Becky. She is too nice, too curious.

"Jo? What's wrong?" Becky faces her and Becky reminds her of someone. Who?

"Nothing's wrong," she says and smiles perfectly.

"Why have you got your ears covered up?" Becky laughs and starts putting on mascara. "Does the radio bother you?"

"No, no reason." Becky doesn't hear it. She is the only one that can hear him and he is doing it on purpose. This is what they did to Beatrice. This is how it all happened and it's going to happen again. Get out! Get out!

"Jo? Where are you going?" Becky stops, the mascara tube poised gracefully in her hand. Jo Spencer has never worn mascara. Why should she?

"Out," she says.

"Well, good!" Becky squeals. "I'll be ready in just a sec. There's this really neat bar where everybody goes!"

"No, I'm going for a walk," she says because she can't go where "everybody" goes. People would see. She must get outside where she can breathe and the air is so cold that it shoots up her nose straight to her brain. She has to walk very very fast; run by dark bushes; run, run fast as you can. Climb a tree, it's safe in trees. Climb it like you climbed the oak tree in Mr. Monroe's yard when his cat got stuck. Hear that cat getting louder and louder. "She'll find her way back down," Mrs. Monroe says. "She's always getting herself in some place that she can't get out of." Yes, she's always getting herself up on some place that she can't get out of. "But she needs help, Mrs. Monroe. I'll climb the tree." And she does, slowly, carefully, put this foot here, grab that limb. Meow! Meow! Higher and higher she climbs and then it is safe; it is warm.

He's not down there; he just called on the telephone from Moon Lake. But, he could be down there; he could've used a phone close by, made it sound long distance, could've lied about Beatrice. She must be very careful. She must recite aloud to silence any noise, any sound. "And all the while, for every grief, each suffering, I craved relief with individual desire; Craved all in vain! And felt fierce, fierce . . ." What are the words? Those words to finish it? Give the correct words and you may climb back down, take kitty home, be safe. "Felt fierce, fierce Fire! about a thousand people crawl; perished with each,—then mourned for all!" Yes, you may go now. Hurry, though because it's spooky here. The big blue eyes just closed and you will be all alone in that room. "Hurry up, please, it's time, Hurry up, please, it's time."

It was a blue Christmas just like Elvis says, like Elvis said. She had seen Elvis just the summer before and it was sad to see him because he looked a little bad, because people talked about how he looked bad. Why did they have to talk about that? Why couldn't they remember how he used to be? Why don't they think of what it took for him to get that way? Why doesn't everyone who says how good Beatrice is looking think about what it took for her to get that way? Jo Spencer looks bad and the blue Christmas didn't help. Everyone kept asking her how she felt and she felt fine! It was none of their business. Everyone at church had stared at her because they knew all about her; God knew and it was depressing. The story about the Virgin Mary was so depressing that she had had to cry and get up and run into that little part that always stays dark, up against the big wooden dark doors where the stained glass is so dark that only specks of light get through. She had waited and watched all the people that she knew crawling like ants for a little piece of bread; a piece of flesh, a drink of blood, bloodthirsty; they are saved. Her brother was there; he was going to be a doctor; he was in love and happy. Little brother was there; he is thirteen, a bad year. Red had been there and it had occurred to her first that it was very funny to see him in a church. Was he repenting? No, no, he was following her. It occurred to her second that she wished his last name was Green and then he could only come out once a year when the colors were right.

Yes, it was a blue Christmas like Elvis always says but now everything is going to be okay. A new semester has begun, a beginning, and she is taking Geology (a necessary lab science), Introduction to Poetry Writing, Philosophy of Religion, English II and French II. She thinks: This is a deadly combination. Je ne sais pas why exactly, why God exists or doesn't exist, why rocks are rocks. In the beginning God created the heavens and the rocks or was it the big bang theory? Can it be encompassed into one thesis, one statement of purpose? Is there a ballad about this? Tout le monde!

Too, things are going to be just fine because she has made new rules to follow. The rules encompass all of the basics and they must be followed to a tee or something awful will happen. She must eat only once a day at exactly five-thirty while Andy Griffith is on T.V. She cannot get off of her bed from the minute that the show begins til the very last whistle of the music at the end. Therefore, she must begin preparations for dinner around five, go to the snack bar and get either one cup of Dannon's yogurt (preferably banana) or one cup of cottage cheese. On special occasions she may get one can of chunky chicken soup and of course, a Tab. These things (one of the foods, a Tab, a pack of cigarettes, an ashtray, and a book to skim while the commercials are on) must be placed right beside the bed, turn on the T.V. at five-twenty-five and wait. She must try not to sleep at night because that is when the dream comes, the dream where she is running, running, running, looking for him because something is wrong but the people that she finds can't hear her; they can't see her. She screams and screams but no one knows that she is alive. No, she must sleep in the afternoons when other people are awake. She must be like a fish and swim around all night with her eyes open, work very hard, make good grades like Bobby so that everyone will know that she is okay. All the while that she is awake, she must think big profound thoughts, points to ponder (except when Andy is on) so that she will stay small and she must write all of these thoughts down in a journal. She must keep a journal for English II but any entry that sounds poetical may be handed in twice, once for English II and once for poetry writing.

For just a quarter, she can get on the bus system and ride all day long around the same loop. If she rides long enough, she can know where she is at any given moment and that is a comfort. It is a very pleasant way to ease the guilt of skipping classes. There are too many people in the classes and they all sit too close together. If she does all of the reading then she can still make good grades. It is just that simple and it is a big secret that only she knows. Becky thinks that she goes to class every day and she does. She goes to English II on Monday, Wednesday and Friday at eight o'clock and she goes to poetry on Tuesdays and Thursdays at nine o'clock. Then she hops a bus and rides all day. She wouldn't even go to English II except that she only gets three cuts and she is saving them for when they are absolutely necessary. Thus far,

English II has not been bad because the reading is very nice. Yes, the man in *Zen and the Art of Motorcycle Maintenance* is a very fine man to read about because he is looking for definitions of things which have no definition and she found *The Bell Jar* terribly amusing. It came as a terrible shock when the professor said that Esther Greenwood was crazy. She had never even considered that Esther was crazy, not really crazy. Beatrice had tried to kill herself and she was not crazy, different but not crazy though that's what everybody says now that it's over, that Beatrice must have been crazy. Nobody wants to believe that someone who is not crazy would try to kill themselves, that they would have a good reason. Who knows what crazy is anyway? The reading is very good and that is why she doesn't mind saving her cuts for a big event when one comes along.

Legally, she could cut poetry writing or at least she could have in the beginning but not now. No, it is a personal rule that she must not cut that class except when absolutely necessary. The poetry professor is very funny and this is why she cannot miss class. Another reason is because he has these piercing steel gray eyes and she knows that he can tell about a person just by looking at them. She must attend regularly so that he will find her worthy of being there. He is very encouraging of what she COULD do even though she is not yet doing it and this is the first time that anyone has ever looked into her Could Be's as opposed to her Already Are's. She must not let this man down on these Could Be's the way that Red let her down. If she does, then the man will hate her the way that she hates Red. She is very pleased with the poem that she has worked on all day on the bus. She began it at ten-fifteen, right after class and it is now five o'clock and time to begin dinner preparations. The poem is called "Amoebae" and there are so many good words about amoebae, slither, slide, shapeless, spineless, splitting. They put a false foot forward and never draw it back. It is a pleasant point to ponder, one that can keep her busy until she sees Andy and Barney.

Jo Spencer wakes late at night; the green hands of the clock show that it is three-fifteen. How did this happen? She has not really been asleep, not really, because she doesn't sleep at night, because the thoughts were there, the panic that will not dissolve in the gray morning as it used to, as it used to be sucked away like a snake's venom, bubbles down the bathtub drain. She wants that Saturday night squeaky clean, skin rubbed to a vigorous pink, wrapped in flannel jammies—sit on the floor and let the big dog Jaspar chew on the fuzzy slippers that came last Christmas—rest your head on Daddy's knee and watch the gray T.V. light flicker on the knotty pine paneling, watch every fear of the day dissolve into the gray, into the hum and the lullaby will hum in the warm bed where only nice dreams are allowed.

Taking a shower is difficult: She must tiptoe down the hall, that fluorescent glaring hall that never changes whether day or night. Quietly, check behind every shower curtain, check every toilet stall for someone lurking there and waiting for this to happen. Do they disappear when she looks only to come back once she is in her shower stall, behind her own curtain, the one at the very end, the last to be gotten should someone come after her?

The water is hot and her skin breathes the stream. Her body becomes full like a plum, rosy and full while it drinks, that thirsty prune. She leans against the side of the stall, now warm, and slowly, ever slowly, slides down and sits in the corner, her feet straddling the drain. From here, she can see; if anyone comes, she will at least see. The water swirls down the rusted hole and is gone like the years of young girls who have been in this same place—the hair that must be squeaky clean on ballgame Saturdays, the legs that must be shaved on those warm days when it is hot enough to lie out, then afterwards to remove suntan oil.

There is one hair and she knows it is there without looking—stuck near the top of the stall where it stays dry, protected—one pubic hair, stripped from its home, isolated, and God only knows WHERE it came from, how it manages to stay there night after night. It is familiar and she can count on it. She cannot imagine what she would do if it was not there.

She turns off the water and waits. The water runs from her body and the cool air seeps through the damp cloth curtain. It should be embroidered like a shroud, that damp cloth. She puts back on her flannel gown and pulls it to her back, her chest to blot the water and tiptoes out, quickly, never looking back to see if there are feet in any of the toilet stalls. It is four-thirty and she is very tired but cannot sleep. She must read in the hall where it is light, where no one is breathing.

Hesiod says that the world order begins with the separation of earth and sky. Anaximander agrees. Isn't that just like him, though?! "The opposites, which are present in the one, are separated out from it. The 'opposites' are the hot, the cold, the dry, the moist, and the rest." It makes sense but how did they separate the earth from the sky. It seems simple but what about the horizon, where one starts and the other ends, that point where they appear to come together and yet you cannot reach that point because of the curve, that constant curve and the very way that the world moves. Way to go Chris! Hesiod says there is a region between the earth and the sky, the chaos, it means "gap." Yes, the inbetween person has a gap. Red is gapped, crapped, but why does his name stay on her brain? Why does every single bus stop remind her to think of him? Why does Hesiod have to be so damned sexual. She cannot escape S-E-X. All beginnings have to depend on S-E-X: Adam and Eve, Hesiod's "wide bosomed earth and Tartarus of the dark mist." Amoebae are not that way: her poem is very important for this reason. Amoebae reproduce themselves; they just slide around having sex with themselves. She has read about people who slide around having sex with themselves, she bets that Red does this often, but a person cannot reproduce themselves by themselves. It is not fair. Only Mary was able to do this and that example is not even worth citing. It is depressing, all of it is very confusing and depressing, but she can't stop reading it because eventually, she thinks, an answer will spring forth. The Old Testament says that the "vital substance" should not be wasted. Red does that, too; he wastes his vital substance. She hopes that he will run out of this fluid at an early age and that his hair will go limp and stringy, his body limp and stringy and that his voice will get real high like the Pardoner in *The Canterbury Tales* and she will say, "I told you so." That merde tête!! Why does he haunt her brain? Why does she have an urge to write a mournful poem for him when she hates his guts? She must do something better, something to lighten her mind. T.V. tunes is the best way to do this. She must think of a show and then hum the music. I Love Lucy—that one is easy; lean against the wall, curl into a ball, you have two hours of solitude before the day begins. Leave It to Beaver—yes, that one is easy because you can see Beaver coming up the walk with his school books, or is he going down the walk with his school books? Who are his parents? That's easy—Ward and June Cleaver. Another one —Bewitched—easy because she is in that black dress like a cartoon; it starts when the frying pan starts smoking and at the end she is a black cat and leaps into Darrin's arms. Oh no, what is Dick Van Dyke? She can hear the little trill where he trips over the stool but what is the part before that? What is it? Her brain is numb, can't think, too late, can't sleep, not yet. With Rose Marie and Morey Amsterdam! She can hear it all except the music. She will go crazy if she can't remember that music. Red will remember! He was always so good at this game.

She must tiptoe into the room, do not disturb Becky or she will want to know what you are doing. Becky must never know what you are doing. Get a dime, carefully; there is one in the pocket of the jeans that you wore last week. Go to the dorm lobby, tiptoe, count the stairs down all four flights. Put in the dime, dial the number. Do you remember the number? Oh yes, that's easy. Ring-ring-ring-ring—it is early so let it ring a long time. "Hello?" Red sounds so sleepy, like a tiny person, a child. "Hello?"

"Hey," she whispers.

"Jo?" It sounds like he is waking up. "What in the hell are you doing. What time is it?"

"I don't know, some time," she whispers.

"What do you want?"

"I've got a problem."

"Yeah, I know," he says.

"You knew?" She asks. Isn't that just like him, though? "Well, what's the music?"

"What?" There is noise at the other end. Is it another person? No, Red is just shifting around.

"Dick Van Dyke, I can't seem to get it. I get this part." She does the little trip over the stool part. "And then I can just hear them saying 'with Rose Marie and Morey Amsterdam' but I can't get all the music."

"I don't know what the hell you're talking about. I can't help you."

"You used to know," she says and cannot help but to cry. Has he forgotten everything?

"That must have been another one of your boyfriends,"

he says. "Maybe it was Pat Reeves. I hear you see right much of him these days."

"No, no I don't," she explains. She doesn't want him to be upset with her. "I haven't seen him in a long time. He's not my boyfriend." Déjà vu. It is a weird feeling.

"Well, I don't know what you're talking about." He gets real quiet, mumbly. "Look, I gotta work tomorrow."

"You don't have to," she says and she doesn't know why. "You don't have to do anything. Just like me. I don't have to do anything except think of the music."

"Look, I gotta . . ."

"No! Don't go! Don't do this to me. You can't go until you tell me the music. Please, please, please."

"Listen, you tell me that you never want to see me again and then you start calling me up because you've forgotten something. Who do you think I am, some kind of nut? I don't have to listen to you; I don't want to listen to you."

"Yes, you do because it's your fault," she screams. "It's all your fault that everything happened and now you act like nothing happened."

"Ah shit, I don't have to listen to you anymore," he says. "Why don't you find somebody that will listen to you. Pat Reeves or hell, anybody. You could probably get some dates. Why don't you?"

"Why don't I?" she yells. "I can get dates anytime that I please. I just don't feel like it right now. I have better things to do."

"Keep doing like you're doing and nobody will ask you out."

"Who asked you anyway, merde tête? merde tête?"
She slams down the phone and runs back up the stairs.
She doesn't have to count them. What did he mean by all
of that? Was he trying to win her back? Well, Ha! She can
get dates! She can do whatever she pleases, anything. Besides, that might not have even been Red. It was someone pretending to be him.

Becky roommate is all aflutter because Jo Spencer has
a date. Jo Spencer does not mention the fact that she herself called up this old friend who goes to Duke and said,
"Long time, no see, friends til the end." She thinks it is a
better idea to let Becky get lots of mileage out of the fact
that her dried up roommate has a date for the first time
since before Thanksgiving.

"This is the same guy that you've been out with before, right?" Becky asks. Jo Spencer nods nonchalantly.
"He asked you out after that but you didn't want to
see him."

"Correctement," she says and fluffs out her long auburn
hair. "I had a change of heart."

"Well, I'm glad to hear it!" Becky squeals. "It's time
that you start having some fun and stop studying so
hard." Becky does not know about the F on the Geology
quiz. Ah well, what she doesn't know can't hurt her now
can it? "You even took down that picture of that old boyfriend of yours."

"Did I have a picture of him?" she asks and giggles a
coy giggle.

"Oh, you!" Becky says and flops down on her bed. "It was right up there on your shelf."

"My, my, the things we forget. Why, I must have put it up there without thinking. Funny, now that it's gone, I can't remember what he looks like." She goes to her closet and starts trying to decide what to wear. It occurs to her that the only thing she has worn in months has been the same pair of levis and a gray sweat shirt that says Blue Springs High. Had she even washed them? No, she couldn't have because the jeans were so big and loose. If she had washed them, they would have fit to a tee just the way her clothes always fit—to a little tee.

"Here, let me help you decide what to wear." Becky jumps up and runs over to the closet. Please, do, since you know so much about these things.

"Okay, I'll let you," she says.

"Did he say what ya'll are going to do?"

"We're going out," she says and she tries to remember what Pat had said. What had he said? Something about a party, going out to eat. "I think we're going to a party."

"Well, he would have told you if it was formal," Becky says. "So, you should go casual. It's better to be underdressed than overdressed."

"Oh, if it was a formal, I'd have the perfect dress to wear. It's emerald green with a slit up the side." She puts her hands on her hips, leans back, sucks in her cheeks like a perfect model. Becky laughs. That is good! Becky thinks she is funny; she can have an effect on people!

"Try these," Becky says and holds out a pair of black

wool pants. Are those her pants? "And this sweater." Becky pulls out a sweater that she has not seen in ages. It is pale blue, fluffy, fuzzy angora, with little pearl buttons up at the neck. She takes off her nightgown and throws it on the bed. It looks lonely without her in it. She puts on a bra first and then the sweater.

"Perfect!" Becky says. "That is a beautiful sweater! Look at all your clothes, Jo. If I had known, I would have been borrowing from you." Becky laughs again. Becky would like to borrow her clothes—HER clothes; share and share alike, like friends. She puts on the pants and they do not look as good as the sweater.

"My God!" Becky says. "When did you buy those pants?"

"I don't remember."

"Well, they're way too big for you." Becky pulls up the pants and clutches a handful of material to make them stay up. "When did you lose so much weight? I mean I knew that you had lost but these things must be two sizes too big."

"Maybe they're my mother's pants."

"Don't you know?" Becky is looking for something else. She finds some navy pants that fit the same way.

"What has happened to all of my clothes?" Jo Spencer asks and Becky looks funny. She is funny, amusing, so entertaining; she has effects.

"How about a skirt?" Becky asks. "If a skirt is too big, you can disguise it by leaving the sweater out."

"Yes, yes, let's disguise it!" she says and puts on a

black skirt. It is a straight skirt and it is hardly noticeable that it is hanging two inches longer than it is meant to hang.

"Hemlines are coming down anyway," Becky says when she steps back to get a good look. "You really should try to gain some weight though, Jo. I didn't realize how skinny you had gotten because you're always in that big gown." It has worked. The gown has worked and now she is so small that she can hardly be seen. She can live without others seeing. "Now, what about makeup?"

"I don't wear makeup," Jo Spencer says because she doesn't need makeup. She has never worn makeup.

"Well, you used to," Becky says. "That picture of you and your brother when you were in high school, you're wearing makeup."

"Was I?"

"Yes," Becky says and begins rummaging through her own drawers. "Here's mascara, eyeliner, blush, lipstick, try them."

"I have some lipstick," she says. "I keep it in my lizard bag. It's called fire engine red."

"Oh, Jo, be serious," Becky laughs again and again. "Have you been drinking this afternoon?" Why does everyone always ask her that, "have you been drinking, Jo?" She has not had anything to drink since that night a long time ago at Moon Lake when she fell in love. Is that what drinking could do, make her fall in love? make good things start happening?

"I don't drink," she says.

"At all?" Becky asks. "I can't believe it. You're the only person I know who doesn't drink and isn't real nerdy. I always thought you did drink."

"Nope," she says and brushes on nice peachy cheeks. "I have before, though. You know," she pauses, the mascara tube poised gracefully in her hand, "it doesn't bother me at all to be around people who do. You know, it doesn't bother me that you do. Actually, I've never even noticed that you did."

"Come on, Jo, all those nights that I've sat here with some of the girls on the hall playing cards and drinking beer?" Becky shakes her head. "You didn't notice? You were sitting right there watching T.V."

"I don't notice a lot of things, Beck," she says just as seriously as she can. She has never called her "Beck" before and that is quite hilarious. Beck thinks so, too.

"You sure could have fooled me," Beck says. "And look at you. Your first date in months and you're not even nervous. Hell, I'm always nervous when I go out."

Beck has told a lie. Why should she ever get nervous? She is most attractive and very smart. She has no reason, no cause, to be nervous. "I have no reason," she says. "Tell you what, Beck, just to show you how I am, I'll drink a beer with you right now."

"You want to?" Becky asks. "Before your date?"

"Sure," she says, "nothing bothers me." She turns around and fluffs her hair out so that it will look like one of those girls on the front of *Cosmopolitan*. It doesn't work quite that way but still she looks good, she hardly recognizes herself.

"You look terrific, Jo. Wish I had a date tonight." Becky opens the small refrigerator and pulls out two Miller Lites. "Guess I'll just go out with the girls."

"I might want to do that one night," she says. "Go out with the girls." That has a nice ring to it. A long time ago, she was "one of the girls" wasn't she? Sure!

"Great!" Beck says and takes a long swallow. "I'm glad to see you finally coming out of your shell."

"Like a turtle?" She is very serious but Beck is not so she takes a long swallow of her own beer. So this is how it is—throw back your head and chug it—you can do whatever you please. Ha! Ha! Red thinks you can't do anything on your own but he is crazy! "Hey, did you used to watch Laugh-In?" she asks and Beck nods. "That part where they say something like If Barbara Bain married John Wayne, she'd be Barbara Bain Wayne and if she divorced him and married Michael Caine, she'd be Barbara Bain Wayne Caine."

"Hey, yeah," Beck says, "I had forgotten all about that. Do another one."

"If Doris Day married Danny Kaye she'd be Doris Day Kaye and if she divorced him and married Zane Grey, she'd be Doris Day Kaye Grey."

"And Dr. Shea! She'd be Doris Day Kaye Grey Shea." Becky finds this terribly funny and gets two more beers out of the refrigerator.

"Who's Dr. Shea?"

"You know, he used to be on As the World Turns."

"I haven't seen that since Lisa and Bob got a divorce," Jo Spencer says. "My mother used to watch that one." It is funny to think of her mother right this second. Her mother has changed since those days when she ironed clothes and watched As the World Turns, not drastically, because basically, she looks the same but there are changes, subtle changes and she cannot pinpoint exactly what they are. Jo Spencer can get a picture, though, the T.V. on, black and white, her mother ironing while she and Bobby eat vanilla wafers and Andy? Is she pregnant in the picture? Yes, wearing an old plaid smock and stretchy pregnant pants and the afternoon light comes through the drapes and casts thin white lines on the pine paneling and the dust rides these stripes of light and she and Bobby try to sweep the specks away but they only come back, slowly move around the room until there is no light left and by that time, her mother is cooking dinner and Andy Griffith is on the T.V. Or was it Huckleberry Hound? When did Huckleberry Hound come on? Quick Draw McGraw?

"Yoo hoo! Earth to Jo," Becky screams and waves her arms. "Lordy, that was ages ago when Lisa and Bob divorced. I can't believe that you never saw Dr. Shea."

It is six o'clock and Jo Spencer has a date at seven. She must look at herself in the mirror again. My yes, she looks like perfection! Like a princess, a May Queen.

"Did I ever tell you that I was the May Queen?"

"Why no!" Beck squeals and kneels.

"Yep," she says and sits back down. She must smooth her skirt very carefully so that it doesn't wrinkle before her date. "What time did Huckleberry Hound come on in the afternoons?"

"I don't know. Why'd you think of that?" Beck puts on an album. It is Boz Scaggs and Jo Spencer approves of this. She likes Boz Scaggs. She loves the song "It's Over"; it makes her feel like she is moving all over even though she is perfectly still. "Why can't you just get it through your head? It's over! It's over!" It is an apropos song to think. Beck is looking at her. What is it that she is supposed to say? Oh yes.

"I think of lots of things."

"Boy, I'll say." Becky is lying flat on her back doing the bicycle exercise. "How can you remember all that stuff when you can't even remember when you bought all that stuff in your closet?"

"Priorities," Jo Spencer says. "Do you remember Milton the Monster? I'm Milton, your brand new son!"

"Hey, yeah!" Becky sits up. "That's the music, too. What about the Jetsons?"

"Meet George Jetson, his boy Elroy, daughter Judy, Jane his wife—du du du du du du." Jo Spencer must move her hands with the proper dus because she does not have a good singing voice. "The music that I can't remember is Dick Van Dyke."

Beck thinks for a minute and then starts doing Lassie. How easy can you get? And that is such a very sad song. She can just see Timmy burying those toys and all of a sudden, woof woof arf arf, and here comes Lassie barrelling down that hill. She and Bobby had watched that one every single time and she had always cried but Bobby hadn't, or had he? Had Bobby ever cried?

"Lassie," she says so that Beck will stop with the sad

songs. "But who was Lassie's owner after Timmy?"

"Oh! I know, it was that ranger," Beck screams.

"But what was his name?" Jo Spencer waits for Beck to answer but Beck can't remember. She really shouldn't tell the answer because that's not the way the game is played but Beck says that she will go crazy if she doesn't know. Jo Spencer cannot carry that burden, the burden of someone's insanity. "It was Corey Stewart."

"That's right!" Beck says and goes to get another beer. "Last one, wanna split it?"

Jo Spencer must think about this. Should she share with Beck, a person that she knows but has never thoroughly exposed herself to? She is feeling good, just like that night at the lake a long time ago. It could even happen again, she could fall in love again, because this is the right feeling; big thoughts are coming in so fast that she can hardly think of them. "Yeah, okay. Let's split it."

While Beck pours half into a plastic cup like the kind that people who go to the football games get and save, Jo Spencer must get up and check the clock and her face once again. Perfect, she still looks perfect and it is just twenty minutes before time for Pat, just twenty minutes before she can test her effects, her charm. She drinks her half fast, faster, fastest and sings along with Boz in spite of the fact that she doesn't know all of the words.

"I'll get it," Beck says when there is a knock on the door. "You just stay cool and calm." There is no need for Beck to tell her this because she is already very cool and calm.

"Why, hi Pat!" she says in such a friendly voice. "Long time, no see." She gives him a hug, a coy, flirtatious hug. "It's so good to see you!"

"Looks like you girls have already started partying," he says and looks around the room. He has yet to look Jo Spencer directly in the face.

"Oh yes," Jo says and giggles. "You know how it is when the girls get together." She punches Beck in the shoulder like all good friends do.

"Are you ready to go?" Pat asks and she gets her coat off the end of the bed. It is the beautiful camel coat that she got just last Christmas before she went on a skiing trip. It seems like she's had it for years. "Nice to have seen you again, Becky." He is so polite! So effective!

"See you later, Beck," she says cooly, calmly. "We'll finish what we were talking about later, okay?"

"Okay," Becky laughs and starts doing Hogan's Heroes. "Ya'll have fun."

"Oh, we will," Jo yells and slams the door. "I just know that we will." She loops her arm through Pat's and they walk side by side all the way down the stairs. It could be happening, she can feel it all over and she wants to talk and talk and talk. She wants to tell Pat about that pubic hair in the shower stall but no, she must save that, she must have some secret all her own. "So, where are we going tonight?" she asks as though they go out every night.

"Some friends of mine are having a party."

"Oh terrific!" she says and hugs his arm. "I've been

wanting to meet your friends." She is very relieved that they are not going out to eat. Why, she has already eaten a can of chunky chicken soup because the night is so special and what would he have thought if he had taken her into an elegant restaurant and she had had to tell him that she had already eaten!

"You have?" he asks in a funny way. He takes her hand off of his arm and opens her car door. While he walks around, she has one split second of dark silence in which she decides that this is the night for Jo Spencer to come out of her shell. "It's been a long time since I've seen you," he says. Yes, she knows that. She knows that she has made him suffer too long. She wishes that she had another beer. "You look so different," he says and stares at her.

"It's the hair," she croons. "See how long." She pulls her hair over one shoulder.

"Yeah, and you've lost weight."

"Just a little," she says. "You know how us girls have to watch our weight. If it's one thing I can't stand, it's a woman who doesn't take care of her body."

"Yeah," he says and stares straight ahead. "So, how's school going?"

"Just fine!" She lights a cigarette and holds it poised so delicately in her fingers. If she glances nonchalantly to one side, she can see the fire twice, the real fire and the reflection in the car window.

"What are you taking?" Pat asks and she can tell by his surface questions that her presence is making him nervous. He cannot control his feelings and thoughts about her and he is building up to serious things. She will make it easy for him; answer the questions.

"French II, English II, Poetry Writing, Philosophy of Religion and Geology."

"Boy, that's a rough schedule."

"Not really," she says very casually and takes a long draw on her cigarette. "You see they all are basically the same course."

Pat Reeves has to laugh at this one, just has to laugh because she is so entertaining, elegant, intelligent. "I don't see that."

"Foundations, structures," she says and uses her hands and eyebrows in a serious yet enticing way. "You see everything has a foundation for the formation. Rock formations, thought formations, word formations. Do you see how it all connects."

"Not really, but I'll take your word for it."

"Really, Pat, I'd think that you could see," she says and pouts a pretty little perfect pout. "Why sometimes I can even use the same material over and over just in different terms, say it in English, say it in French, use geological terms, philosophical terms, poetic devices."

"Give me an example," he says and laughs again, this time an "I'm not believing a word of this but aren't you just cute as a bug" laugh.

"Okay," She clears her throat. "Take for example a word like 'petrify.' You know you can trace it back to a French word meaning stone or something but that's not even important. Think about it, petrified wood, one little piece of wood hardened by years, turned to stone. It's not really wood and not really rock."

"Go on," he says and laughs a "this is nonsense" laugh. "I'm listening."

"Well, don't you see? You could put it into some sort of form and the whole time it would sound like it was about a piece of petrified wood when really it would be about a person. Sort of like 'You can never soften me but do not pine, you may chisel the features you want and they will be mine.'"

"Oh Jo," he says and reaches over and slaps her leg the way that good friends always do. "You had me going for awhile there." He doesn't want to talk about this so she must laugh right along with him like it is all a joke. "Here we are." He stops the car in front of a little white house.

"I thought your friends were students," she says.

"They are!" He gets out and she doesn't wait for him to open her door. "All students don't live in dorms you know."

"I know that, silly," she says and slams her door. "I just like living in a dorm. There are so many different places you can go inside a dorm. It's like not seeing the forest for the trees."

"I'm not even going to ask about that one," he says and opens the door to the house. He doesn't even knock.

"Hi Pat! We were wondering where you were!" This girl wearing a skirt that looks like an old beach towel opens the door. "And you must be Jo."

"That's me," she says and follows Pat Reeves into the room. She smiles and nods at everyone and they go to the kitchen where there is a keg of beer.

"Here you go," Pat says and hands her a cup. It is a big plastic cup all to herself. "Come on and I'll introduce you. Some people from Blue Springs are supposed to be here."

"Who? Who?" she asks in that precious way, half hoping that Red will come, half hoping that he will not. Hoping that he will so that he will see how she doesn't need him—hoping that he will not because he has ruined her life. Love is a rose but you better not pick it, Linda Ronstadt sings.

"Do you remember Nancy Carson and her friend Buffy?"

"Do I remember? My brother dated that whore bag for years."

Pat looks at her real funny and so does the girl in the beach towel skirt, and another girl with long blonde hair who is wearing a bright pink skirt with frogs on it that are blinding. Has she said something wrong? If you can't say anything nice, don't say anything at all. Who the hell said that little tidbit? Had she said something wrong? Heavens no! "Those two are bad news let me tell you!" Again the funny looks. She doesn't have to eat those words. Is this a little faux pas? A little false step? Put a false foot forward and never draw it back!

"Jo's a real kidder. You just got to know her sense of

humor!" Pat slaps her on the back harder than good friends usually do and laughs. "Some people don't know when you're teasing, Jo."

"I'm not kidding at all. Would I kid you, Pat?" she asks, bashfully, spinelessly and it brings a laugh from all. She has effects.

"One of your old loves is going to be here, too," he says when they are seated in the room right beside the stereo. Sing it Linda!

"Red's coming?" she asks and cannot help but laugh at the witty pun that just slid out of her mouth.

"Hell, no," Pat says and he is a little perturbed. "Ray Peters."

"Why would you ask Ray Peters?" she asks and sits back. Build up for a let down. Perturbation sets in. Why was there an initial shock of excitement when she thought that Red might come? It was electrifying, petrifying.

"He goes to school here."

"Ray Peters goes to Duke," she laughs and spills some beer down the front of her sweater. No problem, it soaks right in. "I didn't know he was smart enough."

"Well apparently so. He got in." Pat sits back and puts his arm around the back of the sofa. He is working up his nerve. "Are you okay, Jo?"

"Sure, why do you ask?"

"You just seem different that's all." Pat has that glum worried look on his face that he is so famous for. He looks pitiful but at the same time he looks very much in control, sort of like Bobby.

"It's my hair, I told you. It's so long and do you know

what's funny about that? It's just the way that Red wanted it to grow and now that it's all grown out, he isn't around!" She slaps Pat on the thigh and keeps her hand there. "Isn't that a scream?" Pat wants to kiss her, she can tell and before she knows it, it will be after midnight and they will be kissing and kissing like a pair of gouramis and she will be in love. She leans forward but it is more than Pat can stand. He can't even look into her eyes and see the truth. Instead, he looks around the room, the girl in the beach towel, the girl with the froggy skirt, and then he pushes her away. Isn't that just like him, though? He wants to be subtle, discreet; Pat Reeves hasn't changed a bit.

"Maybe we need to talk, Jo," he says and gets up and pulls her towards the kitchen. They still can't talk because the girl in the froggy skirt is standing by the keg with a boy that isn't wearing socks even though it is February. He has the sense enough to keep his loafers polished to a shiny deep burgundy but he doesn't have sense enough to wear socks in February. The boy can talk; he says, "Hi Pat, where's Trudy?"

"She went home this weekend," Pat says and takes Jo Spencer by the arm. Froggy is staring at Jo Spencer while Pat pulls her away. He pulls her way down the long hall and into the bedroom and closes the door.

"This is breaking a rule," she tells him but she doesn't mind. After the rule has been broken once, it doesn't matter. Isn't that what they say about a virgin? She can do it just once and then she is altered forever; there is no return. "Who's Trudy? Sounds like a cow."

"Trudy is the girl that I'm dating," Pat says and stares at the door.

"No, because I'm the girl that you're dating," she says and looks at the door, too. There is nothing on that door to hold her interest.

"Look, Jo, I just wanted to explain things so that you wouldn't get any wrong ideas." Pat looks at her squarely, straightly, seriously. "I like you a lot, you know that."

"Yes, you've always liked me," she says and squeezes his hand. "You've always been in love with me. I know. I know these things."

"Maybe once I did love you, or thought that I loved you. That was a long time ago." He squeezes her hand and then lets go. "You know we're friends, just like you used to always tell me. We're friends."

"So, why did you ask me out then?" Jo Spencer feels like she has been socked in the stomach. "Why didn't you ask Trudy if that's who you date?"

"I told you, Trudy went home for the weekend. You're the one that called me remember?"

"No, no, I don't remember it being that way at all," she says and gets up to walk around. There are not many places that you can go in this room. There is a beach towel skirt just like the one that that girl is wearing except in different colors, thrown across a chair. She is in that girl's room, alone with Pat Reeves, and she shouldn't be here.

"Yes you do. You called me up and since Trudy was out of town, I thought it would be a good chance for us to get together. You sounded like you needed a friend."

He sounds pitiful, weak. How can he be so controlled?

"I've got loads of friends! All that I need, anyway." She turns around and around and stares at the lightbulb. If she had a broom, she'd throw it down and jump over it. She was always very good at doing that, the best in the neighborhood. "Who needs 'em?"

"Jo, I just wanted to explain, that's all." Pat Reeves makes her stop turning. He holds her arms so tight that she can't feel him holding them. "I'm your friend whether you want me to be or not."

"I know all that! Don't you think I know all that? Do I look like a fool? an idiot?" She asks and Pat shakes his head. "You're the one that looks like a fool, beggarman fool, to sit there and tell me all of that like I was after you or something! You're cocky, that's what you are—to think that you need to let me down easy, to think that I needed to be told all of that. We're just friends that's all." She shakes his hands off of her arms. "Isn't that what I always told you when you used to come around?"

"Yeah, yeah," he says and sits back down on the edge of the beach towel clad girl's bed. "I just wanted to make sure there was no misunderstanding."

"Well, there isn't," she says and that's a lie. Why had he even asked her to this tacky party? Why hadn't he told her about Trudy on the phone? If he was so wild about Trudy the cow, why would he bother to take someone like Jo Spencer out on a date? He wouldn't have even told her about Trudy except that he got nervous that Froggy would tell on him. That was it. Pat Reeves is a chicken.

"Come on, then," he says and takes her arm again like

she can't walk by herself. "Let's join the party and have some fun." Oh, yeah, she is having a ball! "You'd really like Trudy," he says loud enough for Froggy to hear. "Maybe we can all double date one night or something."

"That's a possibility," she says. "It will be difficult for me to decide which of my boyfriends we should go with."

"I'll bet!" Pat says and laughs. "Here, do you need another beer?"

"I don't need anything," she says. "But I'll take one." He laughs again and so does the sockless boy but Froggy doesn't; she stares. Jo Spencer takes her beer and drinks a big swallow fast and even this quick action doesn't make Froggy stop looking.

"I hate Trudy couldn't make the party," Froggy says.

"Yeah, me too," Jo Spencer says. "Of course, I wouldn't be here if Trudy was now would I, and I wouldn't have had the pleasure of meeting you!"

"Jo! I haven't seen you since graduation." Ray Peters comes in and hugs her. She had never allowed him to hug her person before, what makes him think that he can take such a liberty just because he goes to Duke and is all prepped out in bright green pants. "This is my girlfriend, Anna. Anna, this is Jo Spencer. We went to high school together. As a matter of fact . . ." Ray Peters pauses to laugh a very worldly laugh. "Jo was my very first girlfriend."

"Nice to meet you," amiable Anna fille-ami of Ray Peters says. "I've seen your picture in Ray's old yearbook."

"It was just last year," Jo Spencer says and looks to see if Froggy is still staring; Froggy is.

"It was, wasn't it?" Anna asks. "Ray doesn't look at all like he did in his senior picture."

"Oh, I think he looks exactly the same," Jo Spencer says. "Ray will always be Ray."

"Maybe it's because I didn't know him then," Anna says. She is so sweet, so petite. "You were the May Queen and chief cheerleader, weren't you?"

"Jo was everything," Ray Peters says.

"I still am," Jo says. "The only change is my hair, see how long it is."

"I noticed that," Ray says. "It looks real good that way."

"Well, the funny thing about it being this long is that this is how Red always wanted it to get and now it's all long and Red is not around." She looks at Anna. "Red was my old boyfriend in high school."

"I was real surprised when I heard that ya'll had broken up," Ray says. "I thought you were really in love."

"Shoot! I've never been in love!" she says and laughs. "You think I could love him after what happened to Beatrice?" Ray looks funny; maybe he doesn't know what really happened to Beatrice.

"That was really sad," he says.

"What? What?" Anna asks like a little dumb ass.

"This friend of ours, well kind of a friend . . ." Ray Peters wants to drag it into a marathon story.

"Slit her wrists and bled to death," Jo Spencer says and takes a big swallow of beer. That ends that. All's well that ends well. To think that Ray thought that she was in love with Red! What is love anyway? Linda says "love is a rose but you better not pick it." Who the hell wants to pick it?

"No, she didn't die." Ray stares at Jo so Jo stares at his bright green pants. Those pants make her laugh and laugh, make her want to call Ray Peters, Mr. Greenjeans, make her want to call Anna fille-ami, Bunny Rabbit, make her want to call Froggy, Mrs. Moose, no Ms. Moose; Froggy without a doubt would have it no other way than Ms. Moose. "It was close though. They thought at first that she might die." Now Ray is telling all of this to Bunny Rabbit. "If her boyfriend hadn't come in and found her, she might would have died." Let the pingpong balls fall!

"It was like she's dead," Jo Spencer says and stares at Froggy, Ms. Moose. "People were nice to her when they thought she was dead."

Bunny Rabbit stares at Jo Spencer, a blank stare and then turns her attention to Ray. "How sad." She shakes her stupid head like she knows something. "Is she okay, now?"

"Yeah," Ray says and looks back at Jo. "I hear she's doing fine, heard she's going off to school next year, somewhere in Maine. Is that what you heard?"

"You don't always hear what you believe," she says and looks at Ray. He doesn't know what to say. He doesn't know the main reason that she would go to Maine. Maine, pain, rain, sane. Jo Spencer did not believe that so she can't hear it. "Maine has long sleeve weather," she says and again, Ray is dumbfounded. Anna Rabbit fille-ami is dumblosted. Froggy, Ms. Moose, is Miss Piggy in disguise.

Froggy is on the phone. She says, "Oh no, we sure will miss you, Hon." Obviously Froggy is in theatrics and does a poor job at it. "That was Nancy," Froggy says and keeps looking at Jo Spencer. "She can't make it. She and Buffy were all ready to come over and her battery is dead." Ha! Nancy Carson's battery has never been dead. Sounds like a lie; Buffy is probably hot and heavy to see Red.

"Thank God for that," Jo Spencer says and smiles a sweet smile. She has effects! She can make a whole room go silent. Ray Peters finally laughs; he thinks that she is cute; he wants to re-create some past moments, points to ponder, wants to forget Beatrice.

"Do you remember when we went together, Jo?" He laughs, worldly indeed! "And we sat at that ballgame and held hands under your poncho?" Anna thinks this is amusing to hear of her Ray at an earlier day.

"I will never forget it," Jo says. "You picked your nose!"

"What? Come on be serious!" Ray says but it is obvious by the bright red of his face that she is quite serious. Else why would he turn so red? Red and green. Honesty is the best policy. Why should you lie? The truth will set you free. Anna is not amused.

"Think I'll just have another little beer," Jo Spencer says and goes to the keg.

"That's what you need," Pat says. What's wrong with him anyway? He is treating her like a child and he doesn't have that right. Why he's got a girlfriend named Trudy; that doesn't give him any rights, no cause. Froggy is still staring and Ray is trying to change the subject. "Jo always was a big teaser," he says to Anna. "By the way, Jo, whatever happened to Ralph Craig?"

"How would I know?" She asks and takes a big swallow. "I am not my brother's keeper. Besides, I never go to the zoo." Ray and Anna think this is funny because it is about someone else. Froggy laughs and stares and she doesn't even know Ralph Craig. She has no cause.

"Let's go sit down," Pat says so she follows him back into the room and they sit back down by the stereo. "Jo, are you sure everything's okay? You know I'm a good listener." Fill your ears and then fill your pockets. Who does he think he is anyway? Froggy is easing up, slowly, staring, her ears and eyes wide open.

"What's your major, Jo?" Froggy asks.

"I don't have one," Jo Spencer says and lights a cigarette. No one else in the room is smoking and she wants to infect them. "I'm just a freshman."

"You mean you don't have any idea?" Froggy sits on the floor where she belongs and carefully pulls her skirt under her legs. She ought to hide those legs; they are not thin and shapely like Jo Spencer's.

"No idea!" Jo yells because the music has gotten louder. "What's yours?" she asks because it is obvious that Froggy wants to tell.

"I'm in business," she says. "So is Ray and he's a freshman. Guess some people know before others."

"Guess so. Do you go to school here at Duke?"

"Oh, no," Froggy says. "I go to Meredith. That's how I know Buffy and Nancy. You see, Margaret does, and I'm just visiting her for the weekend." Margaret is the girl in the beach towel.

"I didn't think you did," Jo Spencer says and laughs a great big laugh. "I just knew that you must not go to Duke."

"Why?" Froggy asks and her eyes glare up like she's pissed about something. "Why would you think that?"

"It's just obvious, that's all," she says. "Of course, sometimes I'm wrong. I mean I never would have thought that Ray would've gotten in."

"That's not a very nice thing to say," Froggy says and looks at Pat like he's going to say something. He knows better.

"The truth hurts, sometimes." Froggy doesn't have time to reply because Ray and Anna come up and sit on the floor beside her. They are all forming a circle. Any minute now, they will probably grasp hands and begin singing Kum Ba Ya, or Pass It On. She despises both of those songs. She must sing something else so that they won't do this. If she could just remember the music to Dick Van Dyke, she would hum that. But, she still can't remember. Sing something else: "Love is a nose but you better not pick it," she sings and watches Ray turn red again. He is so damn mad! Mad, madder, maddest but he must laugh it off and keep his cool. Why do people do that anyway? Is this what a business major can do? She wants to ponder this but there isn't time; first the circle begins talking about someone that she doesn't know. Do they want to exclude her from the conversation? Well and good because Pass It On will never pass through her lips. Then Margaret comes up to say that there are refreshments over on the table.

"I am refreshed, thank you," Jo Spencer says. "I had a can of chunky chicken soup today."

"I think maybe you ought to eat something," Pat says.

"That's sweet, Patty," she says and Froggy's eyes bulge out of their sockets on "Patty." "But I can't eat except at five-thirty."

"I believe you'd feel better," he says in a concerned fashion. "If that's all you've had, it's no wonder that the beer is affecting you." Affecting? She has effects that affect! "What do you want?" Patty gets up, persistant, resistant rascal.

"I want Doris Day to marry Ted Knight!" Oh, that is so funny! She laughs and laughs and nobody else does because they don't get it. That makes it even funnier! Doris Day Knight! If she wrote it down, the K would screw things up but just saying it is very funny indeed!

"Jo, what do you want to eat? A sandwich?" Pat is standing, his hands in his pockets. Froggy stands beside him. Love is a nose. Froggy whispers in Pat's ear. "It's not polite to tell secrets," Jo Spencer says. She feels so good that she must take off her shoes and prop her feet up on Ray Peters' bright green leg. "You've lost a lot of weight, Ray. You used to be borderline obese."

"I was kind of chubby," Ray says. He is pleased and disturbed by this comment. Pleased that she has noticed that he is trim, disturbed that she remembers how he

200

used to be. Shouldn't you remember how people used to be? Maybe he was disturbed by the single word "obese" for he changed it to chubby which is what any good mother would say about her fat child. A mother would choose "chubby" because she loves that fat dumpling child but she doesn't love Ray Peters so "obese" is perfectly in order.

"You really were chubby," she says. "And what's more, you had great big teeth, remember? How did you ever reduce their size?"

"I wore braces, remember?"

"Yes, yes, come to think of it, I do!" she screams. Pat Reeves hands her a sandwich and she flips it open to see what's in there. It is bologna and cheese. She puts it back together and puts it on top of the stereo. "Why did you think it was so funny that time that you had to kiss Beatrice?"

"What time?" he asks innocently as though he doesn't remember!

"At Lisa Helms' party in the sixth grade. You remember, spin the bottle!" It makes her sad to remember this but she can't stop remembering. "That bottle landed on Beatrice and you laughed! Everybody laughed!"

"I don't remember that," he says. "I remember that we all used to laugh at whoever it landed on. That was a silly game wasn't it?"

"You didn't think it was silly then," she says. "And the way that you laughed at Beatrice was a different kind of laugh. You made fun of her."

"Everyone made fun of her," he says and he is uncomfortable because he shifts his legs around. Jo Spencer must find a new place for her feet. She props them on Froggy who is back on the floor. Froggy doesn't like this but she cannot think of anything to do about it. She must be businesslike and act like Jo Spencer's feet are not there, especially the foot with the hose that is run.

"You know that's what made Beatrice slit her wrists, making fun. Did you laugh when she did that?"

"That's an awful thing to say," Froggy says and pushes her feet away. Where on earth is she going to put them now?

"Yeah, let's get off that subject," Ray says and touches Anna on the shoulder. "Do you want something to eat?" he asks and Anna nods. Run, run, fast as you can! First and ten, do it again.

"The truth hurts!" Jo Spencer yells. "It is just one of those things that will always be that way!"

"Aren't you going to eat your sandwich?" Pat asks.

"Nope, didn't want it to begin with." She can put her feet up on the couch! She can put her head in Pat's lap! She can pretend that she is all by herself in her room in Blue Springs. Big old Jaspar is at the end of her bed and he is such a good dog. When he is on her bed, nothing can get her. "Stay Jaspar," she says. "Stay all night." She can close her eyes with Jaspar there and she can make her breath go in rhythms. She can breathe to Lassie.

Now, she is like that hair on the shower stall wall; way up high, dry and protected. Nothing will ever get her—jamais plus! Now breathe to a good song, a stardust melody, a memory of love's refrain. Meet George Jetson, his boy Elroy. Red is getting in her head. Get out! He is standing there on the pier that first day, swimming out to the tower, that first day. Make him drown. Watch his head go under and stay, little bubbles before the dead man's float. No, sing a song. What is Dick Van Dyke? What was the theme of the May dance? Didn't it have something to do with the universe? "The living creature is a world-order in miniature." She was the queen. She reigned, rained. Say those words out loud. You can't tell the difference can you. Reign? Rain?

"Come on, I think you better go." It is a whisper. She is being lifted up from her warm bed. Or is she on the couch in that pine paneled room and her Daddy has come to take her to that warm bed where only good dreams are dreamed? Open your eyes and see, try to see it all. Pat Reeves is carrying her. They are going to cross the threshold. That shouldn't happen. Why, she can walk by herself. Twist around, get down. There, she is just fine. She wants to stay at the party. All she needed was a little catnap and now, she is just fine.

"Hey, Ray!" she yells. "What was the theme for the May dance?"

"Venus and Mars Are All Right Tonight."

"Just Venus and Mars? Not the whole galaxy?" She didn't vote for that theme. That's a dumb theme. "You know I stuffed Mars, practically all by myself, I stuffed that chicken wire shit full of red paper—RED! paper."

"Come on," Pat says and pulls her to the door. Why is

everyone staring? What do they think that they're doing? Froggy! Look at her sitting there in that tacky skirt like she's somebody!

"Fill your eyes full and then fill your pockets!" Jo Spencer screams and points her finger. "Froggy Frog Face! Croaky bull frog ridden lily white pad!"

Pat Reeves doesn't go up to her room. He leaves her out in the hallway of the dorm all by herself. He says that if she needs a friend to give him a call. To take care, to be cool. She is cool, very cool, poised and sophisticated. Pat says to call if she needs a friend but that they won't be going out anymore.

"That's just hunky-dorey!" she screams and goes up the stairs. First landing—"That's just hunky-dorey!" she screams and she can't wait to get to the third landing to scream it again. Fourth landing—loud, louder, loudest! Roommate Becky wants to hear all about the party.

"It was loads of fun!" she says and takes off that big skirt, that fluffy kitty looking sweater. She must get into that nightgown fast. It has been lying there all night just waiting for her to get back into it. Becky wants to know how she got along with Pat. How did she get along with Pat? She is too tired to think about it. She feels like she can go to sleep even though it's night. She just needed to pat Pat to make sure he was still there, but she didn't pet Pat. There is a difference. Pat is pat and that is that. And now, Jaspar big dog can come back and stay all night long.

It is noon when Jo Spencer wakes up and she has a headache but it doesn't bother her. No, she doesn't mind at all—take two aspirin and call yourself tomorrow. There were no dreams last night. The dream could not get to her because she was so tired. What made her so tired? Going to a party and drinking beer? Drinking not only makes you fall in love but it makes the dream go away. What happened at the party? There are traces of tidbits that resemble nightmares so she must not even think about them. They are not important at all. What is important is that she got a good night's sleep without a dream, and now, she can work very hard. There is so much work to do! A French midterm coming up! A theme to write for English II, a theme of her very own, but right now she must write her poem for next week. She must spend a lot of time on it. She may go out into that bright sunlight and get one Tab and a pack of cigarettes before she begins but then she cannot do anything else until the poem is completed. She cannot take a shower or use the bathroom until the work is done and she already has the beginning figured out, a perfect beginning: I don't dig bloodworms, I buy them packaged like icecream.

All of "the girls" are going out and Jo Spencer has been asked to go with them even though the only girl she knows, really, is Beck. They are going to eat pizza and then they are going to this bar where everybody who is anybody goes. Naturally, this is where Jo Spencer should be! "No thank you," she says when the pizza comes and everyone digs in. "I have already eaten."

"Jo!" Beck says. "All you had was a cup of yogurt! You need to eat!"

"No, Beck," Jo Spencer says. "That yogurt was dessert. I went out to a late lunch today and ate a big salad bar salad, baked potato, steak and cheesecake at Western Sizzlin." That isn't true but it is a necessary lie to get Beck off of her back. It is clear that Beck will not understand about the rules and how they must be followed to a tee or something horrible will happen.

"I thought you studied all day," Beck says. "Who did you go with?" Beck was in the library all day so what she doesn't know can't hurt Jo Spencer.

"I did study most of the day," she says and fills her glass with beer. "Then Pat Reeves stopped by and wanted to take me to lunch."

"Looks serious," Beck says. "Ya'll ought to see this guy that Jo dates. He's so cute!"

"He's all right," Jo Spencer says. "But I told him that I thought we shouldn't go out all the time. You know, I don't want to be tied down."

"And what I want is to be tied down," This girl that Jo Spencer doesn't really know says and laughs. That girl really should not express herself so freely. No, that girl should learn to be subtle, discreet.

"I can't believe that you did that, Jo," Beck says. "I thought you really liked him."

"It's easy to like something if you don't know what else there is to like," Jo Spencer says and she can tell that everyone at the table mulls this one over. It is an effective thing to say.

"So, you just really want to play the field!" This other girl says and Jo Spencer smiles like a good Jo Jo and nods. Now, everyone has forgotten that she is not gorging herself on pizza.

The bar is a nice place to sit. There are lots of little tables and the lights are very dim. There is a band playing at one end and they are very good and very loud. It is a nice feeling the way that the vibrations from the loud sound make Jo Spencer feel like the whole place is rocking. "OOH, that Shakespearian Rag! It's so elegant! So intelligent!" It is too loud to talk and that is fun, too, because she can just drink beer and think, sing along with the band and it doesn't even matter that she does not have a good singing voice because she can't hear herself. As a matter of fact, it is too loud to think and that is a nice feeling, too. People try to talk and sometimes she can read their lips. They say, "Isn't the band good?" Yes, yes, all she has to ever do is nod. Isn't the band good? Yes, nod. "Do you want another beer?" Yes, yes, nod.

When the band takes a break and the lights become brighter, it is like coming out of a good dream and wanting to go back to sleep and have it start all over. Beck wants to introduce Jo Spencer to a friend of hers. "I think you'll really like him," Beck says and nudges her. "Hey, Paul!" Beck waves her hand at this tall boy with dark brown hair. He is cute and his teeth are very nice and straight when he smiles. Beck motions for him to come on over and he has to inch through the crowd at the bar like a worm. He wiggles up and sits down in a chair right across from Jo Spencer. "This is my roommate, Jo," Beck says. "Jo, this is Paul. We went to high school together." He smiles at Jo Spencer and Jo Spencer smiles back. She cannot even feel her lips do that. "Do ya'll need a beer?" Beck asks. Jo has to say something. What was it she had said at that party that got such an effect. Oh, yeah. "I don't need one. But, I'll take one."

"Same goes for me," Paul says and smiles. It worked better the first time. First times are always best.

Jo Spencer thinks that Paul is very nice, too nice, but she must be polite, sophisticated. She asks him why he is in North Carolina if he's from Alabama. She asks him what year he is. He is a sophomore. He is not in a fraternity. He wants to be a lawyer. Jo Spencer wants the music to start back up because Paul is a bore. She wants the music to play loud so that she can look across the room at the boy in the faded denim jacket with a cigarette hanging out of the corner of his mouth. She finds this attractive, the cigarette, the narrow tempting eyes, the bushy blonde hair that you would automatically imagine on a beach bum, a sailor. Where has she seen him before? What did Paul just say?

"Huh," she says in a noncommittal way. She is ready for that beer that Beck is supposed to be bringing. The sailor sees her. He takes a long draw on his cigarette, thumps the ashes to the floor. Is he looking at her? She smiles kind of like she is smiling at him and kind of like she is not. Then she cocks her head like she is so amused by what Paul has just said. What has Paul just said? Who gives a damn? Beck gets back just before the lights go dim and the band starts up. The sailor has taken a seat with several other boys just two tables away. If she makes eye contact, then she is destined to meet him. Maybe if she goes to the bathroom she can get a better look at him.

"Where are you going?" Beck screams.

"To the bathroom!"

"Here," Beck hands her a dollar. "Get me another beer on your way back."

"Me, too," Paul says and fishes around in his pocket for a dollar. Who is she, the waitress? Oh well, she will have an excuse to be up longer, an excused exposure.

She pushes through a crowd of people standing up and slows down when she nears his table. Push slower. Give him time to see you. He does and he smiles the most perfect smile that she has ever seen. His teeth are straight, white parallel. "Hi," he mouths. She nods and then realizes that she is being pushed. The crowd in front of her has moved up a yard. This should never happen so she walks very quickly up to the group. Turn around for a quick peek. Oh no, he saw her look! She must hurry to the bathroom, to the line for the bathroom and that is a good place to be because the light in the hall outside of the bathroom is burned out. It is dark and she can look out into the dim light and see everything and no one can see her.

The bathroom is very small, very nasty. She starts to put toilet paper neatly around the seat like her mother always did at the movie theatre or in service stations but there is no toilet paper. Not any that's dry anyway; all of the toilet paper is in the commode, looks like it's clogged, makes her want to gag. Is this what she missed that time years ago when she would not walk to the latrine? That is a very funny memory and it is funny that she should happen to remember it at this exact time. The mirror is brown looking and warped and she can barely see herself, but she does, and she tells herself that she will remember this moment forever. She will remember being here in this bathroom and she will remember that she remembered about the Girl Scout campout.

That is a big thought about remembering and she must keep thinking about it so that she will not think about sitting on that seat where thousands of butts that belong to people that she doesn't know have sat. "There is no such thing as gravity, the earth sux," the wall says in scribbly blue ink. Who had written that and why? She cannot imagine. It reminds her of Red. He was the kind that would spell things shortened like that, sux for sucks, probably pix for picks, nite for night and lite for light with a long i. It makes her scalp crawl off of her head. He signed a letter with "luv" once and even then, it had made her nauseous. Oh spare me, spare me, she thinks and looks at herself again. "Remember, Jo," she says and leaves. There is no need to flush a latrine.

It is very crowded at the bar and she must wait to give her order. She cannot look anywhere except at the Budweiser clock that goes around and around, big Clydesdales marching in a circle just like the ponies she rode at the fair one time. Andy had slid off of his pony and almost got kicked in the head. What is Andy doing, right this moment? What is her mother doing? Her Daddy? Are they sitting in that pine paneled room with the T.V.

on? Would her mother be here if their roles were reversed? That's a hard one—too hard to think about.

"Hey, aren't you in my chemistry class?" It is him, the sailor looking person and he is standing right beside her.

"I don't take chemistry," she says. But I'm having a reaction right now. Where does that thought come from? Déjà vu.

"You look so familiar," he says. Is this a line? a come on? "Maybe I've just seen you around campus."

"Probably," she says. "I'm around some times." He thinks this is very funny. Is the truth funny?

"My name's Jeff Stevens," he says.

"With a G or a J?" She is hoping that it will be a G because she has never heard of a G Jeff except Chaucer. Just a plain J Jeff. Well, that's okay. "My name's Jo Spencer."

"With a G or a J?" he asks and he seems to think that this is a cute thing to say. She does not think so but she will not hold it against him.

"With a G would be Go," she says. "My whole name is Joslyn so you know it's got to be a J. If it was a G, it would be Goslyn like baby goose."

"I see," he says. "Well, can I buy you a beer Jo with a J?"

"Okay," she says, "and I'll buy my friends' for them."

"You don't have a date do you?" he asks. "I saw you sitting with that guy."

"As a matter of fact, as rare as it is," she says, "I don't have a date tonight. Paul is just a friend of my friend."

"Guess I'm in luck, then," Jeff Stevens says.

"Guess you are," she says and smiles probably the

prettiest smile that has ever been seen. It is happening; there are effects.

Jo Spencer introduces Jeff Stevens to Paul and Becky and then all of them get up to dance. It is a real fast song and Jo Spencer always feels like a fool shaking around. There should be steps, proper steps, rules of the dance but there are not so she makes her own rules: jump side to side, one way your hands are in front, the other way they're behind you. Bob your head.

"Jo's doing the pony!" Beck screams. "I haven't thought of that in ages!" Beck starts doing the pony and even though they are making faces and laughing, Paul and Jeff do the pony. Now, it is fun because it is a real dance that they are engaging in. Jo Spencer wants to try another one: Do the swim! Hold you nose and jump down, come back up. Do the hitchhiker! Lick your thumb and hold it out. Come on baby, let's do the twist. She is having a wonderful time and she knows yet another dance. She can do the four corners. No, make them stop doing that dance. She needs to sit down because everything's spinning. I'm spinning, spinning like a top! No, both of those are bad dances to do; they are Beatrice's dances. Jo Spencer must walk off the floor and get back in her chair, sit very still.

"Hey, are you okay?" Beck asks and follows her. They all follow her. "Jo, you're so white," Beck says. "You must have gotten too hot."

"Yeah, that's it," she says and it is hard to make the room stop moving, to go slower, to let her off.

"Hey, let's go outside for some air," Jeff Stevens says. "How about it?"

"Okay," she says. "I think maybe I'd better go home."

"Sure, Jo," Beck says. "I'll tell the other girls that we're leaving."

"No need for that," Jeff Stevens says. "I'll walk her back. Let me get my coat." He walks back over to the other table where he was sitting earlier.

"Jo, do you know him," Beck asks and squats down beside the chair. "I don't mind leaving now at all."

"I'm fine," she says. "He's real nice, don't you think? He reminds me of someone that I know."

"Well, if you're sure," Beck says and looks intently for an intent answer.

"I'm sure."

It is cool outside and feels good. She must take three deep breaths and every step must be the exact same stride. She holds onto Jeff Stevens' arm and it is a nice way to walk. It makes her feel like she is in another time, another town.

"Feeling better?" he asks and she nods. He puts his arm around her and pulls her up close, closer, closest. He stops and gets her to sit on the old cold steps of one of the campus buildings.

Here, I'll show you where I live before I walk you home," he says. She looks up. How long has she been here? How long has she kissed this person? "Want to?"

"Yeah, all right," she says and they walk for what seems like hours in that cold and her whole body is going to sleep, going numb. Is this what it feels like to die? They are at a house, it must be a fraternity house. She wants to ask which fraternity house but she is too tired, must sit down in that big black chair, be very still, listen to the music from the juke box, watch the last few people leave the room. Red is sitting beside her now, just like all of those nights that they sat at the lake and watched T.V. He is kissing her, again and again. "I better go home," she mumbles and he nods. "In a minute," he says just like he always used to.

"I still love you, Red," she says when he hugs her so close.

"What?" he asks.

"But I'm so tired. You see Jaspar is waiting for me to get home."

"Who's Jaspar?" he whispers in her ear.

"You know Jaspar, my big old dog." It is safe here, warm and the dream can't get her when she is so tired, when she is at home, with Red.

It is gray, early gray, and at first there is that comfort of going back to sleep, dreamless sleep. But there is no comfort, now, only panic. Jo Spencer sits up and freezes as though paralyzed. Where is she? She is under a sheet, in a bed, an exposed ghost. Who is that person? It is a nightmare and she must wake up, she must run through the gray, the early foggy gray so that she will wake up, so that she will lose this thought.

The lobby of the dorm is still dark and she must tiptoe up the stairs until she can see those fluorescent lights outside of her own door. Ease it open without a creak. Beck is asleep, facing the wall. She must put on her nightgown, lie on her own bed. She must stay there but she must not sleep. That nightmare must not come back.

The sun is up and the room is very bright when Beck wakes up. Beck sits on the edge of her bed and whispers, "Jo? Are you awake?"

"Yeah," she says very sleepily even though it has been hours since she slept.

"You had a late night," Beck says. "I got up to use the bathroom around five and you weren't here. I was sort of worried."

"Oh, I was fine," she says. "I wasn't tired so I sat down in the lobby and watched T.V." Beck looks like she doesn't believe this. It must appear real. "It was one of those old science fiction movies."

"Oh," Beck says and runs her fingers through her hair. "I had a great time last night. It's always so good to see Paul."

Paul? "Oh yeah, he's a real nice guy."

"Yeah, he really liked you," Beck says. "I told him that you weren't dating anyone in particular. Hope you don't mind cause he might ask you out."

"No, I don't mind," she says and pushes back her quilt. She wants to take a hot shower and sit for awhile.

"You acted like you really liked that Jeff guy?" Beck says like it's not a question but really it is.

"He's all right," she says. "Not really my type."

"What is your type, Jo?" Beck asks and laughs.

She must think about this. It is a question without an answer. "I'm not really sure."

She lets the water run until it is very hot and then she sits in the corner and lathers her legs. The hairs have grown out and she can see where each one comes from, its root, its very own place to stay and live and grow. It was just a nightmare, that's all, the pubic hair is right where it was yesterday, still dry, protected. Nothing has happened. Nothing has changed. She holds her hand up and stares at it. Yes, she would recognize her hand if it was put with thousands of others just because it belongs to her—the little mole right near her thumb, the short square nails, the veins that push up when she does her hand like a claw. She can move her hands many different ways and these have meanings. Yes, the person that she loves must be able to read her hands, to get the meaning. It was all a nightmare and she can call home to Blue Springs and her Mama and Daddy will be coming in from church; Andy will be taking a quick spin on his minibike before lunch—fried chicken, mashed potatoes, garden peas and great big rolls with butter—pecan pie —and a slow sunny Sunday afternoon. She could call Bobby in Winston-Salem and he would be so glad to hear her. He would say, "Can you believe it, Josie? I'm going to graduate in three and a half months. I'm going to med school. Christine says hey. Isn't she great, Josie. She's going to be your sister one of these days soon. I love you, Jo Jo. Buzzy wants to kiss you, Jo Jo." This makes her cry, slowly, silently, spinelessly—as slow and silent as a Sunday in Blue Springs.

Jo Spencer has taken all of her midterms and is flunking Geology. She has a C in French. C'est terrible. She has a C in philosophy and why? Because she wrote that some questions have no answers and if Aristotle and Plato could not find concrete answers, how could she? At the time it had seemed like the right thing to say. She has a B in English II but she has no idea what she is going to make on her theme. She thought that it was a very good idea and also very creative. Her thesis was "We can see all of the changes that our society has undergone by studying television programs of the past and present. From this study I will show how the values and morals of the American population have changed. T.V. is representative of what people want to see, how they want to live." Then she had gone on to explore various aspects. For instance, "I Love Lucy" is about a housewife in the fifties; Ricky works, and Lucy stays home and gets in trouble; they sleep in twin beds, have a kid, and the entertainment world is all elegant and exciting. Then "That Girl" is about a single young girl who goes off to New York City all by herself to seek fame and fortune. New York still resembles the way it was in "Breakfast at Tiffany's" where Audrey Hepburn sits out on her fire escape and sings Moon River. That Girl has boyfriend Donald, but she is not dependent on him as Lucy is on Ricky and Ricky's income. She cites lots of interesting material like the way that Mary Tyler Moore went from Dick Van Dyke, son Richie, and twin beds, to Minnesota where she became a single, on-the-go associate producer of a T.V. station. Now, people sleep in double beds even if they are not married. Nobody makes Westerns. Shows do not have moral endings like Father Knows Best—Ozzie and Harriet—Leave It to Beaver—Andy Griffith—And who would have ever thought that little Opie Taylor would grow up and leave Mayberry, move to Milwaukee to become Richie Cunningham? She ended it all by posing a very philosophical question: "Whatever happened to Alfalfa?" She put a great deal of thought into that question and she did find an answer, there really was an answer.

Whatever happened to Alfalfa? I think about that sometimes and then I turn on the T.V. either early in the morning or late in the afternoon (when the good shows come on) and there he is, preserved in black and white, forever a little boy, a skinny little cowlicked boy who cannot sing worth a damn. He has been that way for years and he will continue to be that way as long as the old shows keep playing. It is all real as long as you don't change the channel, cut it off—real for thirty minutes. It doesn't just work for Alfalfa—Richie Cunningham can go back to being Opie Taylor and yet, he's just Opie Taylor because at the time of the viewing nobody knows (or should know) that he is going to grow up to be Richie. Really, they are two different people. Time has not changed them, Alfalfa, Beaver Cleaver, Lucy Ricardo; they live the same episodes again and again—their words and expressions identical each time, every time, a resolution. But life is not that way—you can't preserve yourself that way—can't rewind yourself and do the episode all over. All you can do is think about it over and over and often it is hard to remember exactly how it was. Often, you don't even know whatever happened to so and so, and so you get a picture of the last time that you saw that person.

But then you really see that person and they are so different that they have become a new person and you forget
all about who they used to be. Life is on a reel to reel and
it spins so very fast at times that it can make you dizzy,
things happen over and over but never the same way.
Resolutions are hard to find. This is why people who say
that T.V. is not true to life are correct. If it were true to
life, then they would show the show once and then throw
it away and people would soon forget that Richie Cunningham used to be Opie Taylor. No, T.V. is better than
life because it gives people a chance to go backwards, legally to go backwards, and it is all accepted unlike people
who start to live backwards, old people who think they
are children, or even those people who were born backwards. T.V. captures and preserves, pickles in the pink.
The only other way for this to happen is to die at a very
early age. The End.

She has an A in poetry and that is what makes everything else bearable, especially the nightmare, waking in
strange places, gray places. And why does that of all
things keep happening over and over? Same time—Same
channel—No resolution.

Jo Spencer goes home for spring break and everything
is the same. Andy is trying to make a computer for his
science project. He is too smart for his own good. Bobby
comes home for the weekend and he looks the same but
Jaspar looks very old; his eyes are blueing, blurring and it
makes her very sad. It seems that she has seen those eyes
before, another place, another time, and she cannot help

but cry, to sit on the backporch and cry and the yard looks so small, not at all like it had looked that time that she had sat there with her first period and read *Where the Red Fern Grows* for the fifteenth time.

The house seems silent; when she walks into a room, everything gets silent, dead silent. The feeling is big and scarey and it makes her get her pink rhinocerous off of the shelf and get into her bed. She pulls the covers up over her head so that it is dark, just like nighttime and all that she can see are her hands, her very own hands holding her very own rhino.

"Jo? Honey, aren't you feeling well?" Her mother sits on the bed and pulls back the covers. The light is too bright and she has to close her eyes and see only the blood red patterns stamped on her eyelids. "You only have a week you know." She hates that her mother has said this because she has tried to forget that; she wants to think that she can stay in this house, in this bed forever, this house that she loves, these people. "You haven't even told us about school."

"I have an A in poetry," she says. "The other grades are not so hot. But, I can get them up. Oh yes, I'll get them up."

"You used to never have trouble with your grades in high school," her mother says. "Of course, there's a big difference in college, I know."

"Oh, there is," she says and opens her eyes. Why does it feel like they aren't her eyes.

"Plus being away from home for the first time," her

mother says. "You've had right much to happen, what with Red and Beatrice."

"What about Red and Beatrice?" She has tried to forget all of that. She wants to forget that and the nightmares. They aren't real. She must remember to forget and forget to remember.

"Maybe you need to talk about it," she says. "You know we're always here." Yes, she knows that and it is like a jolt to remember that. It is so big and so real that it makes her cry. It makes her reach up and put her arms around her mother and squeeze, to hide her face. "You know Bobby's a good listener, too. And ya'll have always been so close. Right?"

She nods. "I'm okay, really I am. It's just good to be home, that's all. I think I feel happy, that's all." She says that and now she must be happy; she must be a happy hoppy picture like a good Jo Jo. No sense in making them worry over nothing.

Bobby wants her to go fishing, just the way that they used to. "We don't have to go to the lake," he says. "We can drive down to the beach for the day."

"I don't mind going to the lake," she says. "Come on, Bobby, do you think that will bother me? Nothing bothers me!"

"Do you ever hear from any of your friends?" Bobby asks when they are in the car on the way to the lake.

"Some," she says. "They're real busy, too." No, she hadn't heard from anybody recently and she hadn't tried to get in touch with any of them. They probably were real busy, besides, it hasn't been a good time to see people.

It is a very calm day and Jo Spencer and her brother go out to the end of the pier where she used to lie out in the sun. The watch tower is still there and if the water wasn't so cold, she would jump in and swim out there and dive and flip. She could still do it. The sun is very bright and Bobby pulls out his sunglasses and puts them on. They look so normal on him.

"Hey, Christine left her sunglasses in my car. Wanna wear them?"

"No, they make me feel funny," she says and pulls out a big fat bloodworm and slits him down the middle. He wiggles in three different pieces, still wiggling and looping when she sticks the hook through. She must put her hands in the water fast, get the blood off. "Out! Out! Damn spot!" she says and Bobby smiles but he doesn't laugh the way that she had intended. Then they just sit and stare at their poles. Bobby looks like he always does when he is worried and just about to ask a question. Probably, does she think that Christine really loves him? Should he get married? Yes, she is an Ethiopian Queen, tie the knot, begin to begot. She expects to hear voices any minute, laughs, to feel the pier vibrating and to look up to see Red jogging up to her.

"You thirsty?" Bobby asks.

"Water, water everywhere and not a drop to drink," she says and Bobby doesn't see any humor in this at all.

He pulls a thermos of Tang out of the canvas bag with all their junk and lunch in it.

"Do you want some or not?" Bobby is mad.

"To drink or not to drink . . ." Jo Spencer lifts her hand, one finger pointed upwards and Bobby slaps it; he slaps it hard.

"Cut it out, Jo!" he screams. "Now, what in the hell is bugging you. I'm your brother, remember?" Remember to forget and forget to remember.

"Do you?" he screams.

"I know that," she says. "Yeah, I remember that! Hooray!"

"Jo, listen. I know you're not doing well in school. Probably partying a little too much."

"I never go to parties," she says. "Very rarely do I get invited to parties."

"Well, I know you went to one," he says. "You know Pat Reeves called me because he was a little upset about you."

"Why should he have been upset?" She reels her line in slowly and watches it winding around the reel, around and around.

"He said that you just weren't yourself."

"Who did he say that I was?" That is a very clever thing to say. It is hilarious!

"Look, if something's bugging you, tell me." Bobby pours his cup of Tang into the dark green water and stares behind it as though he can find the orange Tang down in all that green.

"Nothing bothers me—not ever—jamais plus!"

"Josie, you know that I love you don't you?" Bobby looks up and he looks like he is going to cry. It is like waiting for the rain to start at her Grandma Spencer's house where there is a tin awning over the porch and each drop can be heard, one by one, until there is a steady drone, the humming of rain. There, slowly, one drop. She can hear it as it rolls down his face. "I can't stand to see you like this."

"Like what?" she asks and casts her line way out. It's the farthest that she has ever cast a line.

"Pat said that you said all kinds of things. I couldn't believe that you would act like that." Bobby hides his face in his hands. "He said you sort of came on to him but that he knew it wasn't like you at all. He said you had had too much to drink."

"And you believe all that?" she asks. "So what if I did? Haven't you ever done anything like that? Huh? Maybe I just wanted a little of what you've got, you know? You've got everything, Bobby, you've always had everything. Look what you've got right now, you're going to med school, you've got somebody that you love, somebody that loves you! Really loves you! Don't you see how I just wanted to have something like that? What about that time that you took all of my Easter eggs and ate them? You've always had everything!"

"Things haven't always worked out for me," he says. "Don't you remember Nancy Carson?"

"Whore bag."

"Pat said that you said that at the party." Bobby rubs

his hand over his face and half way smiles. "You were probably right about that but you shouldn't have said it." Bobby puts both of his hands on her face and makes her look up. "Things will work out for you, too, Jo. You just have to give it time."

Hurry up please, it's time. "I'm tired of waiting," she says.

"But, you're young."

"But, I feel very old."

"Mom says you're doing real well in poetry."

"I have an A."

"Can I see some of your stuff?" he asks and puts his arm around her.

"Maybe but you'll have to wait until I'm better."

"You mean feeling better?" He gets a serious look again.

"Writing better," she says and laughs. There is a look of relief on Bobby's face and she thinks for a minute that maybe things will get better. Maybe things will get worse. She doesn't know, can't see, because the trees are blocking the horizon. They sit on the pier until late in the afternoon when the sun looks like a big orange ball sinking behind those trees, and it is a sad sight, just the very way that it moves and goes away. They haven't caught any fish but Bobby says that it has been worth the trip. She has not heard or seen Red but his presence has been in every silent moment, every dark green ripple beneath that pier at Moon Lake, and she wishes that he would get out of her head because he has no business being there.

It is the second part of the second semester so she must begin again. The nightmare, that exposed ghost nightmare, has only come to her one early gray morning since spring break and now, she has come up with a solution to keep that nightmare away: She must go back to the original rules except that she will go to all of her classes and make good grades instead of riding the buses. Then, after she eats dinner with Andy, she will stay in that robin egg blue room and study. She will no longer go where everybody goes because right now, she is a no-body and must prove herself otherwise. She must not drink too much. Bobby said that she should not drink too much. "And especially during the week!" he had said. "No wonder you're flunking a subject." But if she doesn't drink, she cannot sleep during the night because that is when the other nightmare comes, the one where she is running through the gray. She must start all over. She must begin by catching up on her English II journal be-cause she is way behind, because she made a C⁻ on her research paper because she didn't DO any REAL re-search because there were no footnotes. "An interesting topic though not what I asked for," the scratchy red ink said. Don't worry about that, look ahead, start over. Wasn't that what Bobby had said?

She must turn to a new clean sheet and begin. She can-not get off of her bed even to use the bathroom until something is done:

Some people think that Columbus was Jewish and I can be-lieve this because I only know a couple of Jews that I think are dumb. The rest are very smart. I heard one time that overall they are the very smartest with Japanese coming in second and I can easily believe this if Chris indeed, was one. Some people think that Jews are trying to take over the world but they aren't. I know who is though. Swinish people whose names are the names of colors; those people (other than Warren Beatty) with sort of simian features. They are the kind of people who will murder and screw anything on two legs. It isn't the Jews. What does that mean anyway? I know a lot of Jews that are better Christians than a lot of Christians but I have never seen a Christian who is a better Jew than a Jew. I am a Christian but not a Christian's Christian. I do not hand out pamphlets at K-Mart's, nor can I abide bumper stickers that say "Honk if you love Jesus," or "Jesus is coming soon." I have never and never intend to give a testimony or to sing "Day by Day" for contributions. So what kind of a Christian am I? If Columbus was or was not Jewish really isn't important. What is important is that he took a chance and I have recently heard that there is no room for chance in a deterministic society. It is all a matter of survival of the fittest and yet, the meek shall inherit the earth? Contradictions upon contradictions and yet, if I could only contradict the contradictions that I made another time, then I would be back where I started from. But sometimes that is more difficult than it sounds. I simply am not certain. Once, a long time ago, someone told me that I was frigid and I contradicted that and now, I will contradict that contradiction. I am that way and it is only during those winter months when the weather outside is colder than I am that I appear to be thawing, to be warm. I'm not. I'm stone cold, stone cold sober and drunk, petrified. The good part is that hair in the bathroom because it is always there everytime that I go in and my hands are there, the same hands that used to catch grasshoppers, only a little bigger, these hands that fingerpainted with a cross eyed girl who it seems got her eyes fixed but could not fix anything else like dying. That's how it seems but these are the same hands. I read a story about hands one time that I liked a lot and I could probably write something about hands, my own hands because I know them so well.

Now, she must sit and think, about hands. Beck has come in and wants to know what she is doing but she cannot let on about the thinking.

"I have to write a poem," she says very intently so that Beck will be quiet.

"Want to go out? Paul and a bunch of us are going bar hopping."

"Thanks," Jo Spencer says. "But I'm behind in my work."

"Maybe you can get it all done," Beck says and gets her books. "I'm going to the library. Be back soon."

"Okay," she says and acts like she will try real hard to get her work done so that she can go, too, when all the time, she knows that she is not going to go. She must concentrate very hard; she must take a chance. You must stay on this bed, in this room. You must not even consider going bar hopping until you gain control, until your false feet make controlled patterned steps, or you will wake up in a place that you don't know, your hands will have touched someone that you don't know. Oh no! Not these hands!

Now, it is dark. Beck left over two hours ago. The light at the window has failed and she cannot see to see. Turn

on a lamp. There, and then there was light! She must sit
with her legs crossed very tightly, endure those little pee
shivers, until she gets the very end for her poem. She
cannot help but wonder what the poetry professor sees in
her poems. What does he think of her? Does he think
that she takes chances? Does he think that she has a
chance? It has become a very important part of her day to
think about this—to think about what he must think. If
she had to pick a new Daddy, she would pick this man.
If she had been born forty years ago and had found herself in a dim smoky room where people were dancing to
the good songs, she would have asked this man to dance.
If she ever had a son, he would be just like this man.

The shivers are getting worse and she must hurry and
finish the poem, read it over very carefully, and if it meets
her approval, she may be excused. It is something to look
forward to. What can she name it? The hardest part about
writing a poem is finding a name for it. The professor
had said that the title is very important, because sometimes the title helps to understand. But some poems don't
have titles and this poem is not difficult to understand. It
is about using your hands to talk, but not sign language,
something bigger than sign langauge. "When someone
holds my hands a certain way, I feel that they are holding
every word that I will ever say." Warm hands/cold heart,
deceptive digits. She will call it "Hands." Now, she can
go to the bathroom so she walks slowly, steadily, down
that fluorescent hall. She can endure the pain now that
she can see relief. That is a very important thought

but she must not think about it until she is seated. It takes a minute for this very natural bodily occurrence to begin because she has waited so long. And then, relief, and it is the first time that she has ever realized what a pleasurable event this can be. It is a part of life that is taken for granted just like hands and it shouldn't be, and even though everyone enjoys this function, hers is isolated from all the others because she sees the pleasure. And why? Because she has suffered through the waiting. Isn't that what they say in philosophy? To know pleasure and truly appreciate it, you must know pain, the opposites, to be happy you must know sadness. To enjoy using the bathroom, you must endure the pain of not going. Yes, and by not eating very much, she will one day find pleasure in devouring a pepperoni pizza! That is what it's all about, the opposites.

By the end of March, it is so warm that everyone starts lying out in the sun. Even Jo Spencer can do this because she has had a great deal of experience. She puts on her old one piece that she was wearing (what was it? two years ago?) when Red came up and introduced himself but she doesn't even think of this because she has remembered to forget him. She is so thin and trim, just the way that a girl of her age should be.

"Jo," Beck squeals. "Aren't you going to shave your legs?" Jo looks down at the hairs that she has so carefully cultivated. Beck has shaved her legs, silky smooth, hairless, but isn't that dishonest? To hide your roots? "I don't have a razor," she says.

"You mean that you've never shaved your legs?" Beck is laughing. "How could you ever sleep with anyone without shaving your legs?" Beck says "ever" like she is horrified. But, Jo Spencer does not sleep with people, so what they don't see can't hurt them.

"I used to," she says and knows that this is true. She doesn't remember when she stopped. She just knows that once she did and now she doesn't.

"Used to what? Shave your legs or sleep with someone without shaving your legs?" Beck finds this terribly funny. C'est terrible.

"Shave," she says. "I don't do the other." This makes Beck laugh even harder.

"So what if you do or don't? It's no big deal." Did Beck really say that? No big deal? "Here, you can use my razor." Beck fishes around in the plastic bucket that she carries to and from the shower.

"Oh no, I couldn't," she says. "I couldn't use another person's razor."

"You think I've got skin disease or something?" Beck laughs again with her head thrown back just the way that people are supposed to laugh. "You're a weird bird, Jo Spencer." Beck picks up her towel and baby oil. "Come on, we're missing the very best sun." Jo Spencer follows Beck down the long flight of stairs and the floor is cool to her bare feet. Outside it is very hot and there are tons of girls like flies in bright bikinis swarming all around. She hopes that Beck will not call one of these girls over to join them.

Jo Spencer spreads out her towel and lies very still. It

feels so good that if she could, she would just go to sleep in this warmth. There is a transistor radio playing somewhere but she can't tell what the song is. She can only hear sparse fragmented notes that occasionally rise above the buzzing.

"I can't stay out here long," Jo Spencer says and rubs some baby oil on her legs. It makes all the hairs stand up like teeny tiny soldiers, an army marching in place to different drummers. "I've got Geology today."

"This is the time of year to cut classes," Beck says. "You've been studying too hard lately. The year's almost over!"

"But, I'm not doing real well in that class," she says and closes her eyes. It is so bright that when she closes her eyes, she sees all the colors and when she opens them, she sees the black spots that grow and grow. She sees that magnolia tree, so green and cool, so different from the way it looks at night.

The Geology professor is boring but she never gets bored because there is too much to think about. The good thing about Geology is the words. The bad part about Geology is defining rocks because there IS a right answer, a correct definition and that is no fun. Who gives a damn? She feels like a fool licking, scratching and sniffing rocks. She must do something else. She must pretend that she is listening and taking good notes, write frantically, though not notes. She can just sit and make a list of the good words, words like erode and debris, lode, core, meandering, silt, buried, glacier, ice, stone, brittle, all of those words that can be so apt if she chooses to describe a person. Yes, those are good words but they make her very tired, the residue, the erosion, and so she must leave class, tiptoe away, get some sleep before it gets too dark.

She is trying to find him because something horrible is going to happen. She is not certain how or when or where; she just knows that it is going to happen and she must find him, warn him. He is so hard to find and it is so gray, gray fog all around, puffs of gray that swirl and swirl over the tall fields of weeds. Her feet are so heavy, her body, so heavy but there is the lake, yes, but she can barely see for the gray. There is a dock at the end of the pier and she must look there, yes, look, but hurry. There is a little house on the dock but it is empty. The wind is whipping faster and faster and the door creaks on its rusty hinges, the windows slam shut, open, shut. There is a buzzing, low at first and then louder, a steady drone getting louder and louder. She runs out of the house to the end of the pier. Wait! Wait! she yells but her voice is swallowed by the drone. There is a boat and she can see the lower half because the fog is clear there. It is a party and everyone that she knows is there. There is Bobby, Andy, Mama and Daddy; Tricia, Cindy, Lisa; Pat Reeves, the Monroes, teachers from kindergarten and grammar school, high school; her poetry professor is serving coffee and he is wearing the most beautiful yellow hat. It looks like he sees her so she waves and yells as loud as she can, but no, he doesn't see her; they can't hear her. They are having a party and throwing confetti and they can't see her. The boat is moving out now, but she can't stop screaming because he is there somewhere. The boat moves further and further away and the fog lifts. The droning is so loud that she has to hold her ears. Now the sky is bright blue and the whistle sounds. Up on the top, leaning over the edge, are Lucille and Bertram. Lucille has her face, the long auburn hair but she knows it is Lucille because Bertram is beside her. She looks up higher on a small platform that was not there before and he is there. He sees her because his hand waves back and forth mechanically and slow motioned. Her grandmother is beside him looking just the way she did in old photographs, waving the same wave. She yells for them to stop, to wait, but they only wave while Beatrice walks very slowly up on the edgerail of the boat. Beatrice sees her and waves like the others while the party goes on and on . . . Stop! Make it stop!

"Jo? Jo?" It is Becky, shaking her. "Wake up, Jo."

She sits suddenly and looks up at the window. It is gray, early morning, not morning; it can't be. "What time is it?"

"Six." Becky is sitting on her bed reading her history. Becky sleeps late in the morning, doesn't she?

"At night?" She runs and turns on the T.V. The news is on. "I missed it."

"What?" Becky asks and looks up over her book.

"Andy Griffith."

"Well, I started to wake you up but I figured that you needed some sleep." She puts down her book and leans forward the way that people always do when they are concerned, when they want to get intent. "You know you look so tired lately and I never even see you, at least I feel like I don't. You're always asleep when I'm awake." She moves up closer, her fuzzy pink slippers inching on the rug, closer and closer. "Is anything wrong?" She doesn't even wait for an answer. "Cause you can talk to me. I wouldn't tell a soul."

She wonders about this. Can she talk to Becky? Does she have anything to say? She starts to pursue the question but the dream comes back like a flash, a jolt. Beatrice, Red, waving—her grandmother, waving, the grandmother that she had never known, the grandmother who had died three years before she was born. Lucille and Bertram were up there, dead, and Beatrice. And Red. Red was up there. "Oh, no," she screams and her scalp feels bristly like it does when something scarey happens— clothes on the closet door when she was five, John Kennedy in the T.V. "It is happening."

"What? What?" Becky jumps up from the bed, her blue eyes wide and almost frightened.

"It's happened, again," she says and runs to the phone. The number is easy to remember; she will never forget that number. It rings, rings, rings, "Hello?" It is him; he's alive. "Hello?" Is it him? "Hello?"

"Red?" she whispers. "Is that you?"

"Yes, who is this?"

"You've forgotten me. Just that easy, you forgot." She wraps the cord around and around her wrist and it looks like a snake bracelet. Yes, you look just like an Ethiopian Princess—goody-goody princess.

"Jo?" At first his voice sounds relieved, saved and then it changes. "What do you want?"

"I had to make sure you were there," she whispers. "I thought you were . . . gone."

"Well, thought wrong," he says and laughs. "You know I'm sort of busy right now, got company."

"Who? Who?" she asks like a precious little hoot owl.

"Look, it doesn't matter." He is getting impatient. He probably has his pants off, bunched up around his ankles and there is a lump in the bed, under the sheet; there is someone in her place. "Look, I don't think you ought to call anymore. You know, you're the one that said that we shouldn't see each other or talk anymore."

"I know," she says. "But don't you see why I had to find out?"

"No, I don't see any of it. So, why don't you just forget it, okay?" He is lying; he used to see it all; he used to understand.

"Don't you remember that time that the lake was so big? Don't you remember how you said that the future was all planned out?" She is screaming and Becky is watching her; Becky is pretending that she is reading history but Becky is listening and watching her.

"Jo, I don't remember any of that." His voice gets real low like he doesn't want anyone to hear. "Look, I'd like to help you out. You know lots of your friends are worried about you; some of them even blame me but that's not it; you know that I've never hurt you. So let's keep it that way? Okay?"

"Nothing's wrong with me," she says. "It was you that

I was worried about. You see, I thought you were dead."
Becky has put down her book now and is staring.

"I think you better go." He laughs and then stops suddenly, cautiously. "I'm fine. Just leave it at that, okay?"

"Does that mean that you don't love me anymore?"

"I've got to go," he says quickly. "You take care of yourself."

She sits, staring at the phone, staring at Becky and she cannot think of one thing that makes sense. He is a liar, a liar. She has warned him, tried to save him so when he dies, it isn't her fault. But, he may need her later; she may have to check again.

"Jo? Is there anything that I can do?" Becky creeps up to her very slowly, like an inchworm, touches her shoulder but it won't stop shaking; she can't stop the shaking.

"Make it stop. Please, make it stop," she sobs and Becky hugs her tighter, tighter and she can see the robin egg blue over Becky's shoulder and it blurs, the drops of water that hit Becky's new pink oxford cloth shirt and spread. "I'm sorry, Becky," she says. "You shouldn't see me."

"That's what friends are for," Becky whispers. Is Becky her friend? She has never done anything for Becky. "What can I do? Please, just tell me what to do." Becky is crying, too, just like Lisa had done that time. And what does crying mean? Does it have anything to do with love? Is that why Red made her cry? Is that why she hadn't ever cried for Beatrice? Or had she, ever so lightly, ever so slightly, silently cried beneath the heavy buzzing, in the hospital, the bathroom, at Holden Beach.

"My Daddy can make it stop," she says. "He loves me."

"Should I call him?" Becky pushes her back and stares at her as if the answer is going to come quickly, precisely.

"Yes," she nods. "He can make it stop." Becky moves away and there is a cold feeling now that she is no longer hanging onto the shoulder of this person that she doesn't even know very well. Becky finds the number up beside the phone and dials slowly. She clears her throat.

"Mrs. Spencer? This is Becky Martin, Jo's roommate." Silence. "No, she's fine, just upset. Just a minute." Becky holds the receiver out into the room but she shakes her head and stretches out on the bed; she is so tired, too tired to sleep even though she needs to. "She wants you and Mr. Spencer to come," Becky whispers as though she can't hear. "Yes, I think so. Oh yes, I'm going to stay right here. Okay, bye." Becky carefully replaces the receiver so that it doesn't make a sound. A girl from down the hall knocks on the door. "I want to borrow Jo's notes from geology," she says.

"Jo isn't feeling well," Becky says without opening the door all the way. "See if you can get them from someone else." Becky closes the door and walks back to sit at the end of Jo Spencer's bed. "She wanted your notes," she says. "I told her that you weren't feeling well," as though Jo Spencer was incapable of hearing the conversation. This is funny, very funny and she must laugh. She must laugh because there are no notes! Ha! Ha! No notes! She laughs and laughs but Becky doesn't. Becky doesn't find this amusing. She wants to sleep, just sleep, but Becky keeps reminding her that her parents are coming. Becky turns on the T.V. Then, Becky wants to play cards. Becky is spending time with her and now she is in control; her parents shouldn't be coming at this time of night! They shouldn't drive at night! There is a knock on the door.

"Let me go," Becky says. "Just in case it isn't them." That is fine with her. She is just about to gin for the third time in a row. Her Daddy comes in first, his eyes warm but dulled, pipe in his pocket. Her mother is behind him and she doesn't even see her until he steps to one side. Wow! Like personalities splitting apart—Ho! Ho! Ho! Her mother's face is white and frightened; her mother tries to smile but it isn't real—peel it away like the skin of an orange.

"What's the matter, honey?" Her Daddy squats right beside her.

"I'm getting ready to gin," she says and smiles but it will not stay. It goes away when she hides her face in his shoulder and he rocks her back and forth like a little baby, a little girl. Her mother is there, too, the hand smoothing her long auburn hair over her shoulder.

It is like a vacation. Her mother gets some clothes out of the closet and packs a little bag. It is too late to go home so they are going to spend the night in a motel and have room service and everything! It is a holiday! Her mother tells Becky that they will talk to her tomorrow; her mother thanks Becky. "Save that hand. I'm getting ready to gin," she tells Becky and they are gone, through the night, driving at night. The room has tacky wallpaper but excellent T.V. reception and she may watch it and she doesn't have to talk at all. She can just watch T.V. while her mother makes some phone calls, while her Daddy tells her some jokes, while he tells her that these things happen, it is nothing to be ashamed of, things just happen and everything will work out, the sun will come back out, you'll see, you'll see.

The next morning, it is like nothing had even happened. What had happened? There were no dreams during the night and the times that she had awakened, her parents had been in the bed beside her. She has reading to do, a poem to write. What was that professor in his beautiful yellow hat going to think of her, skipping class all those times, when she hadn't really wanted to skip. Her mother says that one more day will not matter; she will talk to the professors if Jo Spencer thinks it's necessary. It is Jo Spencer's decision; she is in control. They have an appointment at ten-thirty.

They are the only three people in the waiting room except for the women in little matching tops that are talking on the phone and typing. It is a small room, very small and elevator music plays incessantly. It is dull music and out of this dull music steps a little Phi Delt looking man who laughs and talks to her parents like he knows them or like his best friend is their best friend and the three of them could laugh all night and all day playing the "do you know" game. She is not there, for awhile, and then the laughing stops, surface laughter, surface friendliness, and he asks her to come down this little hall; her parents will be right there waiting for her. Of course!

A waiting room is designed for that! This brings a smile but the others don't find it amusing.

He doesn't talk a lot to her the way that he did to them. He wants her to talk and just the tone of his voice, just the expression on his face makes her cry the whole time that she is in there. She has cried for an hour and it only seems like five minutes. She can cry more day after tomorrow, he tells her, and then she can talk whenever she's ready. Her parents want to stay in the motel with her until day after tomorrow but that isn't necessary. She has work to do, a dorm room, Becky will be worried; Becky might tell everyone that she is crazy and she's not. She had asked the man if she was crazy and he had said, "No, you are not crazy. No, we will have you feeling better." Better? No, No, Best! She must feel best!

She must keep her mind occupied—This is some of his advice—Twice a week, two hours a week, that big black leather chair is all hers and she may say what she pleases. She may say that she hates Claude Williams and that he is dead because of this. No, it seems, it seems that he is dead; it seems that people stare at her for no reason. She would like to be very young again, riding the hobby horses with Bobby, picking up the pecans under Grandma Spencer's pecan tree, sitting in the bathroom where no one can see her, where she is safe, fingerpainting alone without ever knowing Beatrice, or if she knew Beatrice, answering that note years later. Had she mentioned the note? She had never before mentioned that note. She asked him if he was taping her voice, she couldn't talk if he was because it would sound funny, it would not be her voice if he taped it. She had told him that she liked to think big thoughts, like about how shitty most people were! And cuss! She can just cuss and cuss in his presence. She can say "that pecker head! that fuck-up!" and he doesn't even mind. He has secret ways to make her say these things. He has a power almost like God because he is becoming omniscient, with each visit, a little more omniscient. But, he uses tricks, little tricks and she can see them. Ha! Ha! She is too smart for that. If she learns all of the secrets, she won't have to go back anymore. So, if she does know them all, she must pretend that she doesn't so that he will let her come again. She must do like he says and be honest with herself, find out who Jo Spencer really is.

Jo Spencer wants to make good grades, to be smart, so she must study very hard because it is almost time for exams. What is the logical thing to study? Well, the philosophy exam is her first one so she should study for it first. Anaximander says that "the infinite is first and foremost the source of existing things; that out of which they come." She likes Anaximander very much, to have thought to seek out questions which have no true concrete answer except that there is no answer. "Out of which existing things arise can have neither beginning or end." Yes, she likes Anaximander very much. She likes his name. Pronounce it aloud, A-nax-i-man-der. Beck looks at her but Beck doesn't ask her what she is doing. Beck doesn't ask many questions at all since Jo Spencer has started going to the Doctor. It is the X that makes

Anaximander such a nice smart name. Yes, she would like to have a name like that for herself. And that is an honest thought, a thought of her own, and it is so very clear, such a clear, precise thought and she can hardly wait to tell the Doctor about it. He will be so proud of her because she is moving forward—thinking of something that she would like to have, something that she would like to be. He had said, "You've been moving in reverse, you've been trying to go back and change things that have already happened, you can't do that, you can't change it or control it, all you can do is put yourself in forward gear. It's like a car. Most of the time, you're in drive but you must be alert, you must think, be cautious, use your brakes, don't exceed the limit."

"If I play that, I want to be a Mercedes Roadster," she had said.

"Be what you want to be," he had said. "Be yourself."

"I have to be," she had told him. "I'm me."

"And who is that?" he asked. "Who is Jo Spencer? What does she like to do? What does she want to be?" That was a hard question and she had told him so. She wanted to do things that she was good at doing. "What can you do?" Well, she is an excellent swimmer and she knows how to do lots of fancy dives. She is pretty good at tennis. She used to be good at ballet. She would love to be able to draw and sing but she has never been good at either of these. She likes to write poetry. She is very good with dogs. She taught Jaspar all kinds of tricks when he was just a baby, when she was just eleven.

"So, what do you want to be?"

"Happy," she had said. "More than anything, I want to be happy."

"Have you ever been happy?"

"Oh yes, a long time ago."

"When exactly? What can you remember that's happy?"

"Home," she had said but he wanted her to be specific and that was very difficult to remember but once it started, she could do it. She really could think of happy things. Watching T.V. at night and then saying her prayers and then being able to sleep without dreams. Bobby, Bobby and Andy make her very happy and her parents. Picking up pecans under Grandma Spencer's tree, going over to Cindy's house when they were in the second grade.

"And what made you unhappy?"

That was the hard question. What did make her unhappy? For what reason did she become unhappy. "What can you think of that makes you very sad?" His questions were getting harder and harder.

"The dream. The dream where Red is dead. And Beatrice." There, she had said it and she had told him about that other nightmare, the one that really happened over and over again. He had asked lots of questions about the nightmares. He had asked if she felt loved? Had Red loved her? Was she looking for someone else to love her? No, Red hadn't loved her, not really, because he had never made anything stop, the things that made her feel so small. But, yes, she did want to be loved but not by the people of the nightmares. She hates these faceless people of the nightmare. She hates them just the way that she hated Red for doing what he did, for exposing her. Once she wished that Red was dead; she wished that something horrible would happen to make him see what he had done to her, but then something horrible had happened, only not to Red, to Beatrice, and she had wished that, too. She had made that wish that night down at the lake when Beatrice was lying there on the floor of that bathroom. That is why she feels so sad, that is why all the happy went away. She had cried, hadn't she? Really cried? He had told her that that wasn't her fault. "Who do you think you are, God?" he had asked. "Do you think that you have that kind of control, that kind of power?" Had he used the word "guilt" or had she? He had said, "God." Did she think she was God? And this in itself was quite funny, funny enough for her to smile, not even a good smile like a good Jo Jo, just a plain smile for Jo.

"So what do I do?" she had asked. "How can I fix it all?"

"You can't," he had said. "It takes time. Things fix themselves."

That had been just two days ago when they had talked about all that and it had been a very important day because it was the first time that she had really been honest with him, about the real nightmare, about Beatrice. She had felt very good when she left that day but now, it's wearing off, now she's almost out of gas. Still, she has done what he said. She has studied very hard and she has tried to look a little into the future. For instance, she thinks that she would like to think big thoughts like Anaximander, she thinks that she would like to spend the summer at home in Blue Springs even though it's very difficult. She thinks that she might want to run a kennel one day and raise dobermans. She has even written a poem for him, one that she had already turned in for her class. He had told her to write a poem about Jo Spencer but she can't do that yet; she's not good enough, yet. So, she wrote a poem about Beatrice because that's what makes her very sad and she will read it to him when she goes—less than twenty-four hours and she will be in that big black leather chair, her chair, for an hour and she can say whatever she pleases.

Whoever is before her must have loads of problems because they are running overtime. It makes her feel sad that someone would have that much to talk about. She has worked almost the entire crossword puzzle in the newspaper and is just about through with the crypto-quote when he comes out to get her. That person in front of her always slips out the back door but she doesn't, not Jo Spencer, why should she? Some people have problems with an arm or leg, a back, a heart and she has problems with her head, big deal.

Before she even has time to sit down in her chair and pull the Kleenex box closer, he asks about the poem. He is so damn nosey, gets paid to be nosey. He wants her to stand up and read it to him; he says that this will be good practice for the last day of her class when everyone has to stand up and read a sonnet that they have written themselves and then stand there while people say whether or not it's good or bad, or inbetween.

"Here, you read it," she says and digs out the crumpled piece of paper from her pocketbook.

"That's not the deal we made," he says. "You've got to learn to go by the rules and it's my turn to be in charge."

"I always go by rules," she says. "My whole life I have gone by the rules, almost. Almost my whole life I have gone by the rules."

"Your own," he says and gets a very stern look. "To-day we play by mine. Or are you too selfish? think you're too smart?" That is a terrible thing for him to say, a terrible way for him to act after she has been so nice to him, after she has exposed herself. She can read it; she can do whatever she pleases. She straightens out the paper and clears her throat while he sits there staring like he's somebody. He's getting ready to pounce, to go for the jugular, wants to show her what it's going to be like. She can take it. "This doesn't have a title," she says, "but it's about Beatrice. It's about not fitting in."

"You shouldn't tell what it's supposed to be."

"Well, I thought you might need some help!" Jo Spencer snaps but he just smiles at her and motions for her to begin. He smiles like that to make her mad, does it every time and she is not going to let it get to her. "She sits sideways like a crab, seeing two sides." It is difficult to read those words but once she has begun, it gets easier; she pretends that he is not here, pretends that she is on her bed, alone in the room. It makes her want to read loud, louder, loudest. "Blue eyes blur like a blinded dog carried in and out to pee." The picture of Beatrice on that bathroom floor, sick, helpless creature comes to her and she reads faster and faster to make it go away, shakes her head and reads fast, faster, fastest, to the end, the end where it says, "make it go away."

He doesn't even smile, doesn't clap. How humiliating. He could at least say that he thought it was good even if he didn't. "You did write about yourself after all," he says. "I thought you said it was about Beatrice."

"It is!" she screams. "Do I have blue eyes? Tell me, do I?" Ah Ha! She got him on that one. The nerve!

"What don't you like about yourself?" he asks right out of the blue as though that's significant. As though there is something about herself that is not likable! "Come on think. Everybody has something that they don't like about themselves."

"So what don't you like?"

"Patients that ask me questions," he says and laughs. "But if you're so nosey that you must know and if you're so childish that you have to wait until someone has gone first so that you can play follow-the-leader, I'll tell you. I would like to be taller."

"Is that all? That's all you can find wrong with yourself?"

"For the moment," he says and looks stern again. "Now, what about you? Are you going to take a turn or does the game skip you and come back to me?"

"You can quit trying to make me mad. I'm wise to that. I knew from the very first day that you were acting like a real shit on purpose. You were so nice to my parents! Ha!"

"Changing the subject?"

"This fuckin hair, how's that?" she screams and pulls

her hair out to the sides. "I've never had long fuckin hair and I don't want it. It's ugly and it doesn't look like me. It looks like stringy long hair parted down the middle. It looks like I ought to be barefooted and handing out flowers singing 'We Shall Overcome' or 'Pass It On,' and that is not me."

"Cut it then if it makes you so mad," he says and laughs. "There is such a thing as a haircut."

"I don't know how it should be."

"Ask somebody that knows something about hair and just take a chance."

"Just take a chance?" she asks. "Like maybe wearing sunglasses?"

"If you think that's chancy, yes," he says. "But don't do it unless you really want to."

"I don't want to wear bright colors."

"So don't."

"Or paint my nails!"

"Does somebody make you?" He asks and looks at her hands. It looks like she is holding five jelly beans, hot pink jelly beans.

"My roommate says that painting her nails makes her feel good."

"Does it make you feel good?"

"Hell no!" She looks at her watch and realizes that her hour is almost over. Some hour, they didn't even talk about anything.

It is the last day of poetry, her very last class of the year and then exams begin. Before they begin the sonnet reading they must wind up the discussion of William Butler Yeats. The final poem is "Among School Children" and she likes this one very much. The man is remembering, thinking. It is obvious that her professor likes this one very much the way that he reads it aloud, especially the very end: "O chestnut tree, great-rooted blossomer, are you the leaf, the blossom or the bole? O body swayed to music, O brightening glance, How can we know the dancer from the dance." He stops, closes his book and takes a deep breath. "Who wants to explain that?"

She wishes that she knew the answer, that on this last day, she could speak out and tell it. "It's the continuation of life," this boy at the back of the room says. The boy gets a nod and no one else says anything and then so very easily, he tells it, he tells the answer.

"It is the Platonic belief that you cannot tell what something is until it is complete. Once completed, it is immortalized. For example, the dancer cannot be distinguished from the dance until the dance is finished and then the dance is something complete, isolated." She must listen to every word because this is very important to her life in general. "For instance," he glances around the room and then stops on her, "we will never know who Jo Spencer is until she is dead and gone. Then we can see the whole life, know what she was." The whole class laughs at this and she feels her face getting warm. He is picking on her, making fun of her but it doesn't make her mad. He has picked her out of the entire class to make a point, a joke, and he doesn't even know who she is, not entirely and neither does the Doctor and neither does she. It is a big thought to hold onto and her voice doesn't even quiver when she stands to read, even though the professor has announced that he doesn't give final exams, that he will never see them again unless they take one of his courses next year.

It is difficult to stand up beside the desk, difficult to hold the paper steady, to hold her chin steady, all of those good words from Geology seeming to blur and run together. "The title is 'The Beginning of the End,'" she says, her voice sounding so high and unnatural, her voice, the only sound in the room. She does not look up when she finishes but just stands there, folds the paper in and out in teeny folds like an accordian fan. People begin to talk and so she sits back down. It is not good, but it is not bad; it is a good time to be in the middle.

The professor says that it shows a great deal of improvement; she likes the sound of that, improvement; she is getting better but that's not good enough, got to get best. She's got to get better and better, make good solid future steps that can make up for the past false steps, steps so much better that when she has finished her dance, and when people leave her graveside and are sitting with their gin and tonics, they will all say that she has danced a wonderful dance, that there were steps that could have been better but overall, it was a wonderful dance! And what would Beatrice's dance be? It had been awkward from the very beginning and then she almost quit, but it's not over. Even Beatrice has time. Now that she sees all of this, the class is over and that seems very sad. But, too, she can see the class in its entirety because it has ended, a true end, and it has been a very good class. She must tell him.

"I've really enjoyed this class," she says. "I hate to see it end."

"Thank you," he says and he looks like he really means it. She would like to tell him about that wonderful yellow hat that she had seen him wear but he might get the wrong impression, think that she is brown nosing. "You're going to take the next level course next year, aren't you?" He is asking her and she must answer. He must think she's good enough to go on; he must still see the Could Be's in her. Next year seems like a long time away, a very long time away. Once she had even thought that she wouldn't come back, that maybe she'd live at home and go to that technical school where Beatrice had gone and get a quick degree, start over, but there is no starting over, just continuing.

"I don't know, yet," she says and shrugs. "I don't even know what I want to be."

"What are you good in?"

"Swimming," she says and laughs. For some reason this man makes her feel very honest. "Dogs. I know almost all of the tunes to the old T.V. shows."

"And out of all that, you can't find a career?" He laughs and she can just see him in that yellow hat, serving coffee to all the people at the party, the living people, the dancing people. All of the other people in the class have left and she wants to talk to him another minute. It feels like the first time that she has talked in years.

"Hey, do you know the music to Dick Van Dyke? I have tried for months now to remember it." She laughs and it is an honest laugh, a laugh that feels good.

He laughs but then he stops and stares out the window for a minute. He's got it; he remembers the music, the little trip over the stool part and everything. "How's that?"

"That's it!" she screams. "That's it! Thank you. Thanks a lot."

"Have a nice summer," he calls after her. "Think about taking the class." She will think about it.

Jo Spencer has taken all of her exams and now, she is just waiting for the grades to be posted. Becky has already left for the summer and that was sort of sad, sad because a whole school year had ended. They had not said anything like "friends til the end" or "Silly! how could I ever forget you?" Beck had just said, "See you in the fall, Jo. Have a good summer, take care of yourself, write," and Beck had hugged her. Beck had even asked her opinion. She had said, "How do you like my hair parted in the middle?"

"I don't," Jo Spencer had said. "It looks better on the side."

"Well, thanks a lot!" Beck had said and for just a minute Jo had been very scared that she had done the wrong thing, said the wrong thing. "I think you're right," Beck had said and laughed. She had parted her hair back the way that it looks the best and had gone down the stairs with two big bags to where her parents were waiting.

Now, Jo Spencer is left, waiting, because in just two

days, after she has seen her grades and after she has seen the Doctor, she is going to Blue Springs. Bobby is coming to get her and she cannot help but wonder how she will spend the summer. Only Fridays are taken care of because that's the day she will drive up to see the Doctor. She is starting to get tired of sitting in that big black chair but not so tired that she can stop, not yet. She needs to do something to pass the time. The Doctor had said, "Get out. Make some friends. Pick friends who are right for you. Be a friend; be yourself. Don't be hard on yourself; reward yourself." That was it! She can reward herself. She can go outside and walk around. She can walk downtown. She can get a haircut.

The young man standing there with the comb and scissors says that she is the best customer that he has ever had. "Most people tell me exactly how to cut," he says. "Very few people tell me to do what I think will look best."

"I trust you," she says and laughs. "I like to take chances!"

She sits and repeats this to herself over and over while she watches that long auburn hair fall to the speckled floor. It doesn't even look like her hair and she is glad to get rid of it. When he turns her around to the mirror, she can't believe it. Her hair is very short, about a half an inch all over, and it makes her look young, to feel young. She shakes her head back and forth and nothing moves; she can rub her hands all over it and it won't mess up. It will be perfect for swimming and diving.

Next, she must go to the drugstore and look at sunglasses. They have several racks just full of them! She spins one rack around and around. What is she looking for? She takes some great big round buggy looking glasses like what Jackie O. wears and puts them on. No, these make her feel very old. She tries some more but they all make her feel very old; they make her feel funny like she has no purpose, no cause. She doesn't need these anyway. Maybe she will buy some shampoo for her new hair, some real suntan oil that smells like coconuts and bananas, some little plastic disposable razors. They look safe enough and she will have to be very careful, take her time so that she doesn't cut herself in a wrong place. She watches the woman ring up her items and the woman looks hot, miserable, exasperated in those tight stretch pants and that polyester pregnant looking top. She does not want to be like this woman; there is nothing about the woman that she wants to have.

Now, she must go to the grocery store. What does she want? She gets a box of Country Morning Cereal with raisins and dates. It is so good like candy that she starts eating it dry while she waits in line. By the time that she gets out of the store, she has already eaten a third of the box. Well, if she runs out, she will just have to go buy some more, maybe get a half gallon of Breyer's icecream to mix with it.

It is a clear blue day, so sharp that she sees things that she has never noticed. Has that stop sign always been there? Have these people always been here? She sees one person that she recognizes, there, sitting in the window of the coffee shop, sipping coffee and reading. Is that girl always sitting there? The girl with the big brown eyes and does that girl recognize Jo Spencer with short short hair walking by? "Get out, meet people, make some friends," the Doctor had said. She cuts through campus and walks along the brick sidewalks that curve in different directions. There is a girl running around in an open space. She is holding two leather leashes and two blonde cockers are chasing her around, turning, unleashed. That girl has a life just like that girl in the coffee shop, her very own place to live, a chair that she sits in to eat, a bed that she sleeps in; she sleeps—so does the poetry professor, the woman with the sort of wild curly hair and crystal clear blue eyes that she saw tapdancing on a stage one time, the tall thin boy that always wore basic black and always knew the answers in English II, the tall girl with dark curly hair and dark deer eyes that she had just seen in the grocery store. That girl is probably at her home now, putting all of those T.V. dinners in her freezer. Bobby? Andy? Pat Reeves? She is not so different from all of these people. She sleeps; she has her very own place to sleep; she eats, walks, talks, uses the bathroom. Even the Doctor uses the bathroom! He is a person and she is a person. She can make friends just like she used to have. Beck is her friend. She could have walked up to that girl at frozen foods; she could walk up to that girl running around unleashed and talk to her. She could have just said "hello" to that boy in basic black, the girl in the coffee shop, the tapdancer. She can have friends. She can just walk around all day and eat dry cereal if she wants to. She can do anything that she wants to do.

It is the last day, the end, and she has to check the final grade; she has to check Geology. She made an A in poetry, a B in English II, a C in philosophy, a D in French, and maybe an F in Geology. All she wants is a D, a D⁻ even. Maybe they were not all the same course anyway. She has done everything that she can to put off looking. She has even written a note to the poetry professor and if she passes Geology, she can slide it under his office door even though the year is over.

The building is very quiet and it is just as well. It is very dark in here and she can't see well because it was so bright outside. She looks at her watch; Bobby will be coming for her in less than two hours. She looks at her legs, so brown and silky smooth, the pale pink wraparound skirt that she has not worn in years. She has to look. She walks up to the rows and rows of numbers, thank God they don't put names; she finds her number, runs her finger across, slowly, steadily so that she sees it right the first time. There, a D⁻. It is happening.

The campus is empty except for a few people here and there and so she runs as fast as she can, pulls the note out of her pocketbook when she reaches the English building. She gets just outside of his door and stares down at the note, the letters, words, that she had carefully written. "See you next year because I want to take your class. May your dance last a very long time. Joslyn Spencer." She hesitates a minute, her hand by the crack under the door. Would he think that an odd thing to say? A crazy thing? No, she must not think things like that. As long as she knows what she means, it will be okay. As long as she is honest and with that, she pushes the note, now beyond where her fingers could reach if she suddenly wanted to take it back. A decision made. She walks away, down the stairs, through the big glass doors and back to that robin egg blue room that she has come to think of as her room, where Bobby will be in less than two hours and she cannot wait to get in the car and ride through that golden spring day to Blue Springs, North Carolina, where the house will be exactly as she has always remembered.

IV

JUNE 24, 1980

I wake and the room is so dark that at first I cannot remember where I am. I get my bathrobe off of the end of the bed, drape it around my shoulders and go to the window. From there, I can see Moon Lake, a smooth green oval, the reflections from the lights on the pier so clear and so sharp that I think that the real light is coming from beneath the water. The sky is dark gray and misty; it would blend into the dark green of the water and form a perfect rim, that infinite edge of the world if it weren't for the line of spindly pine trees holding it back. I run my fingertip along the pane, up and down, the erratic pattern of the trees against the sky, and it frightens me but I can't stop, not until I have traced it, drawn that fine line that separates the two, connects the two. It is the gray that frightens me, that gradual gray blend that separates night from day and yet, the skies of dawn and dusk are so similar that I am confused, uncertain of what is about to happen, uncertain if I am seeing the beginning or the ending of day. My tongue will not work, my hand will not move from the glass. Then I remember that I sleep at night now, I remember the time, and the fear dissolves in a laugh of relief. I laugh and my hand moves from the window. I laugh because night is almost over. I go into the kitchen, fill the copper kettle, place it on the eye of the stove, put instant coffee in my mug, and then there is nothing, a nothing that I am not even aware of until I am awakened by a shrill hiss, a sudden alarm that sends me, disoriented, into the kitchen where I find the fire-red eye glaring from beneath the empty kettle.

It was only a dream that has prompted me to look back, a dream that like those of the past seemed to slip into reality and I am without knowledge as to when it became real, unaware of the point at which I stopped watching myself and began going through the motions; the questions alone bringing with them that dull sense of dread, the sudden panic of waking. But, I am not there anymore. I am not a child sitting in the bathroom; I am not a college freshman sitting in a shower stall. I am Joslyn Marie Spencer, age twenty-three, spending the summer at Moon Lake, standing in my kitchen with a blackened copper kettle, wondering what to use to boil my water.

When I look back, it seems to me that those last few days of my freshman year when I cut my hair to the scalp and ran around eating dry cereal lasted forever. It's always springtime and there is always that fresh smell of everything thawing, warming. There is always a clear sharp picture as though every day was sharp blue and cloudless, as though the big dorm windows were always thrown open with the smell of near summer sifting through the screens. And it wasn't that way, not always. In the three years to follow, there were long dark winters and rainy nights, occasional nightmares that threw me into the day before I was ready. And yet, glancing back, there is a slow motioned moment when I don't see any of that, as though everything was resolved in those last days. Perhaps several years from now, I will look back and see things more clearly, but for now, I'd rather accept it as a resolution. It is like Pascal's Wager where it is better to believe that there IS a God, since it can't be proven otherwise, so that if indeed it's true, then you would reap all benefits of the afterlife, than to believe that there ISN'T a God and take the chance of going to hell. For now, I would rather accept it all. For now, I choose to believe that life is like a cardiogram where you must always be moving up and down, back and forth, past and future, briefly touching down in the present, coming some distance before a pattern emerges. If you get stuck on any level and stay on the straight and narrow, if your beep beep turns into a low droning monotone and does not veer from that steady gray, then you are a dead duck, so I must look quickly back and wonder where all of the faceless people are, wonder if that pubic hair is still clinging to that shower stall, if there's a young girl sitting there right now, staring up at it, thinking that she is the only person who has ever seen it. But then I must touch down, work a little while on an overdue paper that I am doing for a graduate course, tracing back the witty sayings of the sixteenth century. Then I can look to the future for a brief while; I can think to myself that one day I will really fall in love, that Pat Reeves or someone very much like him will suddenly appear at my door, take me to the movies, tell me about their childhood. I could be anywhere when it happens; I could be here, in this rented house at Moon Lake.

Red Williams is no longer a part of Moon Lake, though sometimes when I look out I expect to see him running back and forth, a bandana trailing from his head. He is not even Red anymore because he has grown into the name Claude, a name that suits him perfectly since he gained weight and married a large lumbering divorcee with bleached hair and two obese (they probably say "chubby") children, and moved to Detroit where he is doing no more work on cars than what he was doing right here at K-Mart's when he was twenty-one. "Pumping gas and a fat ass make you dull," is what I should say if he should ever find his way to my door.

No, I will fall in love with someone who can hold my hands right and I will have a cute, trim, "fit" child named something like Anaximander and we will fingerpaint the walls of his room while my husband is out working and doing other husbandly things. I will paint one of the walls even though I am not artistically inclined; I will paint Noah and the Ark so that Anaximander will learn his animals and get a little Sunday School lesson taboot. Then I will paint the Pinta, the Nina and the Santa Marie so that he will know historical facts. I will not yet tell him that it is believed by many scholars that Chris brought V.D. to the new world. And isn't that something? If it hadn't been for Chris, the father of our country never would have gotten syphilis! How fascinating, the things that hold humanity together, the things that hold people together.

"There stand I like Arctic Pole," Fulke says. Obviously, he has an erection. I am twenty-three so I can say things like that now. I can say anything that I want, tell the truth or tell a lie, but I still can't wear sunglasses. I try to wear them for days just like today when the sun is in the east, well above the pine trees around the lake, and its bright white light makes me see dark spots.

There are other dark spots. Bobby didn't marry Christine. He married Nancy Carson and they are living in Raleigh where he is doing his residency. They are "struggling" since they bought the house, Nanci reported to me in her last letter. (She changed her name to "i" when she developed an interest in "self help" manuals, started wearing beach towel skirts and ultimately went through est training.) Still, we get along quite well. We only disagree on a few issues like clothes, politics, social dos and donts, movies, books, and life in general. The only thing we share is a love for Bobby Spencer. Lisa has already been married and divorced. Cindy is living with a pharmacist in Topeka. Tricia is marrying, of all ironies, Tom Fulton whom she remet in a bar in Charlotte less than a year ago. I am her Maid of Honor and we are wearing these awful purple dresses that are quite similar to the one I wore when I was the maid that fished out baby Moses. Beatrice never left Maine and from what I know has never even been back to Blue Springs, though her parents go to see her. She is married and has a baby. I sent her a Christmas card last year, wrote a note, signed it "your old friend, Jo." When hers came, there was no note and she signed her full name, her new name. It occurred to me that maybe Beatrice doesn't want to look back, doesn't want to remember. I doubt if I'll send a card this year. Andy has been suspended from Blue Springs High three times for saying "shit on that." None of the teachers can believe that he is related to Bobby and myself. He wears a paper clip in his ear and races dirt bikes. People often say that he is going through a phase, "just like Jo went through."

Presently, I have many choices to make. Clearly I am not an "I Love Lucy" nor am I a "That Girl." *The Feminine Mystique* says that you don't have to be an either/or and I am convinced that this is true, that there is a safe inbetween. What I can't help but wonder however, is that if this is true, why did Betty Friedan get a divorce? I am not a Total Woman and I am not a Libber. (I wonder why Marabelle Morgan hasn't gotten a divorce?) I shave my legs and under my arms but I do not wear Saran Wrap. I am smart but I am not Jewish. I am Christian but I am not Catholic and Catholics are Christians. What was Anaximander other than Greek? I used to imagine him being Southern Baptist and then I realized what a ridiculous thought! Anaximander at BTU or VBS, ducking his smart head under water, eating little unsalted saltines. Pat Reeves is an Episcopalian which I suppose would be a nice place to be. I called him not long ago, to tell him that I really am a nice person, to see if he might still care, to see if he looks back, if he would ever come back, though I did not really say any of that. "Take care of yourself," he had said.

On rainy days, I will roll back my nice oriental rugs and little Anaximander and I will roller skate while we watch old reruns on T.V. I will show him Alfalfa and Buckwheat and tell him how they have not changed one bit since I was a child or since his grandparents were coming along. I will show him old pictures of myself so that he can see me another way, a younger me in a cheerleading suit, Most Popular. If I married Pat Reeves, I could show Anaximander the May Queen picture but otherwise, I will have to keep that one hidden. It would upset him; he might draw on Pat's face and for some reason, I would probably switch the hell out of him if he did. I will have a few friends whose company I can truly find pleasure in and we will drink coffee and smoke cigarettes. I will not dress up on these occasions for there would be no need in front of a real friend and I'll just prop my muk-luk bedroom slipper right up on the table if I like.

I really am not close to a lot of people because that is a very frightening thing. The farther you stray, the more people that you become close to, then the higher the probability that you will lose someone. You could hear it on the radio, read it in the paper and all that you could do about it would be to sit and drink a gin and tonic, remember things about this person, the very last time that you saw them, feel that jabbing anger and guilt of things un-said, things undone, helpless to rectify, to get another chance. Besides, Fulke keeps me so busy lately.

When I am thirty and in love, exposed in a favorable light, happy with husband and Anaximander, I'll prob-ably think back to right now, unable to wear sunglasses, working on this paper, sleepwalking and burning my kettle, spending the summer at Moon Lake, and I'll prob-ably think that I was crazy (that I am crazy), and it will probably happen when I am forty, fifty, sixty, seventy, eighty, ninety with fuzzy hair and no teeth, drooling and exposing myself in a childlike way. I will probably be on my deathbed and I will try to peruse my dance before the lights go out, faces coming and going, and I will prob-ably think that the whole damn thing was crazy, up and down, around and around.

But at least I will know that I was moving. At least right now I know that I am moving, sliding, changing. At least right now I know that I am a little bit of everything that I've ever been. I look out at the lake, that cool green water, and I listen to the water in the pot begin to boil, a temporary replacement for the black kettle. The lake is so small now, too small to ever hold all of my Could Be's, all of the single celled creatures. I have gotten so big that the world is getting smaller, or is it that there is some-thing out there so big that it has no answer, definition, beginning or end that makes it all seem so small? It is such a big thought and I really don't have time to think about it all right now. No, for now, I must simply accept it as a question which has no answer because the water is boiling rapidy, spitting itself onto that white surface. I just have to leave it at that for now, touch down in the present and go and fix a cup of coffee. I simply must leave it at that, tell myself that I will return to this thought one day in the future and then I will know. I will know where this unbounded sexless feeling comes from; I will paint by number the hairs on my head; I will count the sexless single celled creatures and I will make sure that each has its very own home, its own life, and I will make the lake grow and grow, to spread and rise, slowly, cautiously, spinelessly, I will make it grow so that it will look just like it used to look, the way that I remember it all. And I will know where the earth and sky meet; I will know what keeps them from running together. I will recognize the beginnings and endings of days, years. I will know the plot of every Andy Griffith show in syndication. Or maybe I'll just live and that will be okay, too, but for now it is the water that I am concerned with, the water that has evaporated right out of the pot and hidden in the air. There is a choice to make, a chance to take. I must either sit and wait for condensation or begin to begin the whole process again and again and again.